*Master Unchained* is a work of fiction. Names, characters, places, and incidents are the products of the author's imagination and are used fictitiously. Any resemblance to actual events, locales, or persons, living or dead, is entirely coincidental.

Published in the United States

Cover design: Damon Za
Author Photo: © Marti Corn Photography

Printed in the United States of America

# BOOKS BY TINA FOLSOM

Prequel Novella: Mortal Wish
Samson's Lovely Mortal (Scanguards Vampires #1)
Amaury's Hellion (Scanguards Vampires #2)
Gabriel's Mate (Scanguards Vampires #3)
Yvette's Haven (Scanguards Vampires #4)
Zane's Redemption (Scanguards Vampires #5)
Quinn's Undying Rose (Scanguards Vampires #6)
Oliver's Hunger (Scanguards Vampires #7)
Thomas's Choice (Scanguards Vampires #8)
Silent Bite (Scanguards Vampires #8 1/2)
Cain's Identity (Scanguards Vampires #9)
Luther's Return (Scanguards Vampires #10)
Blake's Pursuit (Scanguards Vampires #11)
Fateful Reunion (Scanguards Vampires #11 1/2)

Lover Uncloaked (Stealth Guardians #1)
Master Unchained (Stealth Guardians #2)

A Touch of Greek (Out of Olympus #1)
A Scent of Greek (Out of Olympus #2)
A Taste of Greek (Out of Olympus #3)

Lawful Escort
Lawful Lover
Lawful Wife
One Foolish Night
One Long Embrace
One Sizzling Touch

Venice Vampyr

# MASTER UNCHAINED

## STEALTH GUARDIANS #2

# TINA FOLSOM

# 1

*Councilwoman Tessa Wallace* was typewritten on the plain white envelope. No address. No stamp. But when she opened it and read the note inside, Tessa began to tremble. Her breath caught in her throat, and her heartbeat accelerated. Cold sweat began to build on her nape.

*Get out while you still can. You don't want to end up like the last mayor, do you?*

The note wasn't signed. But the threat was clear. Somebody didn't like the fact that she was running for the highest office in the city of Baltimore—an office that had become vacant after the previous mayor, John Yardley, had died two months earlier.

For a moment, she closed her eyes, allowing a shaky sigh to escape. She'd always known that politics was a dirty and dangerous game. But this went too far. The only reason she'd thrown her hat into the ring after the mayor's untimely death was because she believed that the acting mayor, Robert Gunn, wasn't the right man for the job. His incendiary rhetoric only aggravated the civil unrest that currently raged in the city. What this city needed was a peacemaker, not an ambitious politician who had no qualms about issuing executive orders that curbed the rights of minorities. He even went so far as to encourage police brutality against African Americans and Latinos, while white thugs got a free pass. Reports of racially motivated false arrests and illegal seizure of property were piling up, and Gunn didn't see anything wrong with it.

But despite the fact that Gunn was a terrible choice for mayor, she didn't think he'd do something as reckless as threaten her. On the other hand, she wouldn't put it past his many supporters to try and scare her off, thus allowing him to run for mayor unopposed.

A brief knock at the door startled her more than it should have. Before she could answer, the door was ripped open, and Poppy Connor, her campaign manager, charged in. A woman gifted with more energy than an Energizer bunny, the chubby redhead held up a sheet of paper and grinned triumphantly.

"Hot off the press! The latest poll numbers."

Poppy nearly tripped over her own feet on the way to the desk, where she placed the sheet in front of Tessa.

Automatically Tessa glanced at it, but she didn't get a chance to read the numbers, before Poppy announced, "You're up by five points. This calls for a celebratory drink." Excitement spilled from her voice and colored her face. As if Poppy needed a reason to drink. She'd always been a party girl.

Tessa forced a smile. "That's still within the margin of error."

Poppy clicked her tongue. "That's not what you said when Gunn was five points ahead of *you* two weeks ago." She pointed at the sheet again. "I mean, look at it! That's a huge swing in only two weeks. I think our approach is working. You're appealing to the people. They see something in you."

Tessa shrugged, unable to enjoy the good news, the effect of the threatening note still lingering. "Yeah, I guess."

Her campaign manager cast her a questioning look. "You guess? What's wrong? I thought you'd be jumping up and down at that news. Isn't this what you want? Don't you want to win?"

Tessa lifted her eyes. "I do. The people of Baltimore deserve better than Gunn. But…"

"But what? Don't tell me you haven't got the stomach for this. I know people have been attacking you for your youth and inexperience, but you can't let that get to you."

"I'm not." She hesitated, wondering whether to tell Poppy about the note. She took a few breaths. Maybe it was best to just ignore it. So somebody didn't want her to be mayor. Not exactly a surprise.

Tessa pasted a smile on her face. "I'm just a little exhausted." She picked up the piece of paper and studied the poll numbers more closely. "These numbers look really good."

Poppy leaned closer and looked over her shoulder. "And look at the Hispanic and African American voters."

"I'm way ahead with them."

"You're killing it in that demographic!" Poppy confirmed.

"But we have to get the unions on our side. Have you arranged the talk at the—"

"What's that?" Poppy's hand shot past Tessa's shoulder, pointing to the note lying exposed on the desk, now that Tessa had moved the poll sheet.

"That's nothing." Tessa made an attempt to snatch it before Poppy could take it. Too late.

Poppy stepped away, perusing the note, then holding it up. "Nothing? That's a death threat! Jesus Christ, Tessa, when did you get this?"

"It was on my desk when I got back from the council meeting. It's probably just some wacko nutbag." She took the note from Poppy's hand. "I'm not taking it seriously." Even though the threatening words had given her a fright at first, she wasn't going to admit that to Poppy. The less she made of it the better. "If I took every stupid threat seriously, I wouldn't get any work done."

Poppy stilled. "What are you saying?"

"I just told you: I'm not taking it seriously."

Poppy shook her head and gripped Tessa's shoulders, almost pulling her out of her chair. "Look at me." She brought her face closer. "Are you implying that this is not the first threat you've gotten?"

Tessa's breath hitched. She'd never been very good at hiding things—or at lying. Maybe she shouldn't have become a politician. Her father had told her all along that she was too honest for this profession. Too good, whatever that meant.

Poppy's eyes widened. "Oh my God! You've gotten other threats like this, haven't you?"

"I wouldn't call them threats," Tessa said, attempting to diffuse Poppy's concern.

"What would you call them then?"

Tessa shrugged. She had no answer. Instead, she pulled the top drawer of her desk open. Inside were several other notes, all possibly from the same sender, though before today, the messages had been more suggestion than threat.

Poppy pulled a few notes out of the drawer. "Oh crap, Tessa!"

Tessa watched silently as Poppy skimmed the notes.

"When did you get the first one?"

"A couple of weeks after I announced my candidacy for mayor."

Poppy pointed to the remainder of the notes. "I'll take these."

"What are you gonna do with them?"

"Show them to somebody who can help you."

Tessa jumped up. "I can help myself!"

Poppy braced her hands on her hips. "No, you can't. Not when it comes to something as serious as this. You need a professional."

"A professional?"

"Yes, somebody who can protect you, because as your campaign manager, I'm not only responsible for getting you votes, I'm also responsible for your safety." She pointed to the note from today. "I'm not going to stand idly by while somebody clearly wants you dead. I'd be a piss-poor excuse for a friend if I did."

"You can't just go over my head about this!" Tessa protested. "I'm not in danger. This is just some disgruntled voter who'd rather have Gunn as mayor."

"How many disgruntled voters do you know who issue death threats?" Poppy gave her a stern look. "You're getting protection, and that's that."

By now, Tessa was fuming. She jumped up. "If you do that, I'll fire you!"

"Do what you have to, but if you don't accept protection, I'm going to show these to your father. We'll see what he has to say about it."

Tessa's chin dropped. If her father thought she was in danger, he would personally march down to City Hall and put her in protective custody. He'd always looked out for her, though even he hadn't been able to protect her all the time. He'd failed her once, and it had made him even more overprotective. She had no intention of worrying him over something like this. He had enough on his plate. "You wouldn't!"

"Oh, I would, in a heartbeat!" Poppy crossed her arms over her chest. "Your choice."

Tessa pressed her lips together, knowing she'd lost this round. "I should have never hired you. Friendship and business clearly don't mix."

Poppy smiled sweetly. "Honey, hiring me was the best thing you ever did."

# 2

Hamish stepped out of the portal that had brought him from his own compound to one located thousands of miles away. The journey had taken only seconds. It was the Stealth Guardians' primary mode of transportation and enabled them to act quickly in times of crisis. It was also, however, their Achilles' heel: should a demon ever enter one of their portals, he would be able to access any of their race's strongholds and destroy them from within.

Cinead, a member of the Council of Nine, their ruling body, was already waiting for him.

"You came quickly," the elder statesman said in his thick Scottish accent.

"You made it sound urgent."

"It is." He motioned to the hallway. "Walk with me."

As they walked through the maze of corridors, Hamish glanced at the man who'd always been a mentor to him. Dressed in dark slacks and a light Polo shirt, he made a striking figure. In his younger years, Cinead had been a fearless warrior, before deciding to devote his life to guiding his race as a member of the Council of Nine. Today, though, he looked tired and solemn.

"What's on your mind?" Hamish felt compelled to ask.

Cinead smiled, but it was forced. "Many things." He pointed to a door and walked through it, disappearing right in front of Hamish's eyes.

Hamish followed, allowing his body to disintegrate so it could pass through the solid wood and reassemble behind it, an ability singular to his race.

He'd entered a large library with a comfortable seating area and books stacked on shelves as far as the eye could see. Cinead walked to the fireplace, touching the frame of a small picture. Hamish had seen the painting many times: a baby boy stretched out on a bearskin. The dark-haired boy lay on his stomach, stark-naked, a small birthmark the shape of an axe gracing one butt cheek.

"He would be the same age as you, had he lived," Cinead said into the silence. An eerie echo accompanied his words, as if the ghosts of the dead were whispering back.

Hamish swallowed hard, suddenly realizing the significance of today's date. "How long has it been?"

"Two-hundred years to the day," Cinead said, turning toward him, "since the demons killed him. He was just a wee bairn, still in diapers." He walked to the couch and sat down, motioning Hamish to do the same.

He complied.

"I guess I'm getting sentimental in my old age."

Not that Cinead looked old; their race didn't age fast. Even at close to five-hundred years, Cinead didn't look older than a man in his late forties. His eyes, however, reflected the wisdom and experience of his long life and the pain and hardship he'd lived through.

"Is that why you wanted to see me? To reminisce?" If it were so, he wouldn't blame him. Cinead had been like a second father to him after Angus, Cinead's only child, had been killed by the Demons of Fear, their mortal enemies.

The elder Stealth Guardian shook his head. "Although you remind me of him, or rather of how I imagine he would have turned out, had they not taken him. Still, I didn't call you to talk about old times." He smiled. "I'm proud of you, Hamish, for all that you've accomplished as a guardian."

Somewhat embarrassed by the open and unexpected praise, Hamish said, "All thanks to your guidance."

"You're too humble. Another one of your positive traits, like your judgment. You would have made an outstanding member of the Council of Nine and—"

"I told you my reasons for declining a seat on the Council and I thought you underst—"

"I understood." Cinead lifted his hand in a calming gesture. "Don't worry. You're not here so I can talk you into something you clearly don't want. In any case, both vacancies on the Council are being filled as we speak. In fact, I'm glad you decided to remain a guardian. You're more valuable to us out in the field. Particularly now."

Instantly on alert, Hamish felt his spine stiffen. "What do you need?"

Cinead smiled softly. "Ever the eager soldier. That's good. This is a delicate situation, one that requires a man of your judgment and experience. A man who won't let his feelings get in the way of his duty."

Hamish lifted an eyebrow but didn't interrupt. Feelings? He hadn't had feelings in a long time. Feelings had nearly killed him once; since then he'd wrapped a heavy chain around his heart, one he had no intention of ever removing. He was as loyal as ever to his fellow Stealth Guardians, particularly to the men and women of his compound, but every outsider—particularly the charges he was assigned to protect—he treated with cool distance and measured suspicion. Trust was something that he didn't dispense easily these days, because trusting the wrong person could spell the end for him, or for his brothers and sisters.

"... civil unrest and riots. We can't allow this to continue. Do you understand?"

All of a sudden, he realized that Cinead had started talking, and he'd missed half the conversation.

"Yes, sir." He nodded quickly and gave Cinead an expectant look, urging him to elaborate.

"It's all happening in your backyard. We knew there would be problems after the unexpected death of Mayor Yardley, we just couldn't anticipate how bad it would get."

Hamish began to realize what Cinead was talking about: Baltimore, the place he called home. He edged forward on his armchair, genuine interest now surging within him. While he would go anywhere the Council sent him, he preferred missions close to home, because he felt—just like a football team—that it gave him a home field advantage. And over the last two months, things had gotten out of hand there: crime had skyrocketed, demonstrations had turned violent, and riots had erupted.

"You suspect demons are involved in the current unrest?"

After all, it made sense. The Demons of Fear thrived on civil unrest, hate, and fear. It made them stronger. They took every opportunity of inciting violence, so they could feed off the resulting fear. So they could get stronger and one day come out in the open and rule over mankind. And the only thing standing between the humans and their likely fate was the Stealth

Guardians, who'd made it their mission to thwart the demons' plans.

Cinead tapped his fingers against his lips. "I'm not certain. But what I do know is that there is one person who can put an end to this and bring peace to the city again. We have great hopes for her."

"Her?"

Cinead nodded. "Councilwoman Tessa Wallace. She understands the plight of the disadvantaged in the city. They believe in her. She's running for mayor."

Hamish nodded. "I've seen a few news reports. She's certainly a better choice than Gunn." Then he shrugged. "And I believe the voters know that. Nothing for us to do."

"On the contrary."

Hamish cocked an eyebrow.

"One of our *emissarii* sent word that the councilwoman has received death threats."

"From the demons?"

"We're not sure. In any case, if she exits the race, it will only play into the demons' hands. We can't let that happen. In his two months in office as acting mayor, Gunn has already stirred up too much trouble, and he appears to have no intention of calming his constituents. On the contrary: his speeches and his actions only incite more violence, more protests. He divides the various fractions of the city. Race relations are sitting on a powder keg likely to explode at any moment. We fear the worst if he wins the election. But if…"

"… if the councilwoman wins, you think she can turn the city around?"

"With our help, yes." He leaned forward. "That's why I asked you here."

"You want me to protect her and make sure whoever issued those death threats won't get the chance to carry them out," Hamish guessed. "Nothing easier than that." It would be just like any other assignment he'd had in the past. Which begged the question, why Cinead had gone through the trouble of asking him to meet in person, when he just as easily could have sent the assignment through the usual channels.

"Yes, but that's not all. I also want you to make sure she stays on the right path. I want you to lend her strength in the face of the opposition she'll encounter."

Hamish's eyebrows snapped together. "And how am I supposed to do that, considering she won't even know I'm protecting her?"

Cinead smiled, and for a moment, he thought he recognized a tiny glimmer of mischief in the other's eyes. "That's where this assignment will differ from your previous missions. She'll know you're her protector."

Hamish jumped up. "Are you saying she'll know that I'm a Stealth Guardian?"

Cinead chuckled. "Of course not. We're not going that far. She'll believe you're a human bodyguard, hired by a wealthy supporter who wants to make sure nothing happens to her. But that's not all. The people around her can't know who you are. To them, you'll be introduced as her boyfriend. It will give you unprecedented access—"

"Hold it right there!" Hamish shoved a hand through his dark hair. "With all due respect, that's out of the question. I'm not the right person for this kind of assignment."

"On the contrary, you're the perfect person for this assignment."

"Have you forgotten what happened to me?" Because he hadn't. How could he ever forget the betrayal of the woman he'd loved? A betrayal that had nearly cost him his life. And now his elder expected him to pretend to be in love with a human?

Cinead's voice was soft and fatherly, when he continued, "No, I haven't forgotten what you went through. And that's exactly why you're the perfect candidate. You've tasted betrayal. You've seen its signs. You're better prepared than anybody else. Would you really prefer I gave this mission to Manus? Or Logan? They are fine guardians, don't get me wrong. But they wouldn't be able to resist the lure of a woman like Tessa Wallace. Not if they had to pretend to be dating her."

"Lure?" What the hell was Cinead talking about? He'd seen photos of the councilwoman, and while she was certainly very attractive, even beautiful, he didn't understand where the danger lay. Sure, Manus had a reputation for being a philanderer, but he doubted that Cinead knew that. Their compound was a tight-knit group. They didn't kiss and tell.

"It's not her beauty that captivates men, though it certainly draws them to her. It's her soul."

He arched an eyebrow. "Her soul?"

"She's good through and through. Everything she does is for the good of others. She doesn't have a single malicious bone in her body, nor an evil thought in her mind."

"How would you know?"

"Our emissarius has been watching her for many years. I trust him and his judgment. Just like I trust yours." Cinead rose slowly and crossed the distance between them. "I know your heart broke when you lost the woman you loved, and I wish I could make it undone, my son, but I can't. However, maybe that broken heart is the one thing that will help you get through this mission without any emotional involvement. I can't say that for Logan or Manus. Either of them is likely to bring emotions into this mission, jeopardizing our goal. She has to become mayor. Baltimore needs her. Nothing and nobody can be allowed to lead her astray."

Hamish lowered his lids and sighed. He had no intention of falling in love ever again. It was wrought with too much danger. But that didn't mean he liked this assignment. The whole setup was unorthodox. Too many things could go wrong. Stealth Guardians operated in the background. They'd been given skills to make sure that they were never seen: the ability to cloak themselves so they were invisible—something they could extend to their charges either with their minds or their touch, the former requiring more energy than the latter—and the ability to walk through walls so no place was ever inaccessible to them—a skill they could not extend to their charges.

And now Cinead wanted him to operate out in the open? Visible to everybody?

"And the demons?"

"What about them?"

"They'll realize what I am as soon as they see me with her." They would recognize his aura as that of a Stealth Guardian, something only other preternatural creatures could see. Humans didn't have that skill.

"I know. But we don't have a choice. Besides, based on the rumors we hear about their new ruler, we must assume that they're employing different tactics now. Zoltan is more innovative than his predecessor. He'll find out either way that we're protecting her. He's too smart to think we'd leave somebody as valuable as Tessa Wallace unprotected."

Resigned, Hamish looked straight at Cinead. "Who do you want me to choose as my second?"

"Enya. However, I want her to operate in secrecy. Ms. Wallace is not to know about her. Just in case we need an ace up our sleeve."

At least with this order Hamish could agree. "Very well."

Enya, the only female in his compound, would be his backup for those times when he couldn't be with his charge. A wise choice, because despite her prickly nature, Enya was a fine warrior, and as a woman she would be immune to whatever charms Ms. Wallace had.

Just as he would be immune to them.

# 3

"Anton Faldo?" Tessa gaped at Poppy and looked up and down the corridor of the third floor of City Hall, where most of the offices of the council members were located. Seeing that this wasn't the place to discuss such a sensitive topic, she motioned Poppy toward her office, while murmuring through clenched teeth, "Are you out of your mind?"

"He's got the right connections," Poppy said, following her through the door to the antechamber where several assistants for various council members were working frantically, dealing with visitors and busy phone lines.

Tessa rushed past Collette, her own assistant, and flung the door to the office open, charging in. "Connections, my ass!" she hissed as soon as Poppy had stepped into her office. "Faldo is a crook. He's been under investigation several times."

"He's never been convicted," Poppy threw in.

Tessa huffed. "Only because he can afford the best lawyers money can buy. And he probably pays off anybody who gets in his way. The man's bad news."

"He supports your campaign and—"

"What?"

Poppy grimaced. "Don't you look at the donor reports I give you every day? He's one of the biggest contributors to your campaign."

Tessa threw up her hands. "That can't be!" If people found out about this, it would ruin her career.

"I thought you knew."

She fell into her chair, her hands supporting her head. "I can't take his money."

"You'll have to take much more than just his money. You need his help."

Tessa lifted her eyes to look at her campaign manager. They'd gone to college together, and she thought she knew Poppy inside out. Hadn't they always had the same values, the same high moral standards? What had happened to her friend? Had she sold out?

"How can you expect me to accept help from a criminal? He'll want something in return. If and when I'm mayor, he'll want favors. I'm not going to sell my integrity to some crook!"

Poppy leaned over the desk. "You have to be pragmatic. Faldo's donations are routed through one of his companies. Nobody's gonna put two and two together. As for favors: Faldo assured me that his help comes without any strings attached."

"And you believed him?" Because Tessa didn't. After all, there was no such thing as a free lunch. Particularly not in politics, where everything had its price, and everybody was for sale.

But Poppy continued, "Besides, do you really think that Gunn hasn't taken donations from less than savory sources?"

"I don't care what Gunn is doing. I'm not like him."

Poppy sighed. "I know that. But I don't think you recognize the seriousness of your situation. Somebody wants you dead, and I'll be damned if I'm going to reject Faldo's offer to send a bodyguard for you."

"A bodyguard? You mean one of his goons?"

"I've never been called a goon before," a deep voice said from the doorway.

Startled, Tessa jumped up and peered past Poppy. A tall man was leaning casually against the doorframe. He looked to be in his thirties, with thick, dark brown hair and dark stubble on his square chin. His eyes were dark—chocolate brown if she had to describe them. His cargo pants and casual shirt outlined his muscular physique, making him look like he was ready for combat. She ran her eyes over him, unable to look away. She'd never seen a man with such *presence*. Confidence oozed from every pore of his body. There was no doubt that his mere physical proximity could intimidate anybody. Though his photo could just as easily appear next to the word *heartthrob* in any dictionary.

Poppy whirled around. "You must be Mr. MacGregor. Mr. Faldo sent word earlier to expect you."

"I knocked, but I guess nobody heard me." Easing the door shut behind him, the man met Poppy halfway and shook her hand, his gaze straying past her to Tessa. "Hamish MacGregor, at your service. But nobody calls me Mr. MacGregor. I go by Hamish."

Only now could Tessa hear the slight Scottish accent. It made her insides tingle pleasantly, and her pulse kick up a notch.

Poppy gave a soft laugh, one Tessa was only too familiar with: it always surfaced when Poppy was attracted to somebody. And who wouldn't be attracted to Hamish MacGregor? But she wouldn't let a handsome face and a toned physique sway her in her conviction not to accept help from a criminal.

"Mr. Mac—"

"And you must be Miss Wallace," Hamish interrupted, stepping around the desk and offering his hand.

Short of being rude, Tessa felt obliged to shake his hand. "Yes. But as I just told my campaign manager, I don't need a bodyguard."

Hamish lifted one side of his mouth. "From the little I heard, it sounded more like you don't want to be protected by one of Mr. Faldo's goons."

She stiffened. Just how much of her conversation with Poppy had he overheard? "Well, since we're being blunt: I can't be associated with Mr. Faldo's... uh... operation."

He scrutinized her now, looking her up and down. "I'm not in Mr. Faldo's employ, if that's what troubles you."

"Maybe not on a regular basis, but he's footing the bill," she protested. And that meant she'd still be beholden to him in one way or another.

Hamish lifted an eyebrow. "I believe there's been a little misunderstanding. Mr. Faldo is only arranging my services. He's not paying for them."

She stared at Poppy, who nodded. "I thought I told you that I approached the Foodworkers' Union and got them to cover the expense."

Embarrassment swept through Tessa. "Oh. Why didn't you... I... uh..."

"Guess I forgot. I'm juggling way too many things right now," Poppy answered and looked at her watch. "Speaking of juggling, I've got a meeting with a reporter. Gotta go." She marched to the door. "Nice meeting you, Hamish."

"Poppy... That still doesn't mean I can accept..." But Poppy was already gone, leaving her alone with the handsome stranger.

This was never going to work. She couldn't accept this man as her bodyguard. How would she go about her work with him hovering over her? Besides, weren't bodyguards supposed to blend into the background? There was no chance in hell that Hamish MacGregor would ever be able to enter a room without being noticed. On the contrary, all eyes would be on him.

She cleared her throat. "I'm sorry, Mr. MacGregor—"

"Hamish," he corrected immediately, a soft rumbling sound in his voice that sent her off kilter.

"Hamish, I don't think this is going to work."

~ ~ ~

What had Cinead said? *Good through and through?* Not likely! Tessa Wallace was combative, stubborn, and made for sin. The kind of sin that left you sweaty and panting. The kind of sin he'd sworn off. What had Cinead been thinking, assigning him to this battle-ready, high-strung beauty with long dark brown hair and gorgeous lavender eyes?

"You won't be able to blend in," she now said.

Hamish frowned. "Blend in?"

"Everybody will wonder who you are, and I don't want anybody to know I have a bodyguard. It's bad enough that I need one."

He shrugged. "That's why you'll tell them I'm your boyfriend."

Panic flashed in her eyes. "What?"

"We discussed that it would be best if I posed as your boyfriend to avoid questions. It will arouse less suspicion."

She swallowed visibly. "We?"

"My superiors and I. We know what we're doing." Even though Hamish didn't agree with Cinead's order. However, the fact that his charge was objecting to the idea, made him involuntarily see the advantages of such an arrangement.

Tessa shook her head. "Nobody will believe it."

"Then we'll just have to make it look believable." At the thought of what that might entail, he felt a jolt of adrenaline rush through his veins. Instantly, he pushed the images from his mind. He wasn't going to make the same mistake his best friend Aiden had made when he'd fallen for his charge Leila. Even though in Aiden's case it had all turned out fine, Hamish knew from his own experience that not everybody was that lucky.

Hamish cleared his throat. "Let's go over the details."

"Details?" Tessa croaked and stared at him like a deer that found itself in the path of a speeding car.

Clearly she liked the idea of a pretend-boyfriend as little as he did. Not that either of them had a choice in the matter. She'd just have to come to terms with it like he had.

"Yes, the quicker we hash out the details, the more smoothly this will go down."

"Mr. MacGregor—"

"Tessa, you'll have to call me Hamish, or nobody will buy that I'm your boyfriend."

He noticed her nervously rub her hand on her pencil skirt, which accentuated her slim waist and long legs. "Hamish, I'm really not sure how this is going to work. I don't know you and you don't know me. There are going to be hundreds of occasions where we can trip each other up."

"We've thought of that, of course." Or rather, Cinead had. "That's why it'll be best for everybody to think that we only just started dating. How about a couple of weeks ago? That way we don't have to know much about each other."

"True," she conceded, "but aren't you supposed to protect me all the time?"

"Yes. So?"

She sighed as if annoyed that he didn't immediately know what she was referring to. "I wouldn't be seeing a guy that frequently if I'd just started dating him. It's not realistic."

"It is, if you're totally into him."

"But—"

He stepped closer so only a foot of space separated them. "Have you never been completely enamored with a man, even though you only just met him?" A flicker in her eyes told him that she'd had that experience previously. "Well, then you'll just have to recall what it felt like and act accordingly. And I'll do the same and pretend I can't bear to be without you. As long as people see us acting like a couple who can't keep their hands off each other, they won't question why I'm not leaving your side."

At least that was the plan. A plan where so many things could go wrong. A harmless touch could lead to something more. A pretend-kiss could kindle a flame that might be hard to put out again. It was better not to go down that road.

"Once the threat is over, we'll have a very public breakup, and everything will go back to how it was." There would be no emotional involvement, and the physical intimacy they'd have to show in the presence of others would only be a well-crafted performance.

"And how do we know when the threat is over?"

He hadn't expected her to ask this question and had no canned answer to it. No answer he could give her anyway. He and his fellow Stealth Guardians would be the ones to assess whether the threat hanging over her had vanished, once her unknown enemy realized that she was no easy target.

"Let that be my problem. You just concentrate on this election. Now I need a copy of your schedule for the next week, including all business and private meetings. I'll need to make sure the venues are safe and conduct background checks on the participants before I can approve your attendance at any event."

"Approve?" She glared at him. "You can't be serious."

He tilted his head to the side. "Do I look like I'm joking?"

"No, you look like you're about to be fired," Tessa grunted, her hands on her hips, her eyes spewing venom. "I decide which events I attend, not you!"

"Wrong."

"Consider yourself relieved of your duty, Mr. MacGregor!"

"You can't do that."

"I can and I will. I'm not dealing with an overpowering chauvinist prick who thinks he can order me around."

He crossed his arms over his chest. "Would you prefer your father finding out what danger you're in and have *him* curb your freedom instead?"

Her mouth opened. "How the f—"

"Whoa, what a nasty word for such a pretty mouth." And she did have a pretty mouth, though at present he didn't appreciate the defiant words coming from it. "I did my homework. And one thing you like even less than having to put up with a bodyguard is having your father find out you're in danger."

She let out an annoyed breath. "You're wrong. I'd rather deal with my father than have to pretend you're my boyfriend."

He gave her a tight smile. "And here I thought you were a good daughter who didn't want to aggravate her father's heart condition."

Caught in her bluff, she glared at him. For several seconds an internal struggle appeared to rage in her. Her chest heaved, her hands clenched, and her shoulders stiffened. Silence stretched between them.

Then she finally gave him an answer. "I can't wait for the day we break up."

"The feeling is mutual." He turned on his heel and stalked to the door. "I'll see myself out. I'll get your schedule from your campaign manager."

After all, there might be events that Tessa didn't feel he should accompany her to, and Poppy was less likely to leave anything off.

"I'll be back when you're ready to leave City Hall."

# 4

Hamish stormed into the men's room—which luckily was empty—and charged into one of the three stalls, slamming the metal door behind him so hard that the entire structure rattled.

"What was all that about?"

He whirled around and found himself face-to-face with Enya, who materialized right in front of him.

"What was what?" he growled. For a moment he'd forgotten that Enya had accompanied him to the initial meeting with his charge—though she had remained invisible the entire time just as Cinead had requested.

Dressed in black shorts and a red, rather tight top, her long blond hair braided and pinned around her head, a casual observer would have never guessed what a magnificent warrior she was—fearless and lethal. Both with her hands and her sharp tongue.

Enya crossed her arms over her chest and slanted him a *don't-bullshit-me* look. "Interesting approach you're taking with your new charge, buddy. Hope it works out."

"You're my second, so don't question my authority." As the sentinel, the lead guardian on the assignment, he was the one who gave the orders. Enya was his backup.

"Wouldn't dream of it," she replied. Her tone said otherwise, however, he had no intention of justifying his actions.

How could Cinead have been so wrong in his assessment of Tessa Wallace? The emissarius who'd claimed she was *good through and through* should have his head examined. Tessa was anything but. She was combative and head-strong. "She's a piece of work, that woman," he ground out.

"Because she didn't fall to your feet and say 'Yes, sir!' to everything you said?" Enya put her finger to her lips in a mock-contemplative gesture. "Hmm. Makes sense."

"What's your fucking problem?"

Enya shrugged. "I have no problem. Because I don't let my emotions get the better of me."

"Neither do I!" Though Tessa's opposition to his suggestions had riled him up. In a purely professional way, of course.

"My bad."

And now Enya was getting on his nerves by making more out of the situation than there was, turning a molehill into Mount Everest. "Don't apologize if you don't mean it."

"You really don't get it, do you?" she asked, shaking her head, her gaze a little softer now.

"Get what?"

She jerked her thumb over her shoulder. "A woman running for mayor isn't gonna be a pushover. Making her comply with certain rules so you can keep her safe will take some finesse. I always thought you of all people had a boatload of that at your fingertips."

"Guess I'm fresh out of finesse."

At that, she chuckled, a sweet sound that reminded him of why he'd always seen and treated her like a younger sister, even though she was practically the same age as he.

"You'd better stock up on it then, because you'll need her cooperation if this whole fake boyfriend-girlfriend scenario is supposed to work. There's only so much I can do in the shadows."

He lifted his hand, stopping her. He knew his duties. "I don't need anybody telling me what I'm supposed to do. Which brings me to your duties." It was best to deflect from him now. Enya had already stirred up too much shit for one morning.

"Don't worry, I know what to do," she said almost bored. "I'll be staying in her office, checking out her visitors and the staff that's coming in and out. I won't leave her side until it's time for you to take over."

"If she makes any appointments or agrees to any events without putting them on the calendar or notifying her campaign manager or me, I'll need to know."

"Understood. But do you honestly think she'd try to sneak past you?"

"She didn't exactly like the idea of me accompanying her to every event."

Enya rolled her eyes. "She's not stupid. She knows that if she wants to be safe, she needs to stick with you. She'll just have to get used to the idea. She strikes me as an independent woman who's not used to asking for permission. Put yourself in her shoes for a moment. Would you like it if some stranger suddenly showed up and said you couldn't do this or that and would need to run every decision about your whereabouts by them? Answer: no, you wouldn't like it at all."

He grunted, but he knew Enya was right.

"So why don't you make it a little easier on her?"

"How?"

"Don't provoke her. She'll only fight back like a caged tigress."

Enya's last words conjured up an image of Tessa dressed in a slinky outfit charging at him and tossing him on a bed, mounting him, mauling him...

Fuck!

He ran a shaky hand through his hair. He hadn't had fantasies like that in a long time. Not since his ill-fated almost-union with Olivia—a woman the demons had manipulated to get to him. And he'd fallen for it, for her. Hard. But it had all been a lie. A lie that had nearly killed him. Was it then a surprise that whenever he saw a woman who stirred any kind of feelings in him, he lashed out in anger, hoping to drive her away before he made the same mistake again? Before he got emotionally involved and let those emotions cloud his decisions.

"... and maybe a box of chocolates. Those always work wonders. Every woman loves them," Enya said.

"What?" How long had he zoned out?

"Why the fuck do I bother giving you advice when you don't even listen?"

"I *was* listening," he lied.

She looked him straight in the eye. "So what did I say then?"

"To give her chocolates."

"And?" She pressed her lips into a thin line.

He scrambled for an answer. "Say something nice to her."

Clearly surprised, Enya arched one eyebrow. "So you do listen occasionally."

*Lucky guess.* After all, he wasn't born yesterday. He had been with enough women to know how to pacify one: pay her compliments, and shower her with gifts. How hard could it be?

"Just don't lay it on too thick. Women can smell it when a man is insincere."

"Enya?"

"Hmm?"

"Get the hell out of here! My capacity for listening to bullshit advice has reached its limit for today."

Chuckling, Enya eased back, walking through the metal door without opening it, while her body turned invisible. "She's got spunk. Maybe I can learn something from her."

He couldn't let her have the last word and swung the stall door open. "You're supposed to just follow my fucking orders. If you can't comply—"

But Enya was already gone. Instead, a man in a suit had entered the restroom and stared at him, shaking his head.

"Man, just do the deed in private. And for God's sake, don't talk to it."

Cursing three ways to heaven, Hamish hurried past him, embarrassment and anger sweeping through him in equal measure. But that wasn't the worst of it. Having to play boyfriend to this bossy woman, who didn't know what real danger she was in, was by far the bigger problem. Cinead had been wrong: the betrayal he'd suffered hadn't inoculated him against being attracted to a woman he had no business desiring.

But he wasn't taking the blame for this. No, he had a very convenient scapegoat up his sleeve: *rasen*. Every Stealth Guardian experienced the mating call the closer he got to his two-hundredth birthday. *Rasen*, the need to find a mate and procreate, influenced a Stealth Guardian much in the same way a dog was affected by a bitch in heat. But Hamish was determined to ignore it—even if that mating call came in the form of the most delectable female he'd ever encountered.

*Rasen* could kiss his bloody ass!

# 5

When her assistant Collette, a leggy black woman in her mid forties, popped her head into the office, Tessa looked up from her files.

"Tessa, I'm leaving now," Collette said. "And so should you if you want to make it to the party on time. Traffic is hell out there. Did you hear they had to close off Park Avenue because of a demonstration?"

"Oh, crap!" Tessa shut the file and jumped up from her armchair, glancing at her wristwatch. "I didn't realize it was that late already. Thank you, Collette. Is Poppy still in the building?" Maybe Poppy could ride with her so she wouldn't have to be alone with her new bodyguard, who'd texted her that afternoon to tell her he'd be picking her up at City Hall to take her to the event.

"No, she left long ago. Said she had meetings outside the office. I believe she was planning to meet you at the party."

Tessa pasted a fake smile on her face to hide her disappointment. "That's perfect, thanks. Have a great night, Collette."

"You, too, Tessa," her assistant replied and left, easing the door shut.

"Damn it," she cursed as she collected her handbag.

It was time to get ready to leave. She quickly checked her clothes, making sure there were no stains on her blouse, then slipped into her gray suit jacket. She'd chosen this outfit especially this morning, because she could wear it both to the office and the event and wouldn't have to waste any time by stopping by at home and getting changed.

Tessa pulled out her compact and perused her reflection. Did her cheeks look a little red? She shrugged. So what if they did. She wasn't going to the event to win a beauty contest.

Her stomach growled. No wonder. She'd skipped lunch in order to receive several concerned constituents who had family members embroiled in the recent riots downtown. They'd been beside themselves, begging her for help, claiming their sons had nothing to do with the fights that had taken place at a demonstration. After two hours of listening to the same story over and over again, she'd been exhausted and close to tears. Something had to change in this city.

Switching off the light on her way out, she closed the door and locked it. The antechamber, which was shared by four assistants, all working for one council member or another, was empty. She was crossing the room when she heard a noise behind her. Spinning around, she instinctively gripped her handbag tighter, hoping to use it as a shield against an attacker. She froze. There was nobody behind her, just the closed door of her office and Collette's tidy desk a few feet to its left.

Heart beating into her throat, she cast frantic looks in every direction, but she was alone.

"Shit!" she cursed under her breath.

She was definitely losing it. She hadn't wanted to acknowledge it until now, but the death threat two days earlier had rattled her, and the arrival of the bodyguard had driven the reality of her situation home. She was in danger because somebody didn't like her political agenda, when all she wanted was to bring peace and prosperity back to this city. The people of Baltimore needed her, and therefore *she* needed to win this election. And that's why—even though she didn't like Hamish's macho attitude—she would just have to play along with her overbearing bodyguard.

And her bodyguard was already waiting for her when she reached the lobby. He'd changed clothes and was now wearing a dark blue suit with a lavender-colored tie. But even the elegant attire couldn't disguise his muscular physique or the fact that he looked like he could overturn a tank singlehanded. To her surprise he smiled at her as she approached him, and when she reached him, he leaned in and kissed her on the cheek.

"You look great, Tessa."

Shocked at the physical intimacy and the compliment, she froze, unable to form a coherent sentence. She felt him lean even closer, his hand on the small of her back now, his mouth near her ear.

"This is where you say, thanks for picking me up, Hamish," he whispered.

He wore no aftershave that she could detect, and he smelled more masculine than any man she'd ever been near. Trying to get her rapidly beating heart under control, she pulled back a few inches and stepped out of his almost-embrace.

"Hi, Hamish, I hope you didn't have to wait long."

He offered his arm, and she had no choice but to accept it, allowing him to walk her past building security to the large double doors leading out of the building.

"You're worth waiting for," he said.

She cast him a sideways look and lowered her voice to a whisper. "You don't have to lay it on that thick. Nobody's watching us."

He graced her with a devastatingly charming smile. "You never know." Then he winked at her. "Besides, I need the practice. We both do."

She had no comeback for this.

At the bottom of the stairs, he let go of her arm and opened the passenger door of a black Mercedes and helped her in. She slunk into the elegant interior. Moments later, Hamish got in on the driver's side and started the engine.

He motioned to the controls. "If you want the air condition on, feel free. Or if you're too cold, I can switch on the seat warmer."

She raised an eyebrow. "Why so friendly all of a sudden?"

He pulled away from the curb and eased into the evening traffic. "I think you got the wrong impression of me earlier."

"Did I?"

"Apparently. And I know that's partially my fault. I'm not used to my charges refusing protection."

"And I'm not used to somebody telling me where I can and cannot go."

"I realize that. That's why I propose a truce."

"What kind of truce?"

He looked at her briefly. "The only kind of truce there is: where both parties lay down their arms and agree not to start a fight."

She shrugged. "I never started a fight with you."

He opened his mouth, but then closed it again. For a moment he said nothing, then, "Well, then I guess it's up to me to apologize for the argument in your office."

"Guess it is." She wasn't going to make this easy on him, because she had to set one thing straight: she was the client.

"I'm sorry if I came on a little strong earlier," he started, his voice a little gruff, as if it irked him that he had to apologize—or as if he'd never done it before and was entirely unfamiliar with the concept. "But all I'm concerned about is your safety, and I'm not going to make any compromises when it comes to that. As you may have guessed, I'm not too wild about having to pretend to be your boyfriend, but from now on neither you nor anybody else will notice that. I guarantee it."

While she appreciated his apology, he'd practically negated it with his last words. He wasn't too wild about being her pretend-boyfriend? "And you think *I'm* wild about it?" She blew out an outraged breath and looked out the side window. "If I had time to date, you wouldn't be my first choice either."

"Ouch," he said, accompanied by a barely suppressed chuckle.

She whirled her head to him and saw him grinning. Damn, why did that annoy her so much? Or was it not the smile that riled her up, but the fact that he didn't like the idea of dating her? As if she wasn't good enough for him. Or pretty enough. Or—oh screw it! Why did she even care? Well, she didn't!

"Hmm, now that we've cleared that up, I'm sure we'll get on famously," he prophesized. "Nothing helps a relationship flourish like low expectations."

"Aren't I lucky?"

# 6

Hamish took a deep, calming breath, stopping himself from replying to Tessa's comment.

*Keep it together, man!*

Fuck, he wasn't good at this. It had been hard enough to apologize, and he'd be damned if he made any more concessions. Maybe she could treat a real boyfriend like this, but not him. And everything had started so well. He'd paid her a compliment, kissed her on the cheek, led her to the car like a gentleman. He'd even opened the car door for her. What else did she want from him?

*If I had time to date, you wouldn't be my first choice either.*

Her cold words echoed in his mind. She'd made it pretty clear that she didn't like him. He should be happy about it. After all, didn't that make things easier? At least he wouldn't be tempted to act on his inexplicable attraction to her, knowing she would reject any advances anyway. But instead of welcoming her indifference toward him, it pissed him off.

"We'll be there soon," he said into the silence.

"There's a lot of traffic," Tessa said, her voice sounding doubtful as she pointed to the intersection ahead of them.

By the time they reached it, it was clear why no one was getting through. On the street to their left, an angry mob had formed. What or whom they were angry at wasn't immediately discernible. After all, random riots seemed to break out pretty much every other day lately. And this mob was armed with baseball bats and stones.

"Shit!" Hamish cursed and looked for an escape route. He was already blocked in by traffic behind him. And while he had enough space in front to do a U-turn, oncoming traffic had blocked that lane too, preventing him from turning around the way they came.

Crossing the intersection wasn't an option. The police had already barricaded the street. His only option was to turn right. When he glanced at Tessa, he noticed her apprehensive look.

"It's getting worse every day," she murmured.

"I'll get us out of here."

Turning the wheel sharply to the right, he pulled them out of traffic and jumped the curb. They drove down the broad sidewalk, two wheels on the street, two on the sidewalk. Good thing that all the pedestrians had fled, not wanting to be caught up in the angry mob that was now bashing in windows and throwing rocks at cars, shouting and yelling unintelligible things.

The moment he saw an alley to his right, he took it and raced through it faster than he should. But he'd managed to get his precious passenger out of the danger zone. That was all that mattered.

Now his mind was free again to think of other things. Such as how lovely Tessa had looked when she'd walked toward him in the lobby. There'd been a glow about her, and her lavender eyes had looked even more brilliant than they had earlier in the day. And the closer she'd gotten, the more vibrant they'd become. At that thought he caught his own reflection in the windshield and noticed the same color reflecting back at him. But the color didn't come from Tessa's eyes, it came from his tie.

He did a double-take. Had he accidentally chosen a tie to match her eyes? What the fuck was wrong with him?

Annoyed at himself for not making more of an effort to suppress the effect *rasen* was clearly having on him, he tried to concentrate on driving until they arrived at the event.

Just barely on time, he pulled up to the curb where a valet was already waiting to take the car keys. He jumped out and snatched the ticket from the guy, grunted a quick "Thank you" and walked around the car. But he wasn't quick enough. Tessa had already gotten out. He closed the car door behind her and took her elbow.

She whipped her head around to him. "What?"

"Careful, the stairs are uneven, and there isn't really enough light." He pointed to the steps that led up to the entrance of the industrial-looking building. This was definitely not one of those fancy hotel fundraiser events that politicians liked to attend. This looked a lot less elegant. "Take my arm, please," he said in a softer tone, back in pretend-boyfriend mode now.

When she finally hooked her arm under his, he placed his hand over hers, pressing down gently. He felt a corresponding shiver race up his arm and down his spine, reminding him of how long it had been since he'd touched a woman.

"When we're in there, I'm going to have to mingle," she said.

"No worries, I won't be in your way." He could just as easily watch her from a little distance. Maybe that would be better anyway.

"Good."

They arrived at the entrance, where a young Asian woman in her early twenties stood waiting with a clipboard. "Name, please."

"Tessa Wallace," Tessa replied.

"Oh, Miss Wallace, I'm sorry I didn't immediately recognize you. It's just so dark out here. You know, something went wrong with the lights earlier, and the electricians haven't been able to fix it yet," she babbled excitedly.

"That's alright," Tessa said in a friendly tone.

The woman leaned in a little, putting Hamish on alert immediately. "And just so you know, you have my vote. We need somebody like you."

Tessa beamed at her and reached her hand out. "That's so sweet of you to say. Thank you, I really appreciate your support."

They shook hands, and the woman looked back at her clipboard. "Odd, you RSVP'd for only one person. Hmm."

"I'm sorry," Hamish interrupted and smiled at the woman. "That's entirely my mistake. I didn't think I could make it tonight, but then something got cancelled and I was able to accompany Tessa after all. I hope that won't be a problem."

She gave him a hushed glance, her cheeks turning a darker shade of red, before she smiled back. "No, of course not, any guest of Miss Wallace is welcome." She stared at the spot where Tessa's arm was still linked with his. "I'll just have to make a note of who you are and in what capacity you're here tonight."

"Hamish MacGregor. Just put me down as the lucky guy who's dating Miss Wallace." He winked at her.

"Oh, yes, of course, Mr. MacGregor. Have a great night." She shifted her gaze back to Tessa. "Both of you I mean."

As he ushered Tessa inside, he glanced back. More people were lined up behind them, waiting to be let in. Hamish let his gaze roam, assessing his surroundings. There was a stage at one end, high tables with drinks and canapés along the walls, and a small dance floor off to one side. A tacky 80s disco ball hung over the center of the dance floor. It turned, reflecting light from several colored spotlights onto the walls and ceiling, as well as the guests. Music was piping in from somewhere. An abundance of sparkling lights provided for a ritzy party atmosphere in the large, industrial-style hall with its exposed ducts and beams running along the high ceiling.

He looked at Tessa, whose eyes were already roaming to ascertain who was in attendance.

"What kind of event is this anyway?" he asked.

"I thought you looked at my schedule."

"It looks like your campaign manager only sent me the abbreviated version." Something he had to remedy later. "It only gave me the location and the time."

"Must have been an oversight."

Hamish cocked an eyebrow. Oversight, his ass! "Yeah, sure." Then he motioned to the crowd in the large hall. "So, what's this all about?"

"It's the opening of the new drug rehabilitation center."

"The one the City Council opposed so staunchly?"

She nodded. "You know your city politics. I was able to push it through, but one of the concessions was that they had to establish it out here."

He looked at her, understanding what she meant. "Not exactly the best part of town. Not a good place for getting addicts away from bad influences."

Her face lit up. "That's exactly what I told the other council members. But they refused to see my point."

"Let me guess: they didn't want it in their backyard, or the backyard of their constituents."

She sighed. "But the center was needed so badly, I had to make compromises. I just hope we don't end up paying for it later."

"It's a start. You should be proud of it."

"I am." She looked around, motioning to the crowd. "I just wish I could have done more. But Gunn was opposing me all the way."

"The acting mayor?"

"He wasn't acting mayor then. He was just a council member like myself. And his district was where the center was supposed to be located. They'd already secured a building. But he mobilized the council to oppose the application." She suddenly looked past Hamish, her eyes widening, her mouth dropping open. "Oh that little shit! What is he doing here?"

Hamish spun his head in the direction of Tessa's gaze. There, only a few yards away, Robert Gunn, the acting mayor, was shaking hands with another man.

"Who is Gunn talking to?" Hamish asked, motioning to the well-dressed older man with the dark hair which, judging by his gray eyebrows, was dyed.

Tessa shot him a look, anger spewing from her eyes now. "Bill Mantle, the director of the center."

Suddenly there was a lull in the music and Mantle could be heard saying to Gunn, "Without you supporting us, we would have never gotten this off the ground. How can I ever thank you?"

Gunn laughed. "Well, not that I'd ever wanted anything in return, but since you're asking..."

Just then the music got louder again, drowning out the rest of Gunn's reply. Hamish looked back at Tessa, whose jaw was clenching.

"He's taking credit even though he opposed the center all along. That jerk," she murmured, outrage in her voice, and pushed past him.

But Hamish grabbed her arm, holding her back.

"Let me go!"

He pulled her closer, sliding one arm around her waist. "Don't! You going and accusing him of stealing your thunder won't help now."

"But—"

"Trust me, Tessa, you don't want people to remember you as the hysterical bitch who started a pissing match with the acting mayor. It'll only play into his hands."

"I'm not hysterical! He opposed the center, and now he's pretending to be for it."

Hamish steered her in the opposite direction, guiding her to the dance floor, while she continued her protests. After all, Cinead's directive had been to keep her on the right path, and starting a brawl was definitely not the way to go, as much as he understood her anger.

Once on the dance floor, he pulled her into his arms and started to dance.

"What are you doing?" she protested.

"Stopping you from doing something stupid."

"How dare you?" she hissed and tried to get out of his arms. Without success.

He drew her closer so her body was flush to his, their chests, hips, and thighs touching. She drew in a sharp breath as if only now realizing the intimacy of their situation.

Hamish bent his head to her ear. "Now pretend you actually enjoy dancing with your boyfriend, and don't look like you'd rather be somewhere else. People are watching."

She grumbled indistinctly, but fell into step with him. After a few moments, he eased up on his tight grip, but Tessa continued to follow his lead with such grace, it felt like they'd practiced together many hours.

"You dance very well," he murmured, enjoying the moment. How long exactly had it been since he'd danced with a woman?

"So do you." She lifted her eyes to look at him. "But you don't have to do this. I'm calmer now. I promise. I'm not gonna start a fight with Gunn."

He chuckled. "Right."

She stiffened slightly, making him stroke his hand gently along her lower back.

"Hamish," she ground out under her breath, her eyes darting to the side as if checking if anybody was close enough to hear her. "I said you can let me go now."

"No, you said I don't have to do this."

"Same thing. We don't need to dance."

"Why?" he asked, pinning her with his eyes. "What are you afraid of? That you might actually have fun?"

Goddamn it! Before picking her up, he'd resolved to use his charm to make her comply with his commands—just like Enya had suggested (though he would never admit that to his fellow guardian.) And everything had been going well enough so far. So why was he getting annoyed with her again? Was it because she was so adamantly against being touched by him? Did she find him that revolting? And what if that was the case? Why should that bother him? This was just an assignment like any other. She was a human woman, and he'd sworn off human women, not wanting to fall into the same trap a second time.

"I don't... I'm not..." she stammered, appearing embarrassed.

Despite her words and against his better judgment, he led her into another turn, twirling her, then bringing her back to him. She gasped, and her chest heaved. Her cheeks seemed flushed all of a sudden, a shy smile forming on her lips. For a moment he forgot what he was here for. He only saw her red cheeks, her sparkling lavender eyes, and her plump lips—lips he liked to imagine were parted in invitation. How long had it been since he'd accepted such an invitation? How long since he'd kissed a woman? Did he even remember what the lips of a woman tasted like?

All he had to do was lean in closer...

"Tessa, there you are!"

# 7

Tessa looked in the direction of the voice and instinctively stopped dancing, easing herself out of Hamish's arms—arms that had felt far too tempting. She'd nearly forgotten why she was at this event. The person now standing only a few feet away from her reminded her of the purpose of this evening.

"Gabriella, so nice to see you!" Tessa quickly said to the deputy director of the center, and extended her hand in greeting.

Shaking her hand, Gabriella glanced past her at Hamish, then back at her. "I didn't mean to interrupt, but we wanted to get all the speeches out of the way, so we can all have fun, right?" She giggled like a schoolgirl, her eyes darting past Tessa once more. "Though it looks like you started already."

At Gabriella's obvious hint, Tessa turned and motioned to Hamish. "Gabriella, this is Hamish MacGregor, my, uh, boyfriend." God, that sounded so strange, though she didn't know whether that was because she hated lying or because having a boyfriend seemed such a distant memory. "Hamish, this is Gabriella VanSant, the deputy director of the new center."

Hamish shook her hand and unleashed a devastatingly charming smile. "What a pleasure to finally meet you. Tessa speaks very highly of you."

Tessa nearly choked at the ease with which the lie rolled over Hamish's lips. What if Gabriella started asking questions about just what Tessa had presumably said about her?

"The pleasure is all mine." Gabriella giggled again, making her look at least ten years younger. Clearly, even a woman in her sixties could still be charmed by a handsome man, even if that man was a good twenty-five years younger than her. What did they call women like that again? Oh right, *cougars*.

Just then Gabriella cast her a chastising look. "Where have you been hiding this man all these months?"

"Uh, oh, I didn't. It's just, I—"

Hamish took Tessa's hand. "Tessa and I haven't been dating for very long." He smiled at her, then looked back at their host. "Though we are quite inseparable these days. I'm sure a woman like you, Ms. VanSant, knows all about the excitement of new love."

Gabriella blushed furiously. Hamish had managed to make her a compliment by alluding that she too was desirable and could attract a man who was crazy about her. She was still beautiful despite her age and her wrinkles. Even the extra pounds she carried around her hips and stomach couldn't detract from that.

Laughing, Gabriella playfully slapped her hand against his bicep, before turning back to Tessa. "Tessa, you'd better watch this guy, or any number of women here will try and snatch him away from you."

Hamish laughed. "Not a chance."

*Yeah*, Tessa felt like saying, *because I'm paying him to be by my side.*

Instead, she simply smiled, playing the love-struck girlfriend.

"So, Mr. MacGregor, are you in politics, too?"

"No, far from it. I'm a writer."

Interest spread on Gabriella's face. "Oh, how exciting! What do you write?"

"Instruction manuals for heavy industrial machinery. It's quite fascinating. I'm currently working on a really exciting new machine."

"Oh!" The disappointment in Gabriella's voice was palpable. She tried to hide it with a smile. "Well, that's excellent." Then she looked at her watch. "Tessa, shall we meet at the stage in about five minutes? I'll drum up the other speakers by then."

"Sounds great, I'll be there in a moment," Tessa replied. "Oh, and Gabriella, have you seen my campaign manager? She was supposed to meet me here."

"Poppy is already at the stage," Gabriella said, before addressing Hamish. "It was nice meeting you, Mr. MacGregor."

As soon as she was out of earshot, Tessa turned to Hamish. "Instruction manuals for heavy industrial machinery? Why on earth?"

"In my job, I'm used to blending in. Trust me, nobody wants to talk to me once they hear I write instruction manuals. There can't be anything more boring, and nobody wants to be stuck with a talker who prattles on about some boring technical stuff. Or did you not notice how fast Ms. VanSant lost interest?"

She had to admit he had a point. "I guess."

He leaned in. "Or would you rather your boyfriend were a doctor or a lawyer?"

"I think I can handle a guy who writes instruction manuals just fine." In fact if that were Hamish's real profession, maybe she would find him less intimidating. But as things stood, being in the presence of a bodyguard, even if he was *her* bodyguard, was still something she needed to get used to.

Tessa pointed to the side of the hall where the stage was located. "I should make my way to the stage and get ready to say a few words."

Hamish took her arm. "I'll walk with you." He started guiding her through the crowd. "So what was this building before anyway? Looks pretty industrial."

"It was a tool factory once. But the work was outsourced to a country where labor was cheaper, and since then the space has lain empty. It turned into an eyesore. Gangs hung around here, doing their worst. The owner turned a blind eye."

"So he sold it to the center?" Hamish guessed.

"Not exactly. He donated it. Big tax write-off apparently."

"All's well that ends well."

She shrugged. "I guess so."

Arriving at the stage—a simple wooden construction only about three feet off the floor—Hamish let go of her arm.

"I'll be watching from here."

She nodded and took the three steps leading up to the platform where several people were already assembled. She wasn't surprised to see Gunn there. He was cozying up to the director, Bill Mantle, while Gabriella and a volunteer adjusted the microphone and some cables at the podium. Poppy waved at her, looking all dressed-up and sparkling for the occasion. She wore black pants that flared at her feet and a blouse of the same color covered in silver sequins that reflected the light of the room in rainbow colors. She looked like she'd stepped out of an 80s movie and was going to break into song and dance any second. But before Tessa could go say hi to Poppy, Gunn noticed her, and she had no choice but to greet him.

She nodded to Mantle first. "Nice to see you again, Mr. Mantle." Then she turned to Gunn. "Robert. Didn't realize you were attending this event."

He smiled broadly. "As the mayor—"

"Acting mayor," she corrected him.

"… acting mayor, I have to attend important events like these." His smile didn't waiver. "Besides, I'm a staunch supporter of drug rehabilitation."

That last sentence was clearly added to butter up the director. But Tessa knew better. Gunn didn't care one way or another about drug rehabilitation as long as it didn't take place in his backyard. He didn't represent the underprivileged in this city. He was on the side of the rich.

"And your support is very much appreciated," Mantle said before Tessa could find the right words to refute his claim.

Gabriella joined them at that moment. "We're ready to start. I'll make the introductions, then Mayor Gunn will speak, then Miss Wallace, and you, Bill, will do the closing."

"I insist on Miss Wallace going first," Gunn interrupted. "I don't want to steal her limelight. After all, she worked very hard to get the City Council to approve this center. I really don't need to speak at all. I'm happy with just being here, observing."

Surprised at his words, Tessa raised an eyebrow.

"Are you sure, Mr. Gunn?" Gabriella asked. "We do have enough time allocated for everybody to speak."

Gunn waved her off. "No, no. Please let Miss Wallace have her day in the sun. It's all her achievement."

"That's very generous of you, Mr. Gunn," Mantle said and motioned to Gabriella. "Let's start then."

Tessa glanced back at Gunn. "Thank you, Robert."

But in the back of her mind, questions started to pop up. Since when did Robert Gunn surrender the stage to a political opponent?

# 8

The chatter of the attendees simmered down in anticipation. Hamish listened only halfheartedly while Gabriella introduced the people on the small stage. Instead, he let his eyes roam, perusing the assembled.

He stood near the steps that led up to the stage, where thanks to his height, he had a good view of the crowd. He zoomed in on those in the audience who held cameras in their hands. A few flashes lit up the room. Other people were taking videos with their smart phones. His eyes searched for guns or any other weapons, but he didn't detect anything suspicious.

Nevertheless he remained vigilant, though he doubted the demons were stupid enough to try anything in such a public venue where bystanders were ready to record everything with their cameras. After all, the demons had to worry about exposure too—and unlike Stealth Guardians, they couldn't make themselves invisible. So if a demon was indeed here among the spectators, Hamish would eventually spot him.

People who were planning trouble always gave it away—either by acting suspiciously or by trying too hard to fit in. Either way, they stuck out. So he watched for those who didn't clap when everybody else did, didn't laugh when a speaker cracked a joke. But most of all he watched for those who kept their eyes shielded, either by wearing glasses or by keeping their gaze on the floor, because there was one physical characteristic every demon had: green eyes.

Their eyes and their green blood was the only outward proof of their demonic nature. The aura that surrounded other preternatural creatures—vampires, witches and the like—and made it possible for Stealth Guardians to identify them, was absent in demons. The Stealth Guardians assumed that this was the case because most, if not all, demons had once been human—before they'd committed acts so atrocious that the underworld had claimed their soul. He'd never heard of anyone who'd been redeemed after surrendering to the demons and joining their ranks—ranks that seemed to grow exponentially the more violence and fear ruled the world.

"... without whose help we could have never gotten this far." Tessa's voice penetrated his mind and he glanced at her up on the stage, speaking freely without any notes. "And all of you, who donated so generously to this worthy cause: thank you for your support."

Applause followed Tessa's heartfelt words and grew louder with every second. The noise seemed to turn more grating in his ears, almost metallic. Something didn't feel right.

A prickling sensation traveled up his spine, and he scanned the crowd, then stared back at Tessa who still stood at the lectern, drinking in the adoration of the crowd. Tears seemed to shimmer in her eyes, and she wiped them with her hand. Light was dancing on her face, reflecting off the disco ball that was still turning at the other end of the room. The silver bracelet around her wrist caught some of it, too.

Involuntarily, Hamish looked up at the ceiling.

"Shit!" he cursed and charged up the steps to the podium.

He heard it starting—a ripping sound, metal snapping—and he didn't stop even for a split second. He vaulted toward Tessa, his feet barely touching the ground, his arms stretched out, reaching. He pushed her away from the lectern, hurtling on top of her as she tumbled to the floor. Behind Hamish, metal crashed onto the wooden podium, but Tessa was covered by his body, shielded from falling debris.

Cries of shock and horror echoed in the room as the applause died instantly.

"Tessa, you alright?" he managed to ask.

Beneath him, Tessa trembled. He could feel her heart thundering, or was it his?

"Yes."

"I've got you, lass, I've got you," he murmured in relief.

Slowly he lifted his body off her and looked over his shoulder to where Tessa had stood only seconds earlier. The lectern had been obliterated by a heavy metal duct—probably part of the air conditioning system. Had Tessa been hit, she would have been severely injured, if not killed.

*Shit, shit, shit!*

His heart raced uncontrollably.

He'd been watching the people, but neglected to check whether the stage or its surroundings had been rigged to cause an accident.

"Oh Tessa, no!" Poppy screamed.

"Oh my God, how horrible!" Gabriella cried out, her voice high-pitched and panicking.

"Tessa, are you okay?" It was Gunn who came running now, followed by Mantle. Others climbed onto the stage.

"Stay back!" Hamish ordered, lifting his arm to underscore his command. "I've got her. She's alright."

"You're a hero!" Gabriella exclaimed, and others repeated her words.

But he didn't care about any of that. All he cared about was Tessa's safety. She was still on the ground, trying to sit up now, and he was still crouched down next to her. He reached for her and pulled her into his arms. When she finally met his gaze, sheer fear was reflected in her beautiful lavender eyes.

"Hamish…"

"What a terrible accident!" Gunn said from behind him. "Mr. Mantle, there's no way you can open the center now. You'll need to get all the construction inspected again. I insist. It's not safe."

Hamish couldn't hear the reply as Mantle pulled Gunn to the side, talking to him in hushed tones.

"I'm taking you home."

Tessa didn't protest when he helped her up, but she flinched when he set her back on her feet.

"Are you hurt?"

"Do you need anything, Tessa?" Poppy interrupted. "I can drive you home."

Tessa shook her head. "I'm just a bit bruised."

Hamish looked her up and down and noticed an abrasion on one knee. "You're bleeding."

"It doesn't hurt."

"I'll clean it up for you when we get you home." Then he looked at Poppy. "I'll take care of her. Thanks, Poppy."

He put his arm around Tessa and led her toward the steps. Gabriella walked with them, a worried look on her face.

"We should call an ambulance," she suggested.

"Thanks Ms. VanSant, but I'll take care of Tessa."

Gabriella looked at Tessa for confirmation and received it in the form of a nod.

"I'll call you tomorrow to see how you're doing," Gabriella called after her, "and we'll have an inquiry into how this accident could have happened."

Amidst a few camera flashes, Hamish ushered Tessa from the stage and to the nearest exit as quickly as he could. Time was of the essence now. He needed to contact his colleagues so they could investigate this attempt on Tessa's life before anybody had a chance to destroy evidence.

Because this was no accident.

# 9

Numb, Tessa allowed Hamish to walk her to his car and help her into the passenger seat while bystanders took pictures with their cell phones and talked excitedly. So many voices overlapped each other that she couldn't even hear what they were saying. The resulting noise felt deafening, and only when Hamish finally slunk into the driver's seat and slammed the car door shut, did a semblance of calm settle over her. Only now could she hear her heart beating frantically, and feel the cold sweat that beaded her neck and spine.

She looked at her hands; they were trembling. She clasped them together to make the shaking stop, but it didn't.

"We'll be home soon. You're safe now." Hamish's voice was soothing, but not even his reassuring words could keep the memory of what had just happened at bay.

The images started replaying in front of her eyes. The applauding crowd. Then Hamish slamming into her like a freight train, knocking her off her feet so she crashed hard onto the rough wooden floor. The sound of metal falling onto the lectern. And then, when Hamish had released her, she saw it for the first time: the massive air duct that would have crushed her under its weight, just like it had reduced the wooden lectern to splinters. The recollection of it made her shudder.

"I need to make a phone call," Hamish said, an apologetic tone in his voice.

She nodded automatically, but couldn't get a word past her parched throat for fear it would come out as a sob. Instead she looked out the side window, desperate to push the disturbing images out of her mind. She didn't believe in coincidences, not in coincidences that could have cost her life. Not after the threat she'd received anyway. Until now, she hadn't truly believed that somebody really wanted to harm her, but now she had to face facts.

"Yeah, Enya, we've had an incident," Hamish said into the phone and continued after a few seconds' pause. "A piece of an air duct fell onto the stage where Tessa was speaking tonight. Nearly hit her... yeah, exactly, that's what I think. I need you and the team to go to the new Center for Drug Rehabilitation and check things out... You've got my GPS location from ten minutes ago? Good, just get there as fast as you can. I need to know how it happened. Look at the air conditioning system, electrical, lighting, the works. And check the duct. It looked new to me, but I could be wrong... Yeah, thanks. Oh, and another thing: a lot of the attendees had cameras and were filming the event."

Tessa glanced at him then, surprised by his train of thought. No wonder he was a bodyguard. He remained calm under pressure. Unlike her.

"I need to see the footage. I'm sure everybody's already uploading their videos and photos to social media. Check every platform and copy everything to our servers. Get Pearce on that. I want to review every scrap of evidence. Somebody has to have caught something. That thing didn't just fall down on its own." He paused for a few seconds, casting her a sideways glance, then said into the phone, "Yeah, call me as soon as you've got something. I'll be at Tessa's."

He disconnected the call and dropped his cell phone into the cup holder between their seats.

"Who was that?" she heard herself ask.

"Enya, one of my colleagues. She and the team will figure out how this could have happened."

"I doubt that the center employees will let them snoop around. I'm sure they've called the police by now."

"Don't worry, our company collaborates with the police all the time." He gave her a reassuring look.

"Is there a chance that this was an accident?" Maybe she was just overreacting. Maybe something had gone wrong during the renovation of the space. Perhaps it was shoddy work and not a nefarious plot to eliminate her from the mayoral race.

"There's always a chance," Hamish finally answered, though hesitation laced his voice.

"But you don't think so."

He sighed. "Listen, Tessa, whatever it was, accident or not, you're safe right now. And I'm going to make sure it stays that way. From now on, I'll be checking out every venue you're due to appear at beforehand. Nobody is going to get the chance to do something like this ever again."

She nodded, suddenly realizing how stupid she'd been to revolt against his help. Nothing like a near-death experience to get her to see her protector in a new light. He wasn't trying to boss her around or restrict her movements, he was simply trying to do the job he was hired to do: keep her safe. It was time she showed some gratitude.

"I'm sorry, Hamish, about how I've been behaving," she started.

He turned his head in her direction, a surprised look on his face. "You don't have to apologize for anything. It's not easy to suddenly find yourself in a situation where you have to rely on somebody else—especially when you're used to taking care of yourself."

Surprised that he understood where she was coming from, she nodded and dropped her gaze to her clasped hands. "I don't like being helpless." She'd been helpless before, and she hadn't liked it then either. But she'd been a child and her tormentor had been stronger than her. And for a long time nobody had come to her aid.

"You're not helpless."

"I wish it were true. But I know my own limitations."

"You shouldn't think of it in those terms. Concentrate on what you *can* do. What you're good at."

"It looks like somebody doesn't like what I'm good at."

When Hamish suddenly put his hand on hers, she shrieked. Instantly, he removed his hand. "I'm sorry."

Her heart beat into her throat. "No, I'm sorry. I'm just jumpy. I didn't mean to—"

"It's my fault," he said, interrupting her bumbling apology. "I should know better. You've been through a lot tonight. You need to rest."

She knew he was right.

Hamish fell silent during the remainder of the drive, and she didn't have any words left either. But the silence only led to her mind working overtime. Who had caused this accident? And how had he done it? Had it been on a timer? But if that was the case, how would he have known when exactly she was supposed to speak? After all, Gunn was supposed to speak ahead of her, and anybody who knew Gunn, knew how much he liked the sound of his own voice. He could easily have spoken long enough for the duct to fall on *him*. Had she not been the intended target after all? Was there a target on Gunn's back, too? Or had somebody lain in wait and manually triggered the duct? It would have been the only way to ensure that it hit the right person, if it was indeed a deliberate act and not an accident.

And Gunn: why had he insisted she speak first? Had he known that something would happen? Was he, in fact, behind it all? Would she ever find out?

When the car suddenly came to a stop, Tessa stared out through the windshield, orienting herself. They were stopped behind her apartment building, making her realize something.

"I never gave you my home address."

Hamish met her gaze. "I'd be a poor excuse for a bodyguard if I didn't get all the information on my client before starting my assignment. I was here earlier in the day, checking out your neighborhood and assessing it for any imminent threats."

Slowly she nodded. "And?"

"It's a good building, though I wish you had a doorman."

"Apartments in doorman buildings are expensive."

"I know. We'll make do with what we've got. In any case, they'd have to get past me to get to you. You'll be able to sleep safely tonight."

Was he saying what she thought he was saying?

"You're staying the entire night?"

"That's what you hired me for."

And though intellectually she knew that, reality sank in only just now. Her bodyguard was spending the night in her apartment. Up close and personal.

"I don't have a guestroom."

"I'm not planning on sleeping."

"You'll be watching over me?" The thought was comforting and frightening at the same time. A stranger in her home. A stranger who'd saved her life once already. Would he have to save it again?

# 10

Hamish unlocked the apartment door for Tessa, because he'd noticed that her hands were still shaking. He let her enter ahead of him, then followed her and locked and bolted the door behind them.

He'd been here earlier, not just outside the building to check out the neighborhood like he'd told Tessa, but inside her apartment, too. It was standard procedure when taking on a new charge. He'd checked every egress point and searched her apartment for any potential hazards. Entering her apartment unseen had been child's play—he'd simply cloaked himself and walked through the locked doors. Luckily, demons didn't have those particular skills. They'd have to break in, and risk being seen by a neighbor. He'd found no evidence so far that a demon had been in Tessa's apartment.

"We should take care of that abrasion on your knee before it gets infected," he said to Tessa, as she dropped her handbag onto the coffee table in the living room, which connected to the open-plan kitchen.

When she stared down at her knee, he felt her stiffen visibly as if every mention of what had happened tonight tossed her back into a pit of despair. She turned abruptly, avoiding his gaze.

"I need to take a shower."

"Let me check the bathroom first." He stepped past her and opened the door to the bathroom, inspecting it. The window was closed and locked, and there were no places where anybody could hide. The apartment was on the third floor, and there was no fire escape on this side of the building. Nobody would be able to get into the bathroom from the outside. He turned around. "It's all good. Take your time."

Tessa forced a smile and disappeared into the bathroom. Hamish heard the lock click shut a moment later. He couldn't blame her for feeling she needed to lock herself in the bathroom.

She was vulnerable right now, and he was a stranger to her. If locking the door made her feel safer, so be it.

Knowing he couldn't do anything productive until he got word back from his fellow guardians, he marched into the kitchen, took off his jacket, and opened the refrigerator. There were enough supplies to whip up a simple meal. Since Tessa hadn't had a chance to eat anything at the event, she would probably be hungry. And the forlorn look she'd given him told him she needed comfort. At least he could give her that in the form of food, since his touch earlier had clearly rattled her—although he'd meant it to be reassuring.

Hamish found white wine, cream, some tomatoes and onions in the fridge, as well as pasta and olive oil in one of the hanging cabinets, and went to work. He was no stranger to cooking. After all, at the compound, where he lived with several other Stealth Guardians assigned to Baltimore, everybody fended for themselves when it came to food. Though he had to admit, ever since Aiden had bonded with a human, the lovely Dr. Leila Cruikshank, the quality of the food at the compound had improved vastly.

He'd spent many evenings gathered around the dining table with the other guardians, devouring Leila's delicious dinners. He'd learned a thing or two from her, and hoped that what he was throwing together for Tessa was edible. And would soothe her nerves a little.

While the pasta and the sauce boiled, he walked to the bathroom door and listened. The water was still running. He held his breath, listening more intently. There was another sound, too. He couldn't be one hundred percent certain, but his sensitive hearing picked up sobbing. He cursed under his breath, wishing he could walk in there and comfort her, but doing so would only frighten her more. Clearly she'd kept it together in his presence, not wanting to appear weak, but the moment she was alone, she broke like a twig in the wind.

Frustrated that he couldn't do anything for his charge, he walked back into the kitchen and set two places on the kitchen island. Then he checked his cell phone and sent a message to Enya.

*Anything yet?*

A few seconds later, she texted back. *Manus and I just got to the location. Keep you posted.*

He put the cell phone back in his pocket and tasted the pasta, then drained it and poured it into the pot with the sauce. He covered it with a lid, then leaned against the island and waited.

The minutes ticked by, but finally the bathroom door opened. Slowly he turned around and watched Tessa walk into the living room. She wore a long, fluffy white bathrobe. At her neckline he saw something lavender-colored peek through—a negligee. Her feet were bare. She'd combed her hair, but it was still damp. Her face looked flushed from the hot shower, and if she'd indeed cried, she'd hidden the fact well, maybe by splashing cold water around her eyes.

"I made us dinner. You must be hungry," he said, pointing to the place settings, before he turned back to the stove, grabbed the pot and serving spoons, and placed the dish on a pot holder on the island.

"You didn't have to do that."

"I didn't just do it for you. I'm hungry, too," he deflected, although he could have easily gone without dinner.

"Thank you." She approached and sat down on one of the barstools.

"I hope you like pasta with tomato sauce. There wasn't really much else in your fridge."

She pasted a smile on her lips and lifted her eyes to meet his gaze. "Pasta sounds great."

He served them both, then took the seat next to her. Tessa started eating quietly, and he did the same.

"Do you do this often?" she suddenly asked.

"Do what?"

"Cook dinner for your clients?"

"Not really." In general, his clients, or rather his charges, didn't even know he was there.

"Hmm." She fell silent again.

He wanted to bridge the silence with something, but was afraid that any mention of the incident at the center would upset her again. Searching for a safe topic of conversation, he went through the obvious subjects in his mind. The weather—nothing to talk about there. It was neither too warm, nor too cold. Current events—not a safe topic considering Tessa was running for mayor and the current events included riots and demonstrations, events fraught with danger. Her appearance—women liked compliments, but he was staying far away from that minefield, particularly since it was nighttime, they were alone, and Tessa was dressed rather enticingly. She might interpret his words as a come-on, which was not his intention.

This left precisely nothing to talk about. Nothing but the food.

"I hope the pasta isn't too hard. I like it al dente."

"Me, too." Her voice was barely audible. She continued eating until her plate was empty. When she pushed it aside and turned to hop off the barstool, Hamish glanced at her. His eyes caught a splash of red on her white robe.

"Oh, some sauce splattered onto your bathrobe." He took his napkin and stood up. "Let me get some water." He was at the sink, wetting his napkin, when he heard a sob behind him.

He whirled around and saw tears streaming down her face. "Tessa, what's wrong?"

She pointed to the red spot on her bathrobe and sobbed. "Everything. Everything is wrong. I almost died tonight."

He dropped the napkin in the sink and rushed to her, pulling her off the barstool and into his arms without thinking. She clung to him then, shaking, so he lifted her up and carried her to the couch, sitting down with her in his lap.

"I'm sorry, lass," he cooed and stroked his hand over her hair. "I'm sorry you had to experience that."

"If you hadn't been there—"

"But I was there," he interrupted her, refusing to let her finish that thought. "And I'm here now. Nothing is gonna happen from now on. I promise."

"How can you be so sure?" she asked through her tears.

"Because I won't let it happen." He drew her closer to underscore his promise.

Maybe he shouldn't have, because now he felt her body more intensely. He smelled the sweet scent of her freshly washed skin, felt the warmth of her breath brush against his neck and her hands clawing into his shirt as if her life depended on it.

"Lass," he murmured and couldn't stop himself from pressing a kiss into her hair.

Instead, he should lift her off his lap and stick his head in the freezer to stop himself from doing something stupid. Anything to distract himself from the delectable woman in his arms. But no distraction was forthcoming. And with every second, his willpower to stop this madness waned. When she lifted her head and looked at him with her tearstained eyes, he couldn't resist wiping the moisture away with his thumb. But what was meant as a gentle, soothing gesture, one he'd often used on his friends' children when they'd gotten into scrapes, was anything but innocent now.

"Hamish?"

Had she just whispered his name, or was he hallucinating?

He blamed his long abstinence from women for what he was about to do. Blamed *rasen* and all it entailed. He even blamed Cinead for having chosen him to protect Tessa. But he couldn't blame her, because all she was looking for was a place to feel safe. She would be safe in his arms. But would he be safe in hers?

Despite the fact that the answer to this question eluded him, he dipped his face to hers and brushed his lips against hers. Gently, softly at first. But when she inhaled sharply, everything primal in him took over, and he captured her lips like a wolf captured the helpless deer caught in a trap. He knew what he was doing was wrong. But it didn't stop him from pressing his mouth to hers and dipping his tongue between her parted lips, exploring her. And God, she tasted good. Sweet, innocent, yet not inexperienced. She responded to his kiss, not only by swiping her tongue against his and angling her head to invite him in, but also by putting her arms around his neck and holding him close.

He sensed her need—the need to forget. And he couldn't deny her this little pleasure. And just like Tessa, he wanted to forget and experience a few moments of abandon. A few moments of pure lust. Because that was all this could be: lust between two adults who needed to *feel* instead of think.

The way she kissed him back, the way she held him, made him want more. Hunger grew inside him, and while his hands had been idle until now, they couldn't remain so. Without thinking where this might lead, he felt for the belt of her robe and tore it open. He slid his hand inside, gliding against the silken fabric of her negligee. From beneath it, her body's heat radiated as if he'd dipped his hand into a vat of boiling liquid. He knew he'd get burned, but he didn't care, because the reward was worth it.

The longer he kissed her and the more intense the kiss became, the more his need to feel her naked skin under his palm grew. He slid his hand higher up, to just under her breast, and felt her gasp into his mouth. But she didn't push him away, didn't pull back her head to stop the kiss, so he moved higher, until he held her breast in the palm of his hand. He loved the weight of it, the roundness and firmness. He squeezed it and felt her shift on his lap, making him aware of that part of his anatomy which he'd been so ardently ignoring, but couldn't ignore any longer—for the damn thing was growing at an alarming speed.

He ripped his mouth from hers. He should stop now while he still could, but just then she shifted again, and so did the strap of her negligee. As he lifted his hand from her breast, the fabric slid away, revealing one hard nipple surrounded by creamy skin. Too tempting to ignore. He stroked over the hard bud and felt her shudder in his arms. She moaned, her eyes closed, her head falling back.

Goddamn it! To hell with caution!

He dipped his head and sank his lips onto her nipple, sucking it and caressing it with his tongue, while he moved his hand farther south. Over her stomach, down her toned thigh and even farther to the hem of her negligee. He pulled on it, but it was entangled with her bathrobe, so he tugged harder.

"Ouch!" she cried out.

He instantly stopped, his head whipping back, his eyes searching for the cause of her pain. He found it instantly. Blood was seeping from her knee—the very knee that had gotten injured during her fall earlier.

"Shit!" he cursed and stared at her.

Tessa avoided his gaze and nervously pulled her robe over her torso.

"I'm so sorry," he mumbled and lifted her off his lap as quickly and as gently as he could without further injuring her. "I didn't mean to…" Well, he didn't mean to do a lot of things. First and foremost, he hadn't meant to maul her like a hungry beast.

He jumped up. "I shouldn't have done this. It's my fault entirely. It won't happen again." He walked toward the kitchen. "If you tell me where your first aid kit is, I'll bandage you up."

But she was already getting up from the couch. "I can do that myself."

Of course. Why would she risk him touching her again? She was smart.

"I'm tired. I should go to bed. I've got a long day tomorrow," she said.

He didn't turn around when she walked toward her bedroom. "I'll be quiet when I clean up here, so you can sleep." Not that she seemed to be listening to him now.

Shit! Way to screw up on the first day of an assignment!

# 11

Anger and frustration rolling off him in dark waves, Zoltan marched along one of the corridors of his underworld empire, a labyrinth of underground caves. The interconnected chambers covered several square miles. The only way to enter or exit this stronghold was via the vortexes, the swirling portals only a demon's power could open. While in the human world portals could be projected onto practically any surface on ground level, the demon's lair had specific access points that allowed for vortexes. All were guarded by loyal demons.

As he entered the Great Hall, red flames flickered through the cracks of the uneven stone walls, underscoring the fact that this lair was located in the belly of hell. And he was its ruler, the Great One. The king of all demons. Though today he wasn't happy with his subjects. No, in fact, he was furious with them.

The news he'd received from up top—from his network of spies in the human world—was disturbing. And it required an immediate response, one that would teach his subjects that he wasn't to be trifled with. After all, many of them had witnessed not too long ago how he'd killed their previous leader in this very hall and taken the reins of the underworld.

"Who's responsible for this?"

Zoltan tossed the newspaper on the stone floor where two dozen of his demons stood in stoic silence, their shoulders hunched like the cowards they were. Nobody uttered a word. Just like he'd expected. None of them was brave enough to take credit for the incident that was plastered all over the front page.

"When I told you to show initiative, I didn't mean this!" he growled through clenched teeth and pointed to the paper on the floor. "An attack on the life of that councilwoman? What in hell were you thinking, you stupid fucks!"

Clearly they hadn't been thinking at all or they would have known what effect their action would have.

"Do you have any idea the damage you've caused?" He scoffed. "Of course you don't, because you're imbeciles. It's a wonder you can guide your own dicks to piss. Your mothers should have drowned you at birth!"

One of the demons bowed, before taking a step forward and lifting his head. "Oh, Great One, I assure you we had nothing to do with it."

"Liar!"

He charged toward the demon. Instantly the weasel shrank back, trying to hide in the ranks of his brethren, but Zoltan had had enough of the cowardly behavior his underlings exhibited and snatched the demon by the throat. Holding him up in the air and squeezing his windpipe shut, Zoltan glared at the other demons, daring them to help the coward.

"By attacking that councilwoman, all you've done is aid her campaign in becoming mayor. Don't you fucking see that?" No, they were too stupid to make the connection that he could see so clearly. He had to spell it out for them. "Now she's getting the sympathy vote from all those who were still undecided. You fucking idiots!"

The demon in his hold continued to struggle, frantically trying to pry Zoltan's hand off his neck. To no avail. He'd always been stronger than the other demons, even before he'd taken the helm as the new Great One. He'd always felt that he was destined for more. Even from an early age, he'd realized that he was smarter than the other demons. Superior to them.

Zoltan looked at the demon as he choked him, the skin turning green from the blood that collected underneath. He felt his own heart beat an excited tattoo against his ribcage in anticipation of his subject's death. What was one dead demon when he could cement his reign with this display of superiority? After all, they were replaceable—each of them as dumb as the next one.

"Do I have to show you myself how it's done? How you manipulate humans to get them to do what you want? Do you need another lesson?"

He glowered at his demons. Not a single one of them dared look at him. But he'd teach these cowards yet how to rule the world. "Look at me!"

Their heads shot up and they followed his command, afraid of him, just like they should be. It was the only way to rule. By fear and intimidation. And by example.

He pulled his dagger from the sheath at his hip, a weapon forged in the Dark Days, and the only kind of weapon capable of extinguishing the life of a demon, and plunged it in his captive's heart. The gurgling sound coming from the dying demon was accompanied by the gasps of the assembled. With satisfaction that his demonstration was yielding the desired result, Zoltan pulled the dagger from the dead body and wiped the blade on his long black coat. Then he tossed the lifeless shell of the demon into the crowd, watching how they shrank back so as not to be splattered with their comrade's green blood. As if coming in contact with it would seal their fate, too.

"Good, then we understand each other," Zoltan growled. "And the first man who brings me the name of the imbecile who initiated the attack on the councilwoman will be rewarded." He narrowed his eyes at his subjects. "The second will die."

With that threat, he turned on his booted heel and marched out of the Great Hall and toward his private quarters. When he entered, he slammed the door shut so it would echo through the entire labyrinth of tunnels that connected the various caves. Everybody needed to know that the Great One meant business.

Finally alone, he tossed his coat on a bench and exhaled. With it, a wave of pain hit him and he pressed his palms against his temples to ease the pressure in his head. He hated these attacks, always had. But he'd hidden them well for decades, knowing that showing weakness would be his downfall. He knew of no demon who'd ever experienced this kind of pain, which seemed similar to a human's migraine. For all he knew it was common, and he had to assume that just like he hid these episodes, other demons did, too.

For several minutes, he felt paralyzed and utterly helpless, the pain so violent that he couldn't even keep his eyes open. So far, he'd always felt the attacks' approach, which gave him enough time to find a private place so nobody would bear witness to his weakness. He could only hope that it would remain that way.

The attacks had become more frequent ever since he'd taken over as the Great One. More painful, too, as if something inside him was revolting and pushing back against the mounting pressure his position came with. But he wouldn't let this handicap stop him.

When the pain finally eased, Zoltan walked into the bathroom. The floor, walls, and ceiling were of volcanic stone. In one corner, a shower and a tub were molded into the rock, in the other a toilet. The sink was similarly fashioned, but one item from the human world had been added: a mirror. He looked at his reflection now. No outward signs of his debilitating condition showed. He took a deep breath. It was time to mend what his demons had screwed up.

While he had no qualms about killing humans—far from it— he knew that killing Councilwoman Wallace wasn't a smart idea. It would raise too many suspicions and turn her into a martyr. And martyrs were harder to eradicate than humans, who were merely flesh and blood. Because you couldn't kill a martyr; they lingered in the minds of people. It was better to discredit the lovely Tessa Wallace and thus eradicate her chance of becoming mayor, because if she turned the city away from the violence, hatred, and anger that was brewing in Baltimore, the demons would lose ground that they'd fought long and hard for. Finally it was time to claim the city and turn it into a demon stronghold so its policies could infect other cities in the state, then spread farther...

Yeah, he liked that. And if his subjects were too dense to figure out how to accomplish this, he'd have to do it himself.

Satisfied with his plan, Zoltan opened a tall wooden cabinet and inspected its contents. Wigs, beards, and mustaches were on display, as well as molds to slip over his teeth to change his smile. He chose his disguise wisely like he always did when he ventured into the human world, and while he didn't always use all tools of disguise at his disposal, one was essential:

Colored contact lenses to hide his demon eyes. Demons had tried in the past to conceal their eyes with colored lenses, but they'd met with little success. The green in their irises emitted a chemical that burned through any lens within less than an hour, making a permanent disguise impossible.

However, recently Zoltan had come across a talented optometrist who'd been experimenting with different materials for patients who had allergic reactions to regular contact lenses. He'd watched him closely and tested out the various lenses the man was developing, until he found one that lasted several hours before it dissolved and revealed his demonic eyes.

He chuckled to himself. He hadn't shared his discovery with his underlings yet. It was good to always stay one step ahead of everybody, even his own subjects.

# 12

Tessa opened the door to her outer office and entered, but if she'd hoped for a sanctuary after the events of the previous night, this wasn't it. She'd already dodged several reporters when Hamish had dropped her off at a side entrance to City Hall, after she'd spotted a news van parked out front. But apparently a few journalists had made it past security.

Two reporters she recognized jumped up from the visitor chairs and practically pounced on her.

Collette, who'd risen from behind her desk, lifted her arms in defeat. "I'm sorry, Tessa, but..."

Tessa sighed. "Not your fault, Collette."

And not the security people's fault either. After all, as long as prospective visitors didn't carry weapons and could state some legitimate reason—even if it was pretense—security had to admit them to City Hall. And once inside, they could pretty much access any floor and any office. So much for her sanctuary, of which she'd been in dire need. Not only because of the attempt on her life the previous night, but also because of what had happened later in her apartment.

She'd thrown herself at Hamish like a hormonal teenage groupie! Even now, embarrassment ran through her veins and colored her cheeks. How had it even happened? One minute she'd been crying, fear and horror occupying her every thought, the next she'd been in his arms and had let herself sink into the comforting warmth they had provided. Everything had melted into the background and suddenly she'd felt only him: his masculine scent, his strong hands, his gentle words. And when she'd met his gaze, she'd been hypnotized by his eyes, and without thinking she'd moved her head closer and had kissed him.

Of course, he'd responded to her kiss. After all, he was a man, and she didn't know many men who'd turn down a reasonably attractive woman who was coming onto them. But he'd come to his senses quickly. Who knew what else would have happened if he hadn't stopped.

Having to see him this morning had been awkward. And the silence between them when he'd driven her to work had been so thick, she could have cut it with a knife. Was it therefore surprising that all she wanted was to hide in her office and bury herself in her work?

Clearly, it wasn't meant to be. The two reporters bombarding her with questions were making sure of that.

"Miss Wallace, how are you feeling this morning?" Meredith from the Daily Republic asked.

"Are you planning to sue the Center for Drug Rehabilitation for reckless endangerment?" Thom, the journalist working for Online News Blast, interrupted.

"I'm feeling fine." She smiled at Meredith, then looked at Thom. "And no, I'm not planning on suing anybody." She took a few steps toward her office, but the two reporters weren't done yet.

"Who was the hero who saved you from the falling duct?" Thom continued. "Were you at the event together?"

"Do you have a name for us?" Meredith added. "Nobody was able to tell us who he is."

"I'm sorry, I really have lots of work to do," Tessa evaded the question and tried to squeeze past the two insistent reporters.

"Just give us something," Meredith begged. "Speculations are already running wild."

Thom nodded in agreement, pen poised over his notepad. "It's the only way you'll get rid of us."

Collette suddenly shoved herself between Tessa and the two journalists. "The way to get rid of you is to call security. So off you go."

The path to her office clear now, Tessa headed for it and turned the knob.

"If you don't give us his name, we'll just put our bloodhounds on him to find out who he is," Thom announced.

Tessa sighed and turned. She couldn't risk anybody finding out that Hamish was her bodyguard. It was better to give them something. "His name is Hamish MacGregor. And he's my boyfriend."

"How long have you been dating?" Thom shot back, while Meredith asked, "Is this serious? Are you planning on getting married after the mayor's race?"

"No comment," she ground out, already regretting having given the two reporters the information. "Collette, can you please make sure I'm left alone this morning? Thanks."

"Oh, Tessa, I almost forgot, your father—"

"Miss Wallace!" Meredith interrupted, but Tessa was already entering her office and shutting the door behind her. She pressed her forehead against the closed door.

Through it she heard Collette's insistent demands that the two reporters leave or she would indeed call security and have them removed. A few moments later, she heard the opening and closing of the door, then silence.

Finally, she exhaled.

"Tessa!"

She shrieked and spun around. She clasped her chest and gasped for air when she saw her father rising from the wooden bench in the window niche. "Dad!" she choked out, trying to get her breath back.

"I'm sorry, honey, I didn't mean to startle you," he said, approaching her.

Dressed in a business suit and dress shirt, he looked the part of the distinguished businessman he still was, even in his late sixties, though he could have retired years ago. His hair was gray at the temples, but still dark blond everywhere else. His blue eyes were vibrant and his skin tanned as a result of the many hours he spent on the golf course on the weekends. He'd been a strikingly handsome man when he was younger, but even now he was still attractive, could still turn many a head.

Tessa walked into his arms, accepting the hug he offered. And today she really needed it. "It's good to see you, Dad. What are you doing here so early? Shouldn't you be at the office?"

He released her from his embrace, and only now did she notice the deep crease in his forehead. "I would be, if it weren't for this." He reached for the newspaper that lay on Tessa's desk and pointed to the headline.

"Mystery man saves councilwoman from certain death," he read and shook his head, exhaling sharply. "Jesus, Tessa! This is how I have to find out about it? Via the newspaper?"

"Dad, please, as you can see, I'm fine."

"You should have called me last night." He pinned her with his eyes. As a child, that same gaze had always intimidated her and made her confess all her sins. "Your mother and I nearly had heart attacks this morning."

"Mother doesn't have a heart condition," Tessa deflected.

"That doesn't mean that she wasn't worried about you."

Tessa shrugged.

"Well, if you don't care how your mother feels, how about me then? Do you care so little about me that you won't grant me the courtesy of telling me that you're okay?"

"Of course not, Dad. I didn't mean that," she said quickly, realizing that she'd hurt him. And that hadn't been her intention. "It's just... I was in a state of shock last night. Everything happened so fast, and had Hamish not been there, I don't know what would have happened. It never occurred to me—"

"It's alright, honey," he said softly. Then he pointed to the headline again. "So this mystery man's name is Hamish? Who is he? I'd like to thank him for saving my daughter from this terrible accident."

Damn it! This was exactly what she'd wanted to avoid. She hated lying to her father, but if he found out that Hamish was her bodyguard, one question would lead to another, and he wouldn't stop grilling her until he found out that she'd received a death threat. Maybe the lesser evil was to tell him what Hamish and she had discussed.

"We're dating," she said as casually as possible. "Nothing serious."

"You have a boyfriend, and you didn't tell me?" He stared at her as if this was some monumental news. "Why did you keep him a secret?"

"We've really only just started dating. And it's not serious, honestly."

"I want to meet him."

Tessa's shoulders stiffened. "I really don't think that's appropriate at this stage. You know how guys get when you want to introduce them to your parents. I don't really wanna spook him."

"I thought you just said it wasn't serious."

"Yes, so even less of a reason to do the meet-the-parents thing."

"But he saved your life. The guy deserves a medal."

Her father was like a dog with a bone. He wouldn't let go of it.

"I'll tell him you're grateful next time I see him, okay?"

"Don't brush me off like that, Tessa. I'm serious about this. I want to thank the man who saved my daughter."

"But he's a really busy guy."

"What does he do that keeps him so busy?" her father shot back.

"Uh, he writes manuals."

"Manuals?"

"Yeah, you know, instruction manuals for heavy machinery."

Her father lifted one bushy eyebrow. "Sounds, uh, interesting. Well, in any case, even he needs to eat occasionally. Bring him to our house tonight. I'll throw some steaks on the BBQ."

"Dad…"

"No discussion. Tonight, seven o'clock." He turned toward the door. "Your mother will be happy to see you both."

She doubted that, but didn't bother voicing her opinion. Once her father made up his mind about something, there was no swaying him.

"Fine, but I'm not helping with the vegetables!" she called after him as he stalked outside and closed the door behind him, leaving her to stew over the prospect of having to spend an evening playing nice with her mother.

And as if that wasn't bad enough, on top of it she had to pretend to be dating Hamish. Well, wasn't her day starting out just great?

# 13

Hamish stepped into the shower. He'd slept a few hours upon returning to the compound, after dropping Tessa off at City Hall and making sure Enya was there to take over. He should be sufficiently rested after sleeping, but unfortunately, his well-deserved rest had eluded him. Instead, visions of Tessa had plagued his dreams. At first, they'd replayed the incident at the center, but then they'd morphed into something entirely different: a repeat and extension of what had happened at her apartment afterward.

And speaking of extensions... He looked down at his groin where his cock was still standing to attention. He'd woken up like that, which wasn't unusual, but the fact that it hadn't deflated yet was. It appeared that his raging hard-on wasn't going to go away by itself today. Not when he couldn't get Tessa out of his mind. Or her tempting body. Ah, hell, he'd known from the start that this assignment was doomed. He should have refused immediately when Cinead asked him to protect Tessa openly, and insisted on guarding her invisibly from the shadows. At least then, he would never have been tempted to kiss her. Well, maybe still tempted, but at least he would have never had an occasion to act upon it.

Now the damage was done.

And to avoid further harm, he'd have to take care of himself here and now. But the moment he took his hard cock into his right hand and began to tug, he knew that this wouldn't be a routine jerk-off-session where he fantasized about some random non-existent woman with a hot body. No, that fantasy wasn't what popped into his head. Instead, he was met with lavender eyes that looked at him, watched him.

Her hand took over for his, gripping his erection firmly. Up and down she slid on him, her palm moist and warm. He reached for her then and pushed her robe off her shoulders, letting it fall onto the wet shower floor. Her negligee was getting soaked by the water raining down from the showerhead, turning it transparent. Her nipples turned hard and pressed through the fabric in invitation. He reached for one, rolled it between thumb and forefinger and felt her squeeze his cock harder in response.

"Just like that," he murmured and massaged her breast, before he slid his hand down her torso to the juncture of her thighs.

He gathered the fabric with his hand and lifted it up so he could slide his hand between her legs and touch her there. She was wet there, too, not from the shower, but from her own juices. Ready for his touch, his caresses, ready for him. He played with her, diddled her clit to make her even hotter for him, stroked and pinched and caressed her warm folds. Probed at the entrance to her core.

He heard her moans echo against the tile walls and responded to them by sliding his finger into her. Deep and hard. Just the way he wanted to take her. Right here against the wall of his shower, lifted up and supported by his strong arms alone. She lost her hold on his cock, but he didn't mind, because he was ready. Ready to plunge into her. Warmth and wetness welcomed him. Her interior muscles squeezed him to perfection. He began to pound into her, harder and faster, needing more with every second.

"Harder!" he yelled. "Fuck, Tessa!"

She didn't stop him, didn't complain about the rough treatment. Only took what he had to give her. Panting, he felt the pressure in his balls increase, until he could hold back no more. Semen exploded from the tip of his cock and shot not into Tessa, but into nothing. His vision cleared and he found himself with one hand on his cock, the other braced against the tile wall, his semen running down the smooth surface in long, thick streaks.

He dropped his forehead against the wall. Fuck, he'd never had a fantasy that felt so real. And so hot. So hot in fact, that his cock hadn't had enough of it yet. So he kept pumping until finally, after a long while, it deflated and returned to its resting state.

Fuck, if this was what he'd have to do every day just so he wouldn't make another pass at Tessa, then he was grateful that the walls in the compound were made of stone so his fellow Stealth Guardians wouldn't have to bear witness to him slaking his most primal need.

He finished his shower and got dressed quickly, then left his suite of rooms and walked down the corridor leading away from the residential part of the compound. There were no keys or locked doors anywhere in the compound, except to the prison cell on the lowest level—since every Stealth Guardian had the ability to walk through walls and doors—nevertheless they strongly respected each other's privacy. Nobody walked into the rooms of a fellow guardian without being expressively invited to enter.

The building consisted of five levels, three above ground and two below. Its walls were as thick as those of an old castle. Ancient runes, representing the history of the Stealth Guardians, decorated the walls and floors, and charms to ward off evil hung over each door and window.

Many compounds like this existed all over the world. Each of them was protected by *virta*, the collective power of the Stealth Guardians. It, together with an ancient hypnotizing spell, rendered the building invisible to humans and demons alike.

Inside, no humans were allowed. Well, that rule had been broken before, most notably by Aiden's then-charge Leila. He'd brought her to the compound against everybody's better judgment. And she was still at the compound—now as Aiden's wife and mate. And with the blessing of the Council of Nine.

Within the walls of the compound, Stealth Guardians could recharge their energy after each mission. Below, in the vast underground vaults, weapons were stored, weapons that could kill even an immortal Stealth Guardian. Those weapons were guarded diligently, because while no human weapon such as a gun or a knife could permanently injure a Stealth Guardian, the old weapons that had been forged during the Dark Days had the power to kill them. Just like they had the power to kill a demon.

Also in the bowels of the compound, on the lowest level, was the portal that allowed them to travel from one compound to another. Until a few months ago, it had been believed that all portals were located in compounds, however, Hamish had found other portals, which the Council of Nine had named the lost portals. More were being discovered every day, and a special team had started to map them so those portals could be protected from discovery.

The compound also possessed a lead cell from which not even a Stealth Guardian could escape, because lead temporarily stripped them of their powers. However, a prolonged stay in a lead cell could extinguish a Stealth Guardian's powers altogether and thus render him human.

Hamish reached the door to the command center and entered. As expected, Pearce sat at one of the consoles equipped with three screens. Aiden stood behind him, looking over Pearce's shoulder.

Both turned when they heard him.

"Morning, Hamish," Pearce said cheerfully. He was their resident tech guy, the go-to guy for anything to do with computers, though he was just as talented with a dagger as with a keyboard.

"Hey, you're finally up," Aiden greeted him. His oldest friend didn't look too dissimilar from himself: dark brown hair and brown eyes with a small scar over one eyebrow.

"Yeah, can't sleep all day. Got work to do, right?" Hamish pointed to the screens. "Have you reviewed the footage from last night yet?"

"Most of what's been uploaded so far, but every hour I find something new," Pearce confessed. "These days everybody with a smartphone thinks he's an investigative journalist."

Hamish stepped closer. "Which in this case might work to our advantage. Did you find any footage that shows the ceiling?"

Pearce shook his head. "Nope. And we probably won't. Most of the footage being uploaded is of you pushing Tessa out of the way. Nobody's going to upload a failed attempt at videoing the hottest current event to social media."

Aiden jerked his thumb at Pearce. "Pearce's got a point. You're only gonna see those shots that capture the action, featuring you as the hero. Sorry, buddy."

"I guess it was too good to be true." Nevertheless, he wanted to have a look at it himself. "Mind if I take a look? Maybe I'll see something you guys didn't. After all, I met a few of the people on stage, so maybe I'll come across something that doesn't make sense."

Pearce pushed back his chair and stood up. "Knock yourself out. I'm starving anyway. And I hear Leila is cooking today."

"Again?" Hamish asked and stared at his friend Aiden. "You did tell your wife that just because she lives at the compound, doesn't mean she has to play mother hen and feed us all. We did survive without anybody cooking for us for quite a few decades."

Aiden smirked. "Yeah, but you do have to admit that she's turned into a rather good cook. And what else is she gonna do all day? She doesn't have her research anymore."

"Hmm." Hamish nodded. It had been a shame that Leila had had to give up her life's work—finding a cure for Alzheimer's—because it would have inadvertently aided the demons. "But I thought she's decking out a medical center right here at the compound in case any of us gets injured."

"Yeah, and it's fully equipped with the latest gear, but when did one of us last get injured and need a doctor?"

Hamish shrugged. "Guess we're too good at what we do."

Both Pearce and Aiden laughed.

"That's exactly why we need a medical emergency room," Leila's voice suddenly came from the door.

All three turned their heads and looked at her.

"Because you guys all think you're invincible," she continued, shaking her head. "That's when mistakes happen. One of these days, you'll be glad you've got a doctor in the house."

"You tell them, baby," Aiden said and pulled her into his arms.

"I was talking about you, too. You're not any different from your friends."

"Aren't I?" He bent closer and whispered something into her ear.

Leila blushed, and Hamish rolled his eyes.

"May I remind you that you do have private quarters?" Hamish said and motioned toward the door. "I suggest you use them."

"Later," Aiden said. "How about lunch first?"

"That's why I came to find you guys," Leila said. "You should eat something before it gets cold."

"I'm starving," Pearce admitted and marched toward the door.

Leila and Aiden were on his heels. They turned at the door.

"You coming, Hamish?" Aiden asked over his shoulder.

"Leave something for me. I want to look at some of the footage first." Then he remembered something else. "And Aiden."

"Yeah?"

"Has Manus reported yet what he and Enya found at the center last night? I didn't have a chance to speak to Enya this morning."

"I believe he went back there today to listen in on the team the deputy director of the center asked to look into the incident."

"Thanks, I'll call him later then."

A moment later, all three were gone. He heard the sound of their footsteps grow fainter. Alone in the large, cool room, Hamish took Pearce's seat and scrolled through the video files Pearce had assembled in a folder.

Some of the clips were better than others, but not a single one truly showed the entire event unfolding, which perhaps was a good thing: at least nobody had a continuous video of him practically flying across the stage at a speed not even an Olympic sprinter could compete with.

The clips showed Tessa standing at the lectern, with Ms. VanSant, Poppy, Gunn, and Mantle standing farther back and to the side. Then Hamish entered the shot, pushing Tessa out of the way of the falling duct. The camera shook, tilting to one side. The duct had smashed the lectern to pieces and behind it, near the wall stood directors VanSant and Mantle with their mouths gaping open, frozen in shock. Poppy was holding on to VanSant's arm, her eyes squeezed shut. Gunn wasn't at the same spot as before. He'd moved during the rescue. But where to? The camera didn't have him in its viewer. Considering what he knew about Gunn, he'd probably fallen backward on his ass at the moment of impact. Cowardly weasel! And this was the man whose political commercials ran with the slogan *Get your Gunn into City Hall!*

Hamish rubbed his eyes. He wouldn't find the answer he was looking for here. Maybe Manus had come up with something more helpful. And once he'd spoken to Manus, he needed to go see Tessa and clear the air. She'd barely said a word to him this morning, and it was pretty evident that she was pissed at him. However, for the sake of her safety, he couldn't have bad blood between them, because to protect her, he needed her to trust him—and not avoid him.

# 14

Tessa had already heard Poppy outside her door, exchanging a few words with Collette, before her campaign manager gave a brief knock on the door and entered the office.

"Hey, Poppy."

Poppy closed the door behind her and walked to the desk. "How're you feeling this morning? You left so fast, I couldn't even make sure you were okay."

"I'm alright."

Poppy sighed. "I was right to get you a bodyguard."

"I'm really not in the mood for an *I-told-you-so-speech*."

"And you're not getting one. I'm just happy that you're alive."

"Thanks, Poppy."

"So what did I hear from Collette just now? You and Hamish?"

Tessa swallowed. How could anybody know what had happened between her and Hamish last night? It was impossible. They'd been alone. And there was no way Hamish would have said anything to anybody either. Well, at least she thought he wouldn't. Or was he the kind of guy who would brag that he could have gotten her into bed last night?

"Oh my God, you're blushing!" Poppy exclaimed. "Guess something must have happened when he took you home last night, huh? Collette told me he's your boyfriend. You're a fast worker! I'm in awe!"

Tessa sighed, somewhat relieved. Now she knew what Poppy was talking about. She remembered now that Poppy had left before Hamish had explained that he would pose as her boyfriend. "It's nothing like that. Hamish is only my pretend-boyfriend so that people don't get wind of the fact that I have a bodyguard."

"Did he suggest that or did you?"

"He did."

Poppy grinned. "I wonder why. Maybe he's attracted to you and figured he'd kill two birds with one stone."

"Poppy!" Tessa ground out. "Hamish is not attracted to me, and I'm not attracted to him. Period. This is a purely professional arrangement."

Poppy made a dismissive gesture. "So what did it feel like when that hunk was all over you?"

"What?" A jolt of panic shot through her.

"Well, when he practically buried you underneath him to save you from that falling duct." She fanned herself. "Frankly I wouldn't mind being in danger if it meant a hottie like that would protect me with his sexy body. You can't be so blind not to see that, girl! I know your type. Back in college you would have been all over a guy like him."

Tessa sighed, frustration rising, but she knew the only way to stop Poppy was to tell her what she wanted to hear. "Fine. So Hamish is a hot hunk with a sexy body. Happy now?"

"Is this a bad time?" an all too familiar male voice coming from the door said.

Tessa's gaze shot past Poppy. Why had she not heard the door opening? Embarrassment swept through her, and she felt her cheeks heat as she watched Hamish approach. His lips were curved up in a charming smile. Damn it, had he heard her last words? Words she'd said only mockingly to get Poppy off her back. She wanted to sink into a hole and hide.

Poppy suppressed a chuckle. "Oh, hey Hamish, I was just leaving." She glanced back at Tessa.

Tessa hissed underneath her breath. "Don't you leave now, you traitor."

But Poppy was already heading for the door. "See you later."

The door fell shut. Nervously Tessa shifted papers from one side of her desk to the other. "You're too early," she said quickly, avoiding looking at Hamish. "I'm not ready to leave yet."

"I figured that, but I wanted to talk to you about something important. And it can't wait."

She looked up and noticed him staring at the window seat.

"In private, without anybody inadvertently listening in."

In the silence that followed, Tessa heard the floorboards creak, but Hamish wasn't moving. He stood in front of her desk as if waiting for something.

Finally she couldn't take the suspense any longer and said, "If this is about last night..."

~ ~ ~

Hamish waited until Enya had left the room. Despite the fact that she'd been invisible to Tessa, he'd been able to see her since their race had different degrees of cloaking.

"It is," he started. He'd overheard Tessa telling Poppy that she found him sexy. That changed the situation. He tossed his prepared speech out the window and took a slightly different approach.

"I don't want there to be any misunderstandings between us. It could jeopardize your safety. And your safety comes before everything else."

"I think we both knew that this... uh... arrangement could cause problems."

"That's my fault," he admitted.

When she parted her lips to respond, he stopped her by lifting his hand. "No, please let me explain. I've been doing this for a long time: protecting people. And only once have I ever gotten involved with one of my cha—uh, clients. It cost her life." And nearly his, too.

Tessa's eyes widened in shock.

"I won't make the same mistake again, no matter how much I'm attracted to you. I can't risk it. Do you understand?"

She nodded silently.

"I heard what you said to Poppy just now. I'm guessing you're not entirely indifferent to me, or you probably wouldn't have kissed me back when I took advantage of your vulnerability last night."

"You didn't take advantage of me," she said to his surprise. "I wanted you to kiss me."

Her admission made what he had to say even harder. "And I enjoyed kissing you more than I should. But I can't allow myself to do it again." No matter how much he craved a repeat of it. "My job... it's complicated. We have rules and..."

"You don't have to say anything else. Nothing really happened. We're both adults who got lost in the moment."

As much as that might be true for Tessa, it wasn't the case for him, but he didn't contradict her. However, he wanted her to know that this didn't change how serious he was about her safety.

"You have my promise that I'll protect you with my life if I have to. I want you to trust me. You should never have to doubt my commitment to this assignment. And whatever you need me to do to make you feel safe and comfortable, you just have to ask."

Tessa rose slowly, nodding in contemplation. She walked around the desk and approached the window. Glancing outside, she finally spoke.

"It's strange to hear you say that. To hear anybody say that."

He took a few steps toward her. "Why? Don't you believe me?"

"It's not that. I do believe you. And even that is strange. I mean, believing somebody you don't really know. Trusting a stranger."

"But you do."

She nodded, still staring out of the window. Maybe it was easier for her to talk openly without looking at him. "After last night I have no doubt anymore." She sighed. "You reacted so quickly. Without hesitation. I saw some of the video clips people took of the incident."

He noticed her shiver and wanted to put his hand on her shoulder to reassure her, but he didn't. It was too risky, because even jerking off in the shower earlier hadn't dampened his desire for her. On the contrary, it had only shown him what it could be like between them. How good they would be together.

"I reviewed the clips, too," he said instead. "But there was no footage of the ceiling, so I couldn't see how the duct fell."

"Gabriella called me earlier. She said the police were at the scene last night." She looked over her shoulder. "Did your colleague speak to them?"

"Yes, Enya made contact with them," he lied. "But there are no leads yet." Which was the truth.

He'd spoken to Manus earlier. His fellow guardian had taken photographs and swiped the metal for any chemical residue that would suggest an explosive, but the results of the tests weren't back yet.

A knock at the door made him turn.

Tessa glanced past him. "Come in."

The door opened and none other than Robert Gunn entered. When Gunn spotted him, he froze for a moment.

"I hope I'm not interrupting anything."

Tessa walked past Hamish and addressed Gunn, "No, you're not. What can I do for you?"

"I just wanted to check in and see how you're doing after last night." He exhaled. "That was quite horrific."

"It was, but I'm fine."

"Good, good." Gunn smiled and glanced past her, looking straight at Hamish. "I don't believe we've been introduced."

He extended his hand and Hamish had no choice but to shake it.

"Hamish MacGregor."

"Robert Gunn."

"I know who you are."

Gunn shifted, a gesture Hamish could only interpret as nervousness. "Well, I don't want to disturb you any longer." He was already back at the door, when he turned. "Oh, Tessa, before I forget, I was looking for a bunch of files that Yardley was working on before his death."

Hamish recognized the name: John Yardley, the previous mayor, who'd been killed in a still-unsolved hit-and-run two months earlier.

"Yes?" Tessa replied, her eyebrows snapping together.

"I was told you might have taken them to continue where he left off."

"I only took anything related to the Center for Drug Rehabilitation."

"Hmm. Odd. Well, then."

"You might want to try his widow. I know John's assistant packed up his personal stuff. Maybe it accidentally got packed in with it."

"I thought all that stuff was still in police custody."

She shook her head. "No, they sent it to Amanda. She called me just the other day because there was a book in the box that I'd lent him, and she wanted to return it. So she's definitely got the box. Why don't you call her?"

"I will. Thanks!" Gunn smiled and left, shutting the door behind him.

When Tessa turned back to him, Hamish noticed the sad look on her face. "Were you close to the mayor, to Yardley?"

"He was a friend of the family. I was a child when I first met him. He was like an uncle to me. So I guess I knew him well. He was a good man. When I heard of the accident I couldn't believe it at first. We were all devastated." She looked straight at him. "Particularly my father. John and my dad would play golf together and afterwards, there would be a barbeque at our house." She suddenly froze.

"What?"

"I almost forgot. My father invited us for a barbeque at home."

"Us?"

She grimaced. "I'm afraid I had to tell him that you're my boyfriend. And now he wants to meet you. I really don't need this right now."

"You think he won't approve of me?"

"It's not you or him I'm worried about."

"Then what?"

"It's my mother."

# 15

Hamish slowed the car as they approached the address Tessa had given him.

"Are there always this many cars parked on the street?"

Tessa looked around, then shook her head. "Everybody in this area has a two-car garage, plus a spot or two for visitors in their driveway."

"That's what I thought." He didn't like this. Something didn't seem right, and he was trained to spot things that fell outside the norm.

"Maybe one of the neighbors is having a party," Tessa mused.

"Maybe."

He drove up to Tessa's childhood home, intending to turn into the driveway, but stopped. Two cars were already parked in the visitor spots. He cast Tessa a sideways glance and she rolled her eyes at the car's ceiling.

"I'm going to kill her this time, I really am," Tessa groaned.

"May I ask who your intended victim is?"

Tessa met his eyes. "My mother. Why does she keep doing this?"

"I'm going out on a limb here, but I'm assuming the barbeque we're invited to isn't strictly a family affair, is it?"

She huffed angrily. "Apparently not."

Hamish reached over to squeeze her hand, and to his surprise, she laid her other hand over his in a gesture of thanks. "You don't like parties, do you?"

She sighed. "Not particularly. All day at work I have to be *on*; I have to smile, be nice to people, make intelligent conversation, listen intently. You know what I mean?"

He nodded. "A life in the public eye isn't easy."

"And tonight, I would have preferred to chill. Not to have to talk to a bunch of strangers about what happened at the center last night." She took a deep breath. "I'm sorry. I don't mean to bitch, but I just wanted a quiet evening."

"You're not bitching. And I'm gonna make sure nobody bothers you with stupid questions."

A hopeful ray lit up her eyes. "How are you gonna do that?"

"Well, I could just kill anybody who tries to bother you." When her mouth dropped open, he winked. "And I know how to make a body disappear. Comes with the job."

Tessa started to chuckle, and he smiled back at her.

"Thank you, Hamish. I needed that."

Smirking he said, "I meant it!" Then he released her hand and switched off the engine, blocking in the two cars in the driveway. "Now let's go in there and get this over with. We don't have to stay long. I can come up with an excuse so we can leave early. How does that sound?"

She gifted him with a genuine smile, one that made his heart beat excitedly. "That sounds wonderful. You're the best."

"I should hope so," he joked. "After all you should be getting your money's worth."

"Can I even afford you?"

"No, but I'll give you a discount."

He couldn't believe he was actually bantering with Tessa, and she was playing along. And he liked it. In fact, he liked it very much, because she was finally smiling and laughing genuinely, and it made her look even more beautiful. Gods, he was so screwed. Keeping his hands off Tessa would be a struggle for as long as he was assigned to her.

As they walked past the two parked cars in the driveway, the front door was already opening.

"Guess somebody saw us coming," Hamish murmured to Tessa, who was walking next to him.

She waved at the man now emerging from the doorway. "Dad!"

They met halfway and embraced.

"Hey, honey, you made it!" the older man said.

"You didn't tell me this was going to be a big party."

Tessa's father shrugged. "Would you have come if I'd told you?"

When Tessa grimaced, he added, "See, that's exactly why I didn't. Besides, you seem to have forgotten what today's date is. I'm surprised you didn't guess that there would be a big to-do."

Something flickered in Tessa's eyes, as if her father's words had triggered a memory. "Oh."

Her father shifted his gaze and extended his hand toward Hamish. "I'm Philip Wallace."

Hamish shook his hand. "Hamish MacGregor. Pleasure to meet you, sir."

Wallace had a surprisingly firm grip. His body looked trim and toned, indicating that he took care of himself and probably worked out regularly. His dark blond hair was graying at the temples, but showed no bald spots. His eyes were of a vibrant blue, lending him authority. He was a handsome man for his age, but Tessa had not inherited any of his features.

"I wish I could say my daughter told me much about you, but I'm afraid she's been a little tight-lipped."

"Well, we haven't been dating for very long," Hamish said quickly and reached for Tessa's hand to demonstrate that they were indeed together.

"Hmm. I only found out about you when I heard you saved her life last night."

Hamish smiled. "I was at the right place at the right time."

"I'd say! Quite some speed you've got, young man! Can't say I've ever seen anybody react that fast."

Hamish shrugged. So Wallace had checked out the video clips online, no surprise. But there wasn't enough footage to really piece together how quickly Hamish had actually been moving, so he wasn't worried.

Instead he grinned and brought Tessa's hand to his lips, planting a chaste kiss on her knuckles. "Couldn't let anything happen to your beautiful daughter. She's too precious."

"That's what I like to hear. Thank you, Hamish. I may call you Hamish, may I not?"

Wallace graced him with a benevolent nod and smile. Just the reaction he'd expect from a concerned father. It had taken all of two minutes to secure Wallace's good opinion. The man wouldn't question Hamish's devotion to his daughter. One down, more to go.

"Of course, sir, call me Hamish."

"Now, let's go inside, everybody is curious to meet you," Wallace said and turned in the direction of the front door.

Behind his back Hamish exchanged a quick look with Tessa.

She leaned closer and whispered to him, "You're good."

He smirked. "I know." He glanced down at their joined hands, while they followed her father into the house.

The house was a large colonial with a white staircase leading to the second floor, and an expansive entrance hall that opened up into a sitting room, which connected with a dining room. As always when on protective detail, Hamish made a quick assessment of the premises to identify any security risks.

Dozens of people were milling about, all dressed in casual or business casual clothes. Through the large windows in the back of the property, Hamish could see the beautiful yard, where more people mingled with glasses in their hands. A small pool with a Jacuzzi took over a third of the backyard. To one side of it stood a small shed, though it didn't look like a garden shed. Maybe a home office or a little pool house. Grass grew on the other side of the pool, and a large wooden deck provided space for a massive barbeque, as well as ample seating.

Professional catering staff circulated with trays of food and drinks. This was no party planned at the last minute, which made him curious. What exactly were Tessa's parents celebrating?

With Tessa by his side, Hamish followed her father into the large, open-plan kitchen.

"Diane," Wallace called out to a woman giving directions to the catering staff.

She didn't turn, but replied in a tight voice, "Can't you see that I'm busy?"

Next to him, Tessa stiffened. Wallace tossed them an apologetic look, then addressed his wife again, "Tessa and her boyfriend are here."

Diane Wallace whirled around. "Why didn't you say so immediately?" Quickly, she pasted a smile on her face and hurried toward them, arms spread wide. "Tessa, sweetheart, you're finally here."

Mrs. Wallace threw her arms around Tessa, though Hamish couldn't help but notice that Tessa didn't return the overly exuberant hug.

"Mother," was all Tessa pressed out, before she eased back from the embrace. "I see you've outdone yourself again."

Mrs. Wallace didn't comment. Instead she stared at Hamish. "Well, since nobody's introducing us, I guess I'll have to do it myself." She extended her hand. "I'm Diane, Tessa's mother."

Hamish shook her hand. "Hamish. Nice to meet you, and thanks for the invitation. I wish I'd known about it earlier, so I could have changed my plans and we could stay longer." It was a lie, of course, but considering how uncomfortable Tessa seemed to feel in her presence, it was best to line up their exit strategy right now.

"You have other plans?" she asked, her voice sounding almost accusatory.

He tried his most charming smile, and added, "Yes, I'm so sorry, but Tessa has agreed to accompany me to a work event later tonight."

"A work event? Well, if you must."

She turned away, back to the catering personnel in the kitchen, and he caught Tessa and her father exchange knowing glances. Tossing a look back at Mrs. Wallace, who'd moved to the other end of the noisy kitchen, Hamish stepped closer to Tessa and her father.

"You have to forgive her, Tessa," Wallace murmured.

"Do I?" Tessa said in an icy voice.

"The doctor has given her different meds, and I don't think we've got the dosage right yet," he explained, then met Hamish's look. "My wife is bipolar, Hamish. She has a hard time controlling her moods." He gave Tessa a sad smile. "At least we know what it is now, and can treat it. She'll never get as bad again as she once was."

Tessa's lips were pressed into a thin line and she looked away. "Will you excuse me for a moment? I need to wash my hands before I eat."

She rushed out of the room, before either Hamish or her father could respond.

Wallace put a hand on Hamish's shoulder. "How about a drink?"

As much as he could use a stiff drink after all this family drama, he had something more important to do. "I'd love one later. I should wash my hands first too, though."

Wallace pointed to the corridor that led back to the front door. "The door underneath the stairs."

"Thank you."

Hamish walked to it and entered. As soon as he was inside and had locked the door, he cloaked himself and dematerialized, so he could pass through the door and return to the corridor and start his exploration.

He went through the usual routine. First, he went upstairs to check the bedrooms and bathrooms for anything unusual, and to get a sense of what the family was like. Photos, mementos, medications lying around, they all told him a story. He already knew that Tessa was an only child, though the file he'd gotten on her hadn't said much about her parents. He was filling in those blanks now.

The father had a home office, and even on his nightstand there were files with contracts and other notes. Workaholic, no doubt. His wife's closet was filled with designer clothes. Jewelry was strewn around on her nightstand haphazardly, as if the priceless pieces were a dime a dozen. In the drawers he found pills consistent with her husband's claim. As well as miniature bottles of hard liquor. Was she chasing down the pills with booze? Bad combination. Was she the neglected wife who had turned to alcohol for comfort?

He searched on, systematically going through all the rooms. He skipped one: a bathroom. He knew who was inside: Tessa. Only a family member would come upstairs to use the bathroom here instead of the guest bath downstairs.

Knowing he didn't have much time before other guests would find it odd that the guest bathroom was still occupied, he hurried downstairs and continued his quick assessment. But he was already out of time. An impatient woman was knocking at the bathroom door.

"Anybody in there?"

A man walked up to her from the other side. "Maybe it's empty and somebody accidentally locked it." He put his hand on her shoulder. "Let me help you. I know how to open that kind of lock from the outside."

Ah, crap, so much for snooping around unseen.

Hamish charged toward the bathroom, passed through the wall next to it, since the couple was blocking the door, then uncloaked himself inside. Fully visible again, he unlocked the door, and opened it.

"Oh, I'm sorry, were you waiting?" he asked with a smile. "It's all yours."

~ ~ ~

Tessa came down the stairs just as Hamish stepped out of the guest bathroom. Glad she didn't have to walk back into the fray of the party on her own, she called out to him.

"Hamish!"

He turned, smiling, and waited until she'd reached him.

She hooked her arm under his. "Let's go back into the lion's den, shall we?" she said.

He led the way back into the living room. A waiter passed them, offering champagne, and she snatched a glass from the tray. Hamish did likewise.

When they reached the living room, she caught her father's eye on her. He'd been waiting for her to return. He smiled at her from across the room, then tapped a fork against his champagne glass to call for silence.

"Thank you all for coming," her father started, her mother standing next to him, "and helping us celebrate a milestone in our lives."

Hamish leaned closer. "Wedding anniversary?"

Tessa shook her head.

"Thirty-five years ago today we were blessed with our little girl." Philip Wallace lifted his glass toward Tessa, forcing her to reciprocate. "When we finally brought her home with us and were able to call her our own, give her our name, and care for her, our lives became so much richer for it. You, Tessa, have given us so much joy over the years and shown us that although nature denied us the chance to become parents, fate made it possible." He raised his glass again. "Happy adoption day, honey!"

Tears in her eyes, Tessa lifted her glass and locked eyes with her father. The guests repeated the well-wishes. Her gaze drifted to her mother, but she had left her husband's side and snuck out to the kitchen, where one of the waiters was arranging more cocktails on a tray.

"I didn't know you were adopted," Hamish said next to her.

She turned her head. "It makes no difference."

"I didn't mean to imply that it did. I guess that explains why you don't look like your parents at all."

She forced a smile and sipped from her glass. No, she wasn't anything like her mother. And she never wanted to be.

"Your father seems to adore you," Hamish remarked. "That was quite a moving speech."

"He loves me." Maybe too much. Perhaps that had always been the root of her problems.

"I lost my father a long time ago," Hamish said. "You should cherish his love for as long as you can."

"I do," she admitted. Despite everything.

Hamish said, "You don't get along with your mother."

She didn't look at him when she replied, "It's complicated."

Very complicated.

Tessa emptied her glass and let her eyes roam, searching for the waiter. If she was going to get through this evening, she was going to need another drink.

# 16

The vortex, the swirling mass of dark fog and wind he'd used to transport into the human world, closed behind him and vanished without a trace. Zoltan glanced around, making sure nobody had witnessed his entrance, but the bushes and trees in the residential neighborhood had hidden him well.

He'd donned a beard, brown contact lenses, and dark blond hair that reached over his ears and curled at his nape, the facial hair helping him blend in with the fashions young humans seemed to favor these days. He'd drawn the line at the man-bun though. How any self-respecting man could wear such an emasculating hairdo was beyond him, and he certainly wasn't going to sink that low.

He only had to walk two blocks to reach the house in question. The many cars parked on the curb on both sides of the street, as well as in the driveway, indicated that the homeowners had guests. Lots of them. But he wasn't going to let that stop him from doing what he'd come to do. He was sure there was a way in without being noticed.

A whiff of cigarette smoke blew in his direction. He looked around for its origin and saw a young man standing next to a bush, smoking. He wore the outfit of a catering company, a white shirt, black slacks, and a red bowtie. Perfect.

Zoltan walked casually as he approached the young man, who couldn't be older than twenty-five.

"Evening," Zoltan greeted him with a grin, then motioned to the house behind him. "No smoking inside, huh?"

The kid made a motion to extinguish his cigarette, but Zoltan stopped him. "No, don't put it out for my sake. Actually I was hoping I could bum one off you." He jerked his thumb to the house. "Before I join the party."

The young man grinned and dug into his pocket, pulling out a pack. Zoltan reached for it and helped himself to a cigarette. But he didn't light it immediately.

"What's your name?"

"Kevin."

"I'm Harry, nice to meet you," he lied. Lying was second nature to him. As was the use of force. "Must be hard working these parties. Hope you're not short-staffed. These people can be like piranhas, working you guys to the bone."

Kevin gave a long suffering sigh. "Right? Well, at least they hired five of us. So it's not too bad."

Zoltan lit his cigarette and took a drag from the disgusting thing. "That's cool. When I used to work in catering, I found it a great way to meet people. You know? Every party was a different crew. I rarely worked with the same colleagues more than once."

"Same here," Kevin agreed. "I don't know the other four. The boss just schedules us, you know. You can't really choose who you work with."

Zoltan nodded as if he cared. "Yeah, true. So, what company do you work for?" He glanced around. "I don't see a catering truck."

Kevin motioned to the house. "Oh, we parked in the alley behind the property. Didn't wanna occupy any parking spots meant for the guests."

"Yeah, makes sense." Though the kid still hadn't answered his question. "So what company was that again?"

"A Class of its Own Catering."

"What a coincidence! Is John still running the joint?"

"John?" Kevin furrowed his forehead. "I don't know a John in management. Bruce does the scheduling."

"Oh, Bruce, right," Zoltan said, slapping his hand against his forehead, pretending to know who Kevin was talking about. "John is in accounting. Of course you wouldn't know him."

He took another drag from his cigarette, then threw it to the ground and extinguished it with his shoe. "Well then, off to the party."

"Have fun."

Zoltan faked a motion to the opposite side, then wrapped his arms around Kevin's neck and jerked him back, before the kid even realized what was happening to him. He started to struggle, but Zoltan was many times stronger and dragged him behind the bushes.

"Now tell me, how bad are you, huh? Ever stolen anything? Ever beaten somebody up?" Zoltan whispered into his captive's ear, hoping he was right about the kid. "Yeah, you're no choirboy, are you?"

Kevin fought, his fear rising with every second. Perfect. Underneath it was something else. Kevin wasn't innocent. He'd committed crimes, petty crimes, but that would do. Zoltan tossed his victim to the ground and pinned him there, one hand around his throat so he couldn't scream. Savoring the moment, Zoltan bent closer and opened his mouth, sucking in a deep breath, then another. A light mist started escaping through Kevin's nostrils. Zoltan sucked harder and slowly eased up on his grip around his victim's throat. More mist rose, turning a darker shade, first gray, then black.

Yes, that's what he needed. This would be a good feeding, a rich one. The young man at his mercy had done bad things, and now Zoltan reaped the benefits. With every breath, he sucked in more fear and evil from his victim, and felt his own strength growing. His cells replenished, filled with power. In the last few months he'd come across many rich feasts like this. There was more and more evil in the world, and it tasted good.

Renewed and strengthened, Zoltan let go of his captive. Kevin was unconscious now.

"Thanks for everything, Kevin."

The hapless human had given him all he needed. And now Kevin deserved his rest. In a few hours, he'd wake up with a headache the likes of which he'd never known before. He could kill him of course. For a brief moment he considered it. But that could be messy, and he didn't want to get any blood on Kevin's clothes.

"It's your lucky day."

Moments later, Zoltan emerged wearing Kevin's white shirt, black slacks, and that ridiculous red bowtie. Not even his mother—if he had one—would recognize him now.

"Showtime."

Zoltan entered the house via the tradesmen's entrance to the side. Kevin had propped the gate open, so he could enter after his smoke break. Zoltan now closed it behind him and walked to the door at the end of the walkway and peered inside. The kitchen. Several catering personnel were busy with drinks and food. Time to establish his credentials so he could move freely within the house.

He stepped inside and addressed a woman who was filling flutes with champagne. "Hey, sorry, uh, Bruce sent me."

She stared at him. "Yeah, why?"

"He said the clients requested six staff, not five, so he sent me to chip in last minute before the homeowners think they're getting shortchanged."

She shrugged. "Fine by me. It's a little crazy here right now anyway." She turned to one of the others, a young man who was just picking up a platter with canapés. "Hey, Mike, have you seen Kevin? He was supposed to do the cocktails." She motioned to a tray with various pre-mixed drinks.

The guy shrugged. "Nope."

"I saw somebody smoking outside," Zoltan offered. "Maybe that's him."

"Figures," the woman said. "What's your name?"

"Greg." The name *Harry* had already outlived its usefulness.

"I'm Cathy. Can you take the cocktails?"

"Sure. No problem."

It would give him a good cover to check out not only the house itself, but also the homeowners and the guests. Nobody in these circles ever noticed a servant. By the time Kevin woke up and somebody realized that a stranger had been able to move within the house unimpeded, he'd be long gone. Nobody would be able to give an accurate description of him. And even if they did, it would lead nowhere. Because the human world didn't have any record of him.

With ease, Zoltan moved through the ranks of the city's upper crust, and made his way to the person he wanted to look at more closely: Tessa Wallace, the councilwoman. She'd just walked up to a woman who looked vaguely familiar, and hugged her. The woman was a good twenty to twenty-five years older than Tessa.

Zoltan moved closer.

"Amanda, I'm so glad to see you," Tessa chirped. "How have you been holding up?"

A sad look crossed the other woman's face. He'd seen that look before. Yes, at a funeral. He loved going to funerals, loved watching humans mourn their loved ones. The pain that saturated the air at a funeral was so heavy, so thick, that he could practically snatch it out of the air and swallow it down, to feed that part of him that gave him his demonic strength. After a funeral he always felt invigorated, replenished. And this woman had suffered: Amanda Yardley, the widow of the former mayor. Even now, pain radiated from her, and though pain was not as powerful as fear, he was drawn to it nevertheless.

"I'm coping," Amanda said in reply to Tessa's question. "Every day gets a little easier."

"We all miss him terribly."

"Thank you. By the way, I brought the book you lent him. I left it with my jacket." She pointed toward the front of the house. "Remind me before I leave."

"I was actually just talking about that today. Gunn is looking for some files, and it's possible that they were accidentally packed in with John's personal stuff. He might call you."

Amanda tossed her a confused look. "There were no files in the box they sent to my house. Just some awards, a few trinkets and personal papers, and his appointment book." She smiled wistfully. "I hung the awards on the wall of his study."

A tap on his shoulder made Zoltan turn.

"I'll take one of those," the tall man said and pointed to a glass on Zoltan's tray.

"Of course, sir," Zoltan answered, managing to keep his cool. He wasn't easily rattled, but suddenly coming face to face with a Stealth Guardian was nevertheless a bit of a surprise. Not that it was totally unexpected.

Although one thing did come as a surprise: the man, whose distinct aura identified him as a Stealth Guardian, was no stranger to him. In fact, a few months earlier, in an old farmhouse in California, he and two of his demons had fought against two Stealth Guardians—and come away empty handed. This man had been one of them. And one other thing immediately became clear. He was the same man the newspapers and social media channels had identified as the hero from the night before. An online article he'd seen that afternoon had claimed that Hamish MacGregor was Tessa's boyfriend.

"Thank you," Hamish said, snatching a glass, before brushing past Zoltan to join Tessa.

So the Stealth Guardians hadn't lost any time assigning a guardian to the councilwoman—a guardian who'd then promptly saved her life. However, one thing was odd: did the charge know she was being protected? Did she know who her boyfriend was? Had the Stealth Guardians suddenly changed strategy and started working out in the open?

In any case, with Hamish in the picture, right now wasn't the right time to act. He would have to change his plans. No matter. He was flexible. There were plenty of other routes to get to Tessa and destroy her.

Without drawing any attention to himself, he moved away from his primary target and surveyed the scene. It wasn't hard to spot who the hosts were: Tessa's parents, Philip and Diane Wallace. Philip Wallace seemed to be a strong-willed individual, his posture and poise indicating determination, whereas his wife was anything but. Her body language revealed her insecurity, which she tried to hide beneath expensive jewelry and designer clothes.

But Zoltan sensed something else, too. There was a scent about her, faint, but undeniable. An alcoholic, for sure. Drugs probably weren't too much of a stretch either. Whatever she was using to get through the day, and through this party, it made her an easy target. Ah, how he loved the upper crust with their insecurities and their lack of restraint! It made them just as easy to manipulate as a drug addict on the street corner.

Diane Wallace was his way in.

He just had to get her alone.

# 17

Hamish walked around the car and helped Tessa out of it. Her cheeks were flushed, and her lavender eyes sparkled like two stars in the night sky.

When he closed the car door behind her, she giggled. "I can't believe how you made Mrs. Cranston run for cover when you were going on and on about how exciting instruction manuals were."

He grinned. "Serves her right for peppering you with questions about the incident at the center last night."

"Thanks for saving me. Both from Mrs. Cranston and from the falling duct."

Tessa leaned in, and the temptation to pull her against his body rose. But he knew he couldn't act on it. He'd made a promise to her and to himself. And he was going to keep it. *Rasen* be damned.

"How many glasses of champagne have you had?" he asked, smirking.

"Are you suggesting that I'm drunk?"

Hamish chuckled. "Not drunk. Just a little tipsy." And it was kind of endearing to see her so carefree.

"Well, you would be too if you had to make nice with my mother for an entire evening."

"I thought she was rather—"

A sound coming from behind him made him spin around.

"Shit!"

Two intimidating looking men were charging toward him. Sharp blades glinted in their hands, making their intentions clear in a split second; their green eyes flashing in the dark confirmed it.

Instantly cloaking Tessa with his mind, Hamish ordered her, "Run inside, now!"

He shoved her in the direction of the front door to her apartment building, then bent down and pulled his dagger from his boot, dropping the car keys in the process. One of the demons jumped him, while the other raced toward the front door, guided by Tessa's screams.

Hamish crashed to the floor, his demonic attacker landing on top of him. Hamish kicked him off, rolled away, and cloaked himself in the next instant. But the demon was good. He'd anticipated the evasive move and swiped Hamish's arm with his dagger. He cried out, uncloaking himself in the melee, before kicking out at his attacker. The demon tumbled backwards, giving Hamish a chance to get to his feet.

He tossed a quick sideways glance toward the front door. Tessa had reached it now, but she was digging in her handbag, trying to find her keys, panic making her clumsy.

"Fuck!" he cursed and rammed into the demon, catapulting him into the air so he crashed against a car on his way down.

But the asshole wasn't giving up. He got up, aiming his dagger at Hamish, and threw it with a quick flick of his wrist. Hamish dove away and cloaked himself again. The dagger landed harmlessly on the sidewalk. The demon was pulling another dagger from his belt, when Hamish came at him invisibly, kicked it from his hand, and rammed his own blade into the demon's side.

The demon cried out, green blood splattering onto the sidewalk like confetti at a carnival. Some of it splashed on Hamish. It stuck to his clothes and remained visible, disclosing his location to the demon.

"Gotcha!" the demon grunted triumphantly and barreled toward him, another dagger in his hand.

Shit! Just how many weapons did this fucker have?

A cry from Tessa made Hamish whirl his head in her direction. Fuck! The other demon had her pinned against the front door, even though she was still cloaked. Still invisible to anybody but Hamish.

Hamish spun around and raced toward her, the first demon right behind him.

"Let go of her!" he screamed.

The demon holding Tessa captive looked over his shoulder. An evil grin spread on his face. "Too late, guardian."

"Noooooo!" Hamish screamed as he felt strong hands grip him from behind. The demon he'd stabbed pulled him back and tossed him against the wall of the apartment building. His head whipped back, pain radiating through his entire body. But he couldn't let such a small thing stop him. Not when Tessa was struggling to fight off the demon who was trying to drag her away, while she held on to the door handle for dear life.

"Hold on, Tessa!" he managed to cry out, while he tried to twist his arm so he could fend off his attacker. To no avail. The demon had him pinned.

"Good night, guardian," the demon grunted.

Hamish felt the blade at his neck and knew there was only one way out. He dematerialized and passed through the wall, materializing in a closet next to the entry hall. Spinning around, he gripped his dagger tightly with his right hand and passed through the wall again, dagger aimed at the demon's chest, reappearing in front of him, just as the demon was hitting his fist against the wall in frustration.

Before the asshole even realized what was happening, Hamish plunged his dagger into the demon's heart and sliced upward, killing him with one swipe of his blade. But there was no time to celebrate. He whirled his head toward Tessa. The demon had managed to pry her away from the door and was dragging her, kicking and screaming, away from the building.

Hamish jumped him from behind and tore him off Tessa. The demon had no chance. Hamish's dagger found its target with furious precision. Full of rage, Hamish drove his blade into the helpless creature, watching with satisfaction as his guts spilled onto the street, painting it green. But even when he knew the demon's life force was already extinguished, he couldn't stop. With one last swipe, he severed the demon's head from its body and watched it roll a few yards away until it was caught by the grid of a drain.

Only then did he turn around to where Tessa had landed on the sidewalk. But she wasn't there anymore. She was running toward the Mercedes; in fact, had reached it already.

"Tessa! Stop!"

He charged after her.

"Get away from me!" she screamed, frantically looking around as if searching for an escape route, when she suddenly bent down and picked something up.

Shit! His car keys!

She charged around the back of the car and got in. The engine revved just as Hamish reached the passenger side door and gripped the handle. Too late. The doors had locked, and Tessa was racing away.

Bracing his hands on his knees, he cursed. "Fuck!"

Now that Tessa was fleeing in his car, she wasn't cloaked anymore—she was outside his range, and if those two demons weren't the only ones trying to get to her tonight, she would be exposed.

Frantic, Hamish pulled his cell phone from his pocket and pressed the number of the compound's command center.

Logan picked up. "Hey, buddy, what's up?"

"I need you to remotely disable my car right now, and give me its location."

"Okay, give me a sec." He heard Logan typing away on his keyboard.

"And I need a cleanup crew outside Tessa's apartment. Two dead demons."

"Whoa! What the fuck happened?"

"Ambush!"

"And your charge? Is she okay?" Logan asked.

"She fled with my car."

"Smart cookie, trying to escape the demons, huh?"

"She fled from me. *After* I'd already killed the demons." Maybe beheading the one who'd attacked her had been a bit too much for her sensitive nature. But when he'd seen the asshole's hands on her, he'd seen red.

"Why the fuck?"

"Hell if I know." However, he had his suspicions: what if she'd seen too much? After all he'd had to use his preternatural skills to free himself from the demon's hold. What if she'd looked in his direction just then? If that was the case, he had a problem on his hands. But first he had to find her. "Have you located the car yet?"

"Hmm. Working on it." A short pause. "Ah, just got a lock on it. Disabling now. She's at the corner of Elm and Thirty-seventh."

"Thanks. And send the cleanup crew right now. Tell them to make sure they don't leave any body parts behind."

Logan groaned. "You went all machete on them, didn't you?"

As if Logan would have acted any differently in the same situation.

"They had it coming!" For touching Tessa. Hamish pocketed the phone and started running. She hadn't gotten far. He should be able to catch her.

# 18

The car's engine suddenly began to sputter. Tessa punched the gas pedal of the Mercedes down harder, but the car slowed.

"No!" she ground out, looking at the gas gauge, but to her astonishment, the tank was nearly full.

"What the...?"

The engine noise ceased, and the steering wheel locked. The car had stalled.

"So much for German engineering!" she cursed. She put her foot on the brake and pressed the starter button. Nothing! Frustrated, she hit her fists against the steering wheel. "Damn it! Start already!" When she hit the starter button again, her eyes fell on the gearstick. No wonder the engine wasn't starting: she was still in drive. She put the car in park and tried again. All she heard was a click.

"Please, please!" she begged, but the engine didn't respond. "Shit, shit, shit!"

She couldn't stay here like a sitting duck. She had to get away. Oh God, what she'd seen back there had terrified her down to the marrow of her bones. She didn't want to think about it, not now, or it would paralyze her.

She reached for the door handle and yanked at it. It wouldn't open. "No!" she screamed and yanked again frantically. She slammed both her fists against the door, even rammed it with her shoulder, then noticed the button for the locking mechanism. Feeling suddenly foolish, and praying that it worked, she pushed it and tried the door again. She almost fell out of the car when the door opened.

The moment she disentangled her feet from the pedals and was outside, she began to run.

She'd lost her handbag in the fight with her attacker, and therefore had no cell phone to call for help. But she knew there was a police station only four or five blocks from here. She had to make it there. Her life depended on it.

As she ran, the attack replayed in her mind, assaulting her with images that couldn't possibly be real. Images that had no basis in nature or science. She knew she'd had a few glasses of champagne, and maybe she was even over the legal limit for driving, but she wasn't drunk, and knew for sure she wasn't hallucinating.

Two men had attacked them out of the blue, and while Hamish had fought off one of them, the other had chased her. And caught her. Clumsily at first, but then she'd been in his grip and hadn't been able to escape him. She'd tried to hold on to the door so he couldn't drag her away, and had been forced to watch in horror as Hamish tried to fight off the other thug.

That's when she'd seen it: Hamish had suddenly disappeared before her very eyes, only to reappear in a different spot. Like a genie in a bottle. She'd blinked at first, thinking her fear was causing her vision to blur, but there'd been nothing wrong with her eyesight.

Hamish had disappeared several times. And then reappeared. Stunned and paralyzed, her strength had started to wane. When his attacker had suddenly slammed Hamish against the wall of the building and pinned him there, she'd thought it was over. And then Hamish's body had sunk *into* the wall, faded right through it and disappeared completely, only to return a second later, stepping back out *through* the wall, and ramming his knife into his attacker.

She should have been relieved at this point, but when she saw the green blood that spilled from the dead thug, the last ounce of her strength left her, and her attacker had dragged her away from the door. Green blood! It was impossible. But she'd seen it.

Hamish hadn't even flinched at the sight of it. As if he'd expected it! As if he'd seen it before! Then she'd seen the streaks of green on his clothes. Did it belong to his attacker, or was it Hamish's? Was he the same as them?

When she'd witnessed him massacre the second assailant with so much rage, fear and horror had gripped her, and she'd nearly thrown up. She'd never seen such fury in anybody's eyes. Such bloodlust. She'd seen a monster in those eyes. An untamed beast. And all she'd been able to think was: *Run! Get somewhere safe!* For all she knew, those two thugs had unleashed something so evil in Hamish, something so uncontrollable, that it would lash out at her next. And whatever it was, it wasn't human.

Survival instinct had overridden any rational thought. Yes, Hamish was her bodyguard, but what did she really know about him? Sure, he'd saved her life, not once, but twice, but what if that had all been part of a bigger plan?

No, her best chance of survival was to get to the police. They'd help her. And once they found the two dead bodies, they would start a manhunt for Hamish.

She turned a corner, and there, on the next block, she saw the lights of the police station. She was almost there. Just a few more steps. She gasped for air and begged her tired legs not to desert her now.

"Almost," she murmured breathlessly as she reached the steps leading up to the station door. She stretched her arm out toward the handrail. But it slipped from her grip as she was suddenly ripped backwards.

An arm wrapped around her waist, lifting her off her feet, while simultaneously a hand clamped her mouth shut, before she could take a breath to scream.

Her assailant yanked her back away from the station and dragged her around a corner. A block from the station, he turned and carried her down a side alley next to an auto repair shop. She kicked at him with her legs and struck out with her arms, but to no avail. He didn't slow down, until he pulled her into the yard of the auto repair shop, where he finally stopped.

"Stop kicking me, Tessa!"

It was Hamish, but instinctively she'd known that already.

"Now calm down. I'm gonna take my hand off your mouth, as long as you promise not to scream."

Fat chance!

"Nod to tell me you'll cooperate."

She nodded.

Hamish took his hand off her mouth, and she screamed as loud as her lungs allowed. A split second later, his hand was back on her mouth.

"Bad move, Tessa. I expected better from you. I thought we'd been through this once already and established that you're following my commands."

She grunted and kicked her leg back to hit him in the shin.

"Damn it, Tessa, will you listen to me? You're safe now."

She huffed.

"Those two guys back there are dead. They can't hurt you anymore. I made sure of that."

Yeah, but who would keep her safe from Hamish? She sniffled. What was going to happen to her now?

"Have you calmed down?"

She nodded.

"Good. No more screaming, or I'll have to use other methods to shut you up. So don't try my patience."

This time when he took his hand off her mouth, he spun her around to face him, but didn't let go of her. He looked her up and down.

"Did he hurt you?"

She ignored his question. "Who are you?"

"You know who I am."

"No, I don't. What I saw..." She pointed toward the street. "What you did back there..."

"That's part of my job. To protect you. Even if it means killing an attacker. I know it's hard to accept. But I had no choice."

Tessa shook her head. "I saw you! You disappeared!" She watched his reaction and noticed that he flinched ever so slightly. "You melted into the wall. I saw it with my own eyes. What are you? Because you're sure as hell not human. Just like those two men weren't human. For God's sake, they had green blood. Green! And you, you just vanished and then reappeared, and then you went into that wall, and you came back out as if it were nothing. Damn it, tell me the truth! What are you?"

Hamish exhaled sharply, his eyes searching hers.

"The truth, damn it. I want the truth! Don't I deserve at least that?" She drummed her fists against his chest.

Slowly, almost gently, he wrapped his hands around her wrists to stop her.

"I'm your guardian. And those two dead creatures with the green blood attacking us were demons."

She moved her head from side to side. "No, no."

But Hamish's expression remained sincere. "I'm sorry. You weren't supposed to find out. But if I hadn't used my skills and passed through the wall when that demon pinned me against it, he would have killed me." He paused. "And you would have been next. And I couldn't let that happen, because I promised to protect you."

Tessa panted, trying to make sense of his words. She tried to fill her lungs, tried to send oxygen to her brain, but still, she didn't understand what he was saying. Demons. The word conjured up images of creatures half human, half animal, half ET. But the two attackers had looked entirely human.

"Demons," she murmured to herself. She lifted her eyes back to Hamish. "But they looked human... just like you."

Hamish nodded, easing up his grip on her wrists. "That's what makes them so dangerous."

She had to agree with him. "The green blood. Is that how you knew?"

He shook his head. "I recognized them by their green eyes. It's the only outward sign."

"And you. You said you're a guardian. What does that mean?"

He turned his head toward the alley they'd come from. "Somebody's coming."

"More demons?"

"Somebody must have heard you scream. We've gotta get out of here. Now."

"The only place I'm going to is the police. There's a station just—"

He pulled her against his chest, so her next words were muffled against his shirt. Then he brought his mouth to her ear and whispered, "Not a sound. I'm cloaking us."

She wanted to protest and ask what he meant by that. She lifted her head to speak, but he'd obviously anticipated her move and pressed his lips to hers. Stunned, she froze.

She needed to fight him, because she was scared out of her wits and didn't trust him farther than she could throw him, yet she felt her body respond to him as if she wasn't its master any longer. As if her body knew something her brain didn't.

# 19

The only reason he was kissing Tessa was so she wouldn't scream again.

*Liar!*

Fine, so he was kissing her because he was still riding high on adrenaline after killing those two demons.

*Not true either.*

Okay, realizing how close Tessa had been to being captured and killed by the demons had scared the shit out of him.

*You're getting warmer.*

Damn it! So what if he was kissing her because he wanted to? He didn't have to justify his actions. He'd saved her life two times in as many days. Didn't he deserve a bloody reward for that? So what if that reward wasn't a simple *thank you* from his charge? Who would even know? Just he and Tessa. Who wasn't exactly putting up much of a fight. Sure, at first, she'd remained stiff and had hit him with her fists a few times. But now she was responding to his kiss, going all soft on him. Her head tilted to one side, granting him free access to her mouth. With her lips parted she accepted his invasion and welcomed him.

It was just a short moment they both deserved after the ambush by the demons. Nobody would ever have to find out that he'd broken his vow never to get involved with a human woman again. Besides, he wasn't getting involved with her. It would only be a kiss, nothing more.

"Looks like you found her."

At the sound of Enya's voice, Hamish released Tessa as if he'd burned himself. And maybe he had.

"Shit, Enya! What are you doing here?"

"When the call came in that you and your, uh, client, got attacked, I figured you might need backup."

She looked at Tessa, who nervously adjusted her clothes. Had he pulled her blouse from her skirt, or had that happened during the struggle with the demons?

"But it looks like you've got everything under control."

Hamish sighed and shoved a hand through his hair. Under control? He wouldn't exactly call it that.

"Tessa, meet Enya, my colleague."

Tessa nodded. "Hi."

"Hi," Enya replied.

Tessa fidgeted. "So, are you a... a guardian, too?"

Enya whipped her head in Hamish's direction, bracing her hands on her hips. "What the fuck, Hamish?"

"She knows." He glanced at Tessa. "It's okay, Tessa." Then he addressed Enya again, "Tessa saw me fight the demons. I had to use my... my preternatural skills to survive. I had no choice. The bastards are getting too good."

"Well that's just peachy."

"It is what it is." He shrugged. "Now give me an update. Who's doing the cleanup?"

"Aiden and Pearce are on it. They should be almost done." She pointed to his shirt and pants, which were stained with demon blood. "You should get cleaned up, too."

He nodded. "As soon as I can." He pointed to the stains. "Fucking demon blood can't be cloaked. That's why—"

"Cloaked," Tessa interrupted. "You said that before. What does that mean?"

Enya frowned and tipped her chin up at him. "You just told me she knows."

"I was just about to explain things when you interrupted."

"Didn't look much like explaining to me, but then I could be wrong."

Hamish grabbed her bicep and pulled her a few feet away. "Damn it, Enya," he said in a lowered voice. "Do you have to make Tessa uncomfortable?"

She smirked. "I have the feeling it's not she who's uncomfortable, but you."

Enya had a point, but he wasn't going to admit that. "Drop it! What you saw means nothing, okay? Nothing at all."

She shrugged. "Whatever you say." Then she tossed a pointed look at her bicep. "And now I'd appreciate it if you'd let go of me. I don't like being manhandled."

Hamish released her. "As long as we understand each other. This goes nowhere. You got that?"

"Don't worry, I don't gossip."

He nodded. He believed her. Enya was a straight shooter. At least his compound mates wouldn't have to find out that he'd been playing tonsil tennis with a charge.

"Good. You've got transportation?"

"Yeah."

"Can you drop me and Tessa off at my car?"

"Sure."

Hamish turned back to Tessa and caught her gaze on him. There was something different about her now. She appeared solemn. Maybe the reality of what had happened was only just now sinking in.

The vibrating sound of a cell phone suddenly echoed in the dark yard.

"Mine," Enya announced and pulled it from her pocket. "Yeah, Logan, what's up?" She listened for a few seconds. "Oh shit! Yeah, got it. Sure. I'll tell him." She disconnected the call and put the phone back.

On alert, Hamish looked at her. "What?"

But Enya looked past him at Tessa, taking a few steps closer. "Logan picked up a 9-1-1 call coming from your parents' house."

Tessa slammed her hand over her mouth. "No! Oh God no! Is it my father? His heart?" Panic widened her pupils.

"We don't know. We don't have a recording of it. We just know somebody at your house called 9-1-1, and dispatch sent an ambulance. It's already back en route to the hospital," Enya replied, her voice soothing. "We'll get you to the hospital right away." She tossed him a look. "Right, Hamish?"

He nodded. "Do we know which one?"

"St. Agnes."

Hamish took Tessa's arm. "Let's go. We can talk about everything else later."

He followed Enya with Tessa by his side.

"He looked so well tonight," Tessa lamented. "Damn it, why did they have to throw that party? It was too much stress for him. He needs to take it easy. But he won't listen. He just won't listen."

Hamish squeezed her arm in reassurance. "We don't even know if it's your father's heart. Please don't imagine the worst."

Eyes full of tears looked up at him. "What else would it be?"

"It might not even be him. Maybe one of the guests got sick. Or drank too much and hurt themselves."

He hoped that was the case, because Tessa already had enough to deal with. Finding out that her father had suffered another heart attack would make her crack under the pressure. His first priority now was to keep her strong.

"We'll know in half an hour."

# 20

Tessa stared out the window as if in a trance, while Enya drove them to the abandoned Mercedes. There was too much to process, and she didn't know where to start. To say that she was confused was an understatement.

Demons. Hamish disappearing into the wall. Green blood. Beheaded monsters. Then there was her frantic escape, and Hamish catching her, kissing her, and then proclaiming to Enya that it had meant nothing. Yes, she'd heard it, and it had felt like a stab in the back.

And now this, the worst of all: her father in the hospital. Her night couldn't possibly get any worse. She had a million questions and not a single answer, only a few things she'd pieced together from what she'd seen and heard. And right now her mind was too clouded with worry over her father's health to even recall those things.

"Do you need backup?" Enya suddenly said to Hamish who sat in the passenger seat.

"I'm good. I want you to report the demon attack to the council. Then give Manus a push. I need to know what he found on the duct."

"Sure." She stopped the car next to the Mercedes.

Hamish got out and helped Tessa out of the car. Just as Enya drove off, Tessa realized something.

"Oh no! Get her back! Your car doesn't work. We need hers to get to the hospital." She waved in the direction of Enya's disappearing taillights, but Enya didn't stop and turned right at the end of the block, disappearing from her view.

She suddenly felt Hamish's hand on her shoulder and spun around.

"The car works. I had it disabled remotely earlier, so I could catch up with you."

At his admission, her chin dropped. "You did what?"

Hamish shifted his weight to the other foot. "I had to make sure you didn't get away. I didn't know whether there were more demons following you. I needed to get to you first."

When he opened the passenger door for her, she got in without protest. Numb, stunned. Whatever one might call it. Hamish entered on the other side and pressed against a spot on the dashboard. A panel slid back and revealed a small number pad. He punched several numbers into it, then closed it and pressed the start button. The engine hummed to life.

Tessa leaned back in the seat and tried to calm herself. Maybe figuring out what had happened tonight would take her mind off her worry about her father, because that hurt more than anything else in her life. He was her rock. She couldn't lose him.

"We'll be there in twenty minutes," Hamish said with a sideways glance.

She nodded. "You didn't answer my questions earlier."

"No, I didn't, you're right."

"I need answers now." And when she got them, she would calmly evaluate them from every side, look at everything logically, and decide what to believe—and accept what she must.

"Why don't we talk after the hospital?"

"Why don't we talk now?" she shot back and pinned him with a glare. "Or do you need time to come up with a story first?"

"There is no story. Just the truth."

"Then let me have it. Straight." She folded her hands in her lap to make the shaking stop. "Explain to me what I saw tonight."

Hamish directed his gaze back to the road, and for a moment she wondered if he was going to ignore her, but then he started talking. "The two dead men whose blood is all over my clothes were demons. More specifically, Demons of Fear. Their sole mission in life is to incite violence and fear in the world. They feed off it and it makes them stronger. And one day, when they've reached critical mass, they'll rise up and attempt to rule over mankind."

"How?"

"You don't want to know."

"I do."

"Once knowledge is obtained, it can never be returned. Are you sure you want to know all this?"

She nodded. The more she knew, the better. "I fear the things I don't know more than the things I know."

"Fair enough." He cleared his throat. "They'll manipulate humankind, drain their minds of all independent thought, and turn them into slaves. There will be no free will, no choice, no happiness. Humans will only exist to serve their demon masters."

Tessa shivered involuntarily. Images of apocalyptic movies on foreign planets came to mind, where humans toiled in mines deep underground. The prospect of it made her gasp for air.

"I'm sorry," Hamish said. "But they're as evil as they come."

"And where do you and your colleagues come in? Who are you?"

"We were human once. Just like the demons. But we evolved. Nature gave us certain skills so we could fight the demons."

"Like how you merged with the wall?" She shook her head, still unable to believe what she'd seen.

"I didn't actually merge with it; I passed through it. We're able to disassemble our molecules to pass through solid objects. It gives us access to any place we need. Nobody can lock us out."

"That's how you managed to defeat the demon. He had you pinned against the wall."

"Yes. I had no other way of escaping."

"But what if he'd just followed you through the wall?"

"He couldn't. Demons don't have that skill."

She tucked that fact away for future use. "And earlier, when you were fighting him, you disappeared and then reappeared again at a different spot. What is that? Teleportation?"

To her surprise, he chuckled. "I guess it must look like that. But it's not. I cloaked myself."

"Cloaked? You keep saying that." Would he finally explain what that meant?

"I made myself invisible. And while invisible I changed position to confuse the demon and get the upper hand in the fight."

She furrowed her forehead. "That doesn't make sense. If you can make yourself invisible, then why wouldn't you just fight invisibly all the time?"

"I would, but cloaking takes a lot of energy, and I needed the energy to fight. Demons are incredibly strong. I had to use all my strength to overpower him. I couldn't waste energy on cloaking myself."

"But he got you nevertheless."

Hamish sighed. "Because I used some of my energy to cloak *you* from them."

Had she heard correctly? "What?"

He looked at her then. "When the two demons attacked, I cloaked you with my mind, so they wouldn't see you, so you'd have a chance at escape."

Her heart beat up into her throat now. "But that demon caught me anyway." Even now she could still feel his hands on her.

"Making you invisible doesn't make you disappear. The demons could still hear you."

She slapped her hand over her mouth. "Oh my God. I screamed. He got me because I screamed."

"I had no time to tell you how to act. It's not your fault."

No, it wasn't her fault, but it wasn't Hamish's either. "You tried to protect me, knowing that it would weaken you?"

His shoulders stiffened. "I'm in charge of your safety."

He said it as if it explained everything. Yet it only threw up more questions. "Because I hired you?"

"You didn't hire me. I was assigned to you."

She turned her head fully to him, and he met her gaze for a moment, before turning his attention back to the light nighttime traffic. "But I did. Anton Faldo recommended you. And Poppy practically forced me to hire you. And she got that union to pay for it."

"Faldo is a liaison between the Stealth Guardians and the human world."

"Stealth Guardians? Is that what you and Enya are called?"

"Yes."

"And Faldo, he's one of you? Faldo is a gangster."

Hamish sighed. "Not everything is black and white. Faldo is human. And he might have at one time been less than honest. His methods were certainly shady. But let's just say he's seen the error of his ways, and as penance, he works for us. He reports to us when he sees something that's not right. And his reputation actually helps him. He sees and hears things that other upstanding citizens don't. He let us know about the death threat against you. And we realized immediately that we needed to protect you. So we made it happen."

"But why? I'm nobody special. I could have gotten a security guard from any company—"

"—who would have been ill-equipped to deal with what you're facing. As for not being special. You're wrong. You're very valuable. To us. To this community. You carry a heavy burden on your shoulders. You have to become mayor and turn this city around, or it will fall into the hands of the demons." He locked eyes with her then.

Her heart was beating like a locomotive. She felt as if somebody had dumped a fifty pound sack of potatoes on her chest. "But what if I don't win?"

"The only way you'll lose is if the demons kill you first. And I'm gonna make damn sure that doesn't happen." There was a grim look on his face. She noticed how his jaw clenched and how he gripped the steering wheel tighter, his knuckles turning white.

An odd sense of foreboding washed over her. "They'll try again, won't they?"

He didn't answer, but he didn't have to. She understood now. She was in the demons' way. And the only thing that stood between her and death at their hands was Hamish.

By the time they reached the hospital, Tessa had come to terms with the new situation she found herself in. She was in danger, because the demons didn't want her to become mayor and bring peace and prosperity back to Baltimore. It wasn't really that different from the situation she'd been in before. All she needed to do was to replace the word *demons* with *political opponents*, and she'd be in the same mess. But if she replaced *bodyguard* with *preternatural guardian*, at least it meant she felt a little bit safer. No bodyguard had the kind of out-of-this-world skills she'd seen Hamish use.

Oh God, he was the invisible man who could walk through walls! If she had a chance at survival, then it was because he was watching over her.

Hamish didn't park in front of the main entrance. Instead he drove around the corner, even though there were plenty of free spots in the well-lit parking lot.

"Why don't you park here?"

He pointed to his stained clothes. "I can't go in there like this." He pulled the Mercedes to a stop next to a row of dumpsters. The area was badly lit and away from any windows.

"I'll go in without you."

She opened the car door and got out, but he mimicked her and met her at the trunk as she was rounding the car.

"Oh no, you're not going in there on your own. Not after what happened tonight."

"But you just said you can't go in there like that. I need to see my father."

"I'll only be a sec." He opened the trunk, then started taking off his shirt.

She turned around quickly, not wanting to be caught ogling him. "Why didn't you say you had a change of clothes in the car?"

"Cause I don't."

Her heart drummed violently. "Then what are you doing? You can't go in there naked!"

"I can and I will. But I'll also be invisible." She heard him toss something into the trunk and close it. "Turn around."

"No! If this is some sort of sick—"

She felt his hand on her shoulder, turning her around. She wanted to avert her eyes from his nudity, but she didn't have to. There was nothing to see. While she still felt his hand on her shoulder, she was staring into nothingness. Hamish was invisible.

Curious, she stretched out her hand until it met his naked chest. Instantly she pulled back, sucking in a breath. It was true. He was still there. But he was invisible.

"But why did you have to take your clothes off to do that? When you fought the demons, you didn't have to."

"Normally I wouldn't have to get undressed, because whatever I wear will become invisible with me, but the demon blood on my clothes defies my power. Did you ever watch *The Invisible Man*?"

She nodded.

"Then you probably remember that when he ate colored food, it remained visible in his body. It works the same way with demon blood. It can't be made invisible." He took her elbow. "Now let's go inside. Just behave normally. Don't worry about holding any doors open for me or wondering where I am. I won't let you out of my sight. Okay?"

"Okay."

"And another thing: watch for flickering lights. They indicate the presence of demons."

"How?"

"The aura of the demons reacts with two gases: neon and mercury, which are inside of fluorescent and neon light tubes. If they come too close, the light starts to flicker first, then it burns out. Flickering lights will give us a warning."

She shook her head, stunned about everything she'd learned tonight. "So watch out for flickering lights and for anybody with green eyes."

"Not everybody with green eyes is a demon; it's a very special green. You'll recognize it when you see it."

She swallowed and nodded. "Anything else?"

"Plenty, but right now we don't have time for more."

# 21

Relieved that Tessa had calmed down and seemed to have accepted the explanations he'd given her, Hamish followed her into the main foyer of the hospital. He was dressed in only his boxer briefs and socks—not exactly an appropriate look, but then again, he was invisible, so nobody would have to see him this way. And being invisible afforded him all kinds of advantages. He would be able to snoop around if he needed to without anybody being the wiser. Though his first priority, of course, was to remain with Tessa and make sure nothing happened to her.

In the foyer, Tessa headed straight for the information desk. A TV in the nearby seating area blared, *"Gunshots were exchanged during an altercation in Carroll Park only moments ago. Several civilians are said to have been shot. One police officer is confirmed dead."*

Tessa addressed the person behind the information desk, "My father was admitted just now. Where can I find him?"

The employee looked at her. "Name?"

"Philip Wallace."

The woman typed something on her keyboard, then looked up a moment later, a regretful smile on her lips. "Sorry, ma'am, but I can't find that name. Are you sure he came to this hospital? Maybe he went to County—"

"The ambulance brought him here less than an hour ago," Tessa interrupted, getting more agitated every second.

"Oh, why didn't you say so? Then he wouldn't be in the system yet." She leaned over her desk and pointed to the end of a long hallway. "Go down that way, follow the sign for Emergency, and you'll see the triage desk. They would have checked him in there if he came by ambulance."

With a hurried "Thank you", Tessa ran down the hallway and through the double doors at the end, Hamish following close on her heels.

Around the next corner was what looked like a nurse's station. *Triage,* the sign above it said. Tessa stopped at the desk.

"My father, Philip Wallace, was brought in here less than an hour ago," she said breathlessly.

The male nurse looked at a clipboard on the desk and scanned the list of names. Then he shook his head. "Sorry, he wasn't admitted here."

"Oh no!" Tessa sounded close to tears.

"What's your name, Miss?"

"Tessa Wallace."

The nurse looked back at the clipboard. "I have a Diane Wallace here."

Tessa froze. "My mother?"

"Room three, but you can't go in there right now. There's a waiting room just—"

But Tessa was already spinning around and charging down the short hallway, where long blue curtains reaching from ceiling to floor separated a large room into separate treatment areas.

The nurse hurried after her. "Miss, you can't go down there!" Just in front of the curtained-off area with a large white number three hanging down from the ceiling, he caught up to her. "Miss!"

"Please! I need to know what's going on."

He grabbed her arm, and Hamish felt like punching him, although he knew he couldn't. Luckily, at that moment, a male voice called out from behind the curtain.

"Tessa?"

"Dad!"

The curtain was pulled back and Tessa's father appeared. She practically flew into his arms.

"What are you doing here?" he asked.

The nurse repeated, "She can't be in here."

Hamish passed through the curtain, entering the treatment area, while the doctor who was tending to Diane Wallace walked out, saying to the nurse, "It's fine. Let her in."

As Tessa and her father reentered, Hamish walked to the gurney. Diane lay propped up on it, looking pale. She was hooked up to a monitor and an IV drip. She appeared to have no external injuries. Hamish leaned in closer. Her eyes didn't seem to register anything around her. As if she was zonked out on meds.

"What happened?" Tessa asked her father.

"I was looking for her so we could see our guests off together. I found her upstairs in the bedroom, collapsed. She seemed conscious, but was unresponsive. So I called 9-1-1," her father said.

"She'll be fine," the doctor confirmed. He looked at Tessa, giving her a reassuring nod. "Most likely just a momentary spell of weakness. According to your mother's medical file, she's been on different medications. It's probably an interaction. Her GP should assess her medications again. She's also dehydrated, so I'm giving her fluids." He pointed to the monitor. "Her blood pressure and heart rate are stable now."

Hamish looked at the monitor. Everything looked just as the doctor had said.

"Dr. Hartnell!" came a voice from outside the curtain.

"Yes?"

"We've got two gunshot victims coming in in thirty seconds."

The physician rubbed the bridge of his nose for a moment. "I'm coming. Alert Nellman and Booker."

"Yes, doctor."

Dr. Hartnell nodded at Wallace and Tessa and pulled aside the curtain. "The nurse will check in with you in about half an hour when your wife has had all the fluids. I'll be back after that to see if we can release her or need to keep her overnight." Then he rushed out into the hallway.

Tessa let out a breath and glanced at her mother lying on the gurney. Diane murmured something, and Tessa looked over her shoulder, addressing her father, "What's she saying?"

He shrugged, and they both approached the gurney. Wallace took his wife's hand and held it. "She's been babbling incoherently since the ambulance." He stroked her hand. "I'm here, darling."

Hamish saw the love Wallace had for his wife. True and unconditional love. But he didn't see the same love in Tessa as she looked down at her mother. He'd sensed a calmness come over her the moment she'd realized that her father was okay. She hadn't transferred her worry about her father's health to her mother. As if the woman were a stranger to her. Hamish studied Tessa's face again. No, not a stranger, but somebody she hated.

"I'm sure she'll be fine soon, Dad." The words, obviously meant to calm her father, had a hollow ring to them.

Philip Wallace turned his head to his daughter. "You have to forgive her, Tessa. You can't hold onto the past forever. Forgive her before it's too late." His pleading eyes were brimming with tears.

Forgive her for what?

"That day isn't today, Dad." Tessa turned away.

Just then, more mumbled words came from Diane. Hamish bent down to bring his ear to her mouth.

"The other child... should have taken her, too... belong together... didn't have the strength... couldn't handle both..." Then she broke off.

Hamish looked at her face. Her eyes were closed now. He spun his head to the monitor, but the vital signs were stable and the heart monitor kept beeping at the same rhythm as before. Diane Wallace was asleep.

# 22

Tessa woke late. The night had been exhausting to say the least, and she was glad that it was Saturday and she didn't have to go to the office. But she had responsibilities nevertheless, which forced her to get up when all she wanted was to curl up in a ball and hide.

The doctor had kept her mother in the hospital overnight, and Tessa had promised her father she'd help him bring her mother home in the afternoon and get her settled. She wasn't doing it for her, but for him. He'd looked awfully pale when she'd seen him at the hospital, and she was worried that the stress of having to take care of her mother would take a toll on his health. And that was something she wanted to avoid at all cost.

Tessa swung her legs out of bed and headed for the shower. It felt good to stand under the warm spray and pretend that everything was fine. But too much had changed last night. A new reality had taken hold of her life. She remembered Hamish's words: *Once knowledge is obtained, it can never be returned.* He was right. Now that she knew what the world was really like, she couldn't go back to her old life. She had to try and come to terms with this new one.

When she was dressed, she took a deep breath and walked into the living room. She looked around. Had Hamish left without telling her? The sound of the front door opening made her spin her head in that direction. Hamish walked in, holding a box of pastries.

Her heartbeat kicked up. "You left me alone to go out and get pastries?"

He immediately shook his head. "I had them delivered. But I had to walk downstairs to meet the delivery guy."

Relieved, she exhaled.

"I would never leave you unprotected. Particularly not after last night," he assured her.

"Thank you. I'm sorry I overreacted. It's just... I'm still a little..."

"I know." He smiled, understanding and kindness in his eyes. "Sit down, I made coffee." He placed the box of pastries on the coffee table and walked into the kitchen. A moment later he returned with two steaming mugs, hers with plenty of cream, his black.

She sat down in one corner of the couch, taking a sip of her coffee, while Hamish took the other corner.

"After last night, we need to go over a few things regarding your safety," he started.

She nodded. She'd figured as much.

"You met Enya. She's my second, my backup. But what you don't know is that she's been protecting you all along during the times when I wasn't with you."

"Enya? She was there?" She suddenly remembered the day she'd thought she'd heard something as she was leaving her office. "In my office?"

"Yes. We couldn't leave you unprotected during the day, though the risk while you're at City Hall is obviously lower. Everybody has to go through the metal detectors and be checked in. It limits access somewhat. Nevertheless, we made sure you were never alone."

"And now?" She reached for the box on the coffee table and picked out a pastry.

"Enya and I will still protect you. If I can't be with you, she will be. But now that you know what we are, I need you to promise me that you won't share this knowledge with anybody. Not with your father. Not with Poppy, or anybody else. We've worked like this for centuries, and we can't risk being exposed."

"Enya, is she as good as you? I mean when it comes to fighting demons."

"She's one of the best. I trust her with my life, and so should you. She may not look it, but she's strong. And she's been at this for decades."

Tessa frowned. "Decades? She can't be older than me." She bit into her Danish and chewed.

She noticed Hamish hesitate, running a hand through his thick hair. "I guess I forgot to mention that yesterday."

"Mention what?"

"Stealth Guardians are immortals. We live forever, unless a demon kills us first."

Tessa nearly choked on her pastry, and quickly tried to swallow it down, taking a sip from her coffee to clear her throat.

"Immortal?" She looked him up and down, searching for any sign that he was different. But apparently immortality didn't have any outward signs. "How old is she?"

"Almost two hundred." He met her eyes then. "Same age as I."

Her eyes widened. Thought after thought suddenly charged through her mind. Hamish had lived for two centuries already. He was experienced. He'd seen history happen. And he'd had God-knew how many women. No wonder the kisses they'd shared hadn't meant anything to him. Besides, he knew that a relationship with a human would never work out. She would age and die, and he would live on forever. A human woman would only be a temporary toy for him, gone in the blink of an eye. Now she understood.

"Immortal," she repeated to try to burn it into her mind. So there could never be anything between them, no matter how hot his kisses had been. No matter how much she was attracted to him.

"Yes, but not invulnerable."

She lifted her eyebrows in question.

"The daggers the demons were wielding... they were forged back in the Dark Days, the era when both the Stealth Guardian species and the Demon species were born. Only weapons from back then have the power to kill us."

"What about guns?"

He shook his head. "There were no guns back then. Modern guns can only injure us. It still hurts like a bitch, but a bullet won't kill us."

"You killed the demons with a knife. Was it—"

"Yes."

He set down his coffee cup, bent over, and shoved up the seam of his pant leg to pull something from his boot. He presented it to her on flat palms. A dagger.

"It's beautiful." The blade was shiny and sharp. The handle appeared to be of some sort of obsidian stone and was covered with intricate golden inlays.

"And deadly," he murmured. "It's one of the ironies of our species that what can kill a demon, can also kill a guardian. It shows how our fates are linked."

She looked up. "How many of yours have the demons killed?"

"The number doesn't matter, because each and every one we lost was one too many."

"You said last night that you lost your father. Did the demons..."

Hamish sheathed his dagger, while he answered, "He died fighting. It was because of him that the human he was protecting survived and was able to fulfill his destiny. I'm very proud of him." He rose and picked up his cup. "More coffee?"

"I still have plenty," she said, while Hamish walked back to the kitchen. "I'm sorry about your father. I don't know what I would do if I lost mine. He's all I've got."

"And your mother?"

"We're not close, as you may have guessed."

"That's pretty obvious. Sorry, I don't mean to pry."

Tessa took another gulp from her coffee. "Maybe there's a good reason why nature denies some women motherhood."

"I gather she wasn't the kind of mother you wanted," Hamish said softly as he walked back toward the sofa.

"No, she wasn't." She reached for another pastry. "But I got the father I needed." She was about to take a bite of the donut, when she heard a knock at the door.

"Enya?" Hamish called out, rising.

"Yeah, it's me."

"Coming," he said and marched toward the door, but before he reached it, Enya had already walked through it and entered the apartment.

"Don't bother," Enya said.

Tessa's pulse began to beat frantically, still not used to the preternatural skills of her bodyguards.

Enya nodded at Hamish, then looked past him. "Morning, Tessa. You look better today."

"Morning, Enya," she said.

Enya's gaze fell on the donut in Tessa's hand. "Are those from Mario's?"

"You're early," Hamish replied, ignoring her question.

Enya shrugged and walked to the coffee table, helping herself to a pastry. "Manus wants to show you something. So I figured I'd relieve you early."

Instantly, Hamish's relaxed mood vanished and he was all business. "Where is he?"

"He said to meet him at the center."

Hamish set down his coffee cup and turned to Tessa. "Are you gonna be alright?"

"I'll have to go see my parents later."

"Enya will go with you."

"But how am I gonna explain who she is?"

"You won't have to explain anything. Enya will be invisible."

Tessa sighed. Would she ever get used to this? Would it one day become second nature? "Go. Though I really don't see that it matters now how that duct fell. It must have been the demons. And because they didn't succeed, they came back last night and tried again."

Hamish shook his head. "It still matters. The demons don't always work alone. If we find out who helped them, we'll have a better chance of finding them."

"What are you saying?" she asked, though she was starting to understand where he was going with his reasoning.

"Tessa, the demons use humans to do some of their dirty work."

The revelation made her heart beat into her throat, choking off her air. Irrational fear gripped her.

"Why would anybody help these vile creatures?"

"The demons have their methods: they tempt humans, offer to fulfill their greatest desires. They manipulate them, they blackmail them; anything that works. Most humans are too weak to resist."

Tessa swallowed hard. No matter how strong or how good Enya was, she still felt safest with Hamish. "Can I come with you?"

Hamish and Enya exchanged a look.

"Please," Tessa begged. "Why don't we all go? And if you're not done by the time I have to see my parents, Enya and I can go, and you can stay with Manus." She locked eyes with him. "Please."

Hamish sighed, while Enya shrugged.

"Doesn't bother me," Enya said.

It took a few seconds before Hamish finally replied, "Fine. We'll all go."

# 23

"More bad news, oh Great One," Vintoq, one of Zoltan's personal demon guards, said as he glanced down the long corridor, checking, as he always did, that they weren't overheard.

"I'm on my way up top. What is it now?" Zoltan growled and continued walking toward one of the spots in the vast underground labyrinth where he could cast a vortex to enter the human world.

"Two of your subjects disappeared last night. We fear they were killed."

"So?" That was hardly news. Let alone bad news. If they were indeed so stupid as to have gotten themselves killed, then they didn't deserve to live anyway. Good riddance!

"I have reason to believe that they were up top to mess with your plans."

They'd reached a spot where the corridor widened into a large circle. Yannick, one of his most trusted servants, stood sentry and bowed his head. Zoltan acknowledged him with a nod, then tossed his personal guard a sideways glance. He'd chosen Vintoq because he was smarter than the others. Zoltan contemplated his words for a moment, then let his power rise inside him and opened a vortex of wind and fog in the circle. "Come up top with me."

Once inside the vortex, he added, "What have you heard?"

"Somebody wants to see you fail, so he can take over your position."

"Let him try!" Zoltan laughed. None of those idiots was capable of devising a plan that could derail him. "And when he does, bring me his head."

He stepped out of the vortex, Vintoq on his heels, and looked around the deserted alley they'd been transported to.

Vintoq glanced around. "What are we doing here?"

"You'll see." Zoltan motioned him to follow as he walked to a metal door and entered a run down apartment building through the back entrance.

He marched up stairs that hadn't been cleaned in months. Vintoq's boots made a metallic sound every time he took a step, while Zoltan's own footsteps were virtually silent. Luckily, today, stealth wasn't necessary. The inhabitants of this property were too wasted to hear anybody coming. Such easy prey.

Arriving on the third floor, Zoltan opened the door and walked down the corridor, past several apartments, until he found the number he was looking for. Lucky number seven. Well, lucky for him, not for the occupant.

Without much ado, he kicked the flimsy door in.

Inside, it was dim despite the bright morning sun outside. In front of the windows hung old bed sheets to keep the light out. The studio was a mess, bottles of booze strewn about, drug paraphernalia displayed on a coffee table.

On the bed, a woman slept. Or rather, she'd passed out in a drug-induced stupor on top of the duvet. So pretty. So vulnerable.

Vintoq sidled up to him and pulled in a breath. "Is that—"

"Of course not." Zoltan grinned, satisfied with himself. "But she'll do." In fact, she was perfect. Nobody would notice the difference. Because there would be none.

"Now let's get to work."

~ ~ ~

Hamish suppressed a vile curse and the urge to punch a certain someone. He shouldn't have given in when Tessa had begged him to come to his meeting with Manus. But one pleading look from her lavender-colored eyes, and he hadn't been able to refuse her anything. Now he had to watch as Manus shook Tessa's hand for longer than was necessary and flirted with her like it was an Olympic discipline. And Enya was no help either. She was watching with a smirk.

Manus had entered the building via the usual way—walking through the door—and then unlocked it from the inside upon their arrival. There was nobody in the center today. According to a sign on the door, the opening had been delayed, pending a review of the renovation work. But nobody from the City Building Department would be here on the weekend. The police had made a cursory review on the night of the incident, but not done anything further. They'd left everything in place and cordoned the relevant areas off.

"So what have you got for me?" Hamish interrupted gruffly.

Finally, Manus let go of Tessa's hand and turned to him. "Bad mood?"

Hamish didn't reply, but stared his fellow guardian down.

"Well then, let me give you the short version," Manus said and pulled a laser pointer from his pocket. He pointed it up and the red dot danced around the ceiling. "Voila!"

"What am I looking at?" Hamish asked.

"The only way to access the duct is from down below. Nobody other than a small child would have been able to crawl inside. So whoever touched that duct, had to have done it from the outside." He made a corresponding movement with his pointer. "See the straight edges, where a portion of the duct is missing? That's the part that fell down during Tessa's speech. And those straight edges tell me that the duct didn't get blown from the ceiling by explosives, or the edges would be all jagged and uneven."

Hamish rubbed his chin. "So what are you saying? It was just a malfunction?"

"That's what I wondered myself. So I did a residue test on the duct. It came back negative for explosives. But then I saw the glue."

"What glue?" Hamish asked.

Manus pointed to the duct that still lay on the stage and waved for them to follow him. When he reached the stage, he pointed to one end of the duct.

"Heavy duty tape. But that's not how ducts are normally connected. They usually use a slip joint to hold two pieces together."

Hamish bent closer and examined one end of the duct. Pieces of mangled silver tape seemed burned into the metal. He looked up and met Manus's eyes. "So let's say somebody rigged it so the only thing holding the duct together was this tape. How could that person make sure it fell at the correct moment, so it would hit the right person?"

Immediately after he said it, his gaze shot to Tessa. She shivered. Shit, he hadn't meant it that way. The *right* person wasn't what he'd wanted to say.

Manus pointed to the burnt tape. "The glue melted under extreme heat and the tape started to peel away. It was only a matter of time. Once enough of the tape was off, gravity did the rest."

Hamish shook his head. "But neither the air conditioning system nor the heating was switched on the night of the party. The duct couldn't have gotten hot from the air blowing through it."

"You're right, besides, that would have taken too long to heat up." He switched on his laser pointer again and pointed to one spot, drawing Hamish's gaze to it. "But there are other things that create heat."

Hamish pointed to the red dot. "A laser pointer? That's the most harebrained idea you've had yet."

"Not an ordinary laser pointer." Manus shook his head. "But if you use a small industrial laser, no bigger than an ordinary pen, and point the beam where the ducts are joined by the tape, you'll create sufficient heat to destroy the tape. You just need to be close enough."

"You've gotta be kidding me," Hamish said.

"It's not hard to do. Just search YouTube and you'll find plenty of videos that'll show you how. But you have to be close enough. Considering where the duct is located in relation to the stage and the audience, I'd say only somebody on the stage could have been close enough to point a laser beam at that duct with sufficient accuracy."

Manus motioned to the lights in the room, then the tacky disco ball that hung over the area that had been a dance floor on Thursday night. "I'm assuming that thing was on the night of the party?"

Tessa nodded. "I noticed it when we were dancing. And when I spoke, it was blinding me on and off."

Hamish let out a breath. Damn it, Manus could be right. "It would have made it easy for anybody on stage to use a laser. With all the other lights dancing around the room, nobody would have noticed. I didn't. I was too focused on the crowd taking pictures and videos. There were flashes."

"Exactly," Manus said.

"Which means we have several suspects: VanSant, Mantle, Poppy, and of course Gunn." And Hamish knew exactly where he'd put his money: on the person who had the most to gain from Tessa's death.

"Couldn't it have been a demon?" Tessa asked, looking around nervously.

"That's always a possibility," Hamish admitted, "but since this building uses LED and halogen lighting throughout, we'll never know if a demon was in here. I don't see any neon or fluorescent lights anywhere." He motioned to Manus. "Did you, Manus?"

His colleague shook his head. "Not a one. I think our best bet is to check out the people who were on stage."

"I'll take Gunn," Hamish said immediately.

Enya grunted. "Leave us something to do, will you?"

"You've got enough on your plate," he replied and pointed to Tessa. "You're going to make sure nobody touches a hair on Tessa's head, or—"

Enya lifted her head. "No threats needed. I know my duties." Then she twisted one side of her mouth up and looked at Tessa. "Men think they're the only ones with the brains to execute a plan."

Hamish ignored the hit and looked at Manus. "Manus, why don't you call the compound and have them assign somebody to check out the other people on stage?"

Tessa looked at her watch. "I think it's time to help my dad bring my mother home."

"Let's go then." Enya was already turning around and heading for the door.

Tessa made a motion to follow her, then looked over her shoulder straight at Hamish. "Gunn insisted that night that I speak first. And that's not like him. I have a bad feeling about him. Be careful."

Hamish felt his mouth twist into a smile. Tessa was worried about him? It was an entirely unexpected thing, and he had to admit that he liked it. He liked knowing that there was a woman who cared enough about him to worry about him. Strangely enough he'd never had that same sensation with Olivia. She'd never worried about him. Maybe because she'd never really cared about him.

# 24

Hamish was in luck. Just after he arrived at Gunn's house in the suburbs, the garage opened and a dark SUV backed out. Hamish remained idling at the curb half a block away, waiting for the car to pass him. Gunn was behind the wheel. Perfect. Hamish turned his car around and followed at a distance.

Gunn drove several miles before he stopped at a floral stall outside a small supermarket. He double-parked and jumped out of the car. Within seconds he picked a pre-made bunch of mixed flowers and motioned to the cashier, who took his money and wrapped the flowers in transparent plastic. Flowers in hand, Gunn returned to his car, tossed them on the passenger seat and drove off again.

"What are you up to?" Hamish murmured to himself.

According to his information, Gunn was married, and it didn't appear that he was returning home with the flowers. He was definitely heading in the other direction. Was he visiting someone in a hospital? Or did Gunn have a mistress? Were the flowers for her?

Curious, Hamish continued his pursuit. Busy traffic made sure Gunn didn't notice that he was being followed, but as they got into a more residential area, Hamish had to fall back farther.

The soft music coming from the car's radio was suddenly interrupted. *"Breaking news,"* an announcer said. *"Following the shooting in Carroll Park last night, cell phone videos have surfaced that seem to suggest that the shooting of several intoxicated black teenagers was unprovoked. The two surviving officers involved in the shooting have been suspended. One officer died at the scene last night, and one of the teenagers died during surgery last night. Acting Mayor Gunn has issued a statement asserting that his police force is well trained and that officers are within their right to defend themselves. He went on to question the validity of the video footage—"*

Hamish turned off the radio. He was getting numb to the violence in this city. It was time that somebody did something about the escalating tensions in Baltimore. Gunn was only fanning the flames of discontent and strife, playing right into the demons' hands.

Finally! After another fifteen minutes of driving, Gunn stopped in front of a large suburban home with a neatly kept front yard and got out of the car, flowers in hand. There were few other cars on the street, forcing Hamish to drive past the house, and turn at the next intersection, then parking next to a tree. He glanced around, making sure nobody saw him, and made himself invisible. He exited his car without opening the door, lest any neighbors watching might find it suspicious that a car door opened and closed by itself.

He hurried toward the house where Gunn had stopped. His car was still there, but Gunn himself was nowhere in sight. He had to be inside.

"Well, let's see what you're up to," he murmured to himself and approached the front door.

Behind it, he suddenly heard a dog yapping. He cursed silently. Dogs with their keen sense of smell were bad news. In fact, dogs could be used to sniff out Stealth Guardians while they were invisible. Nevertheless, he had to get in there. Maybe the dog would be too preoccupied with Gunn to pay Hamish any attention.

He waited a few more seconds and listened. The high-pitched barking of the dog moved farther away from the door. Hamish pressed his hand against the door, then passed through it. He found himself in a spacious foyer with stairs to the second floor, a corridor in the middle, and an open archway leading into an elegant sitting room on the right. He heard Gunn's voice and that of a woman coming from the back of the house, where the dog was still yapping intermittently.

Hamish walked along the corridor, treading lightly so he wouldn't be heard.

He reached the kitchen, where Gunn was playing with a white Bichon—the source of the yapping.

"He looks like a puppy. When did you get him?" Gunn asked, rising. The dog barked in protest.

The woman, who'd been arranging the flowers in a vase, turned away from the sink and placed the flowers on the island.

Hamish recognized her immediately. He'd met her at the Wallace's party: Amanda Yardley, the widow of the former mayor.

Was Gunn having an affair with her?

"Only last month," she replied to Gunn. "You know, after John's death, I felt very lonely, so my sister suggested I'd get a dog."

The dog suddenly left Gunn, raced around the island, and barked loudly in Hamish's direction, his bark taking on a vicious growling tone.

"Damn it, Diggi! Stop barking! There's nothing there," Amanda admonished the dog, before she addressed Gunn again. "But he's driving me batty. He's not trained yet, you know. And he constantly barks. I mean, look at him! Now he's barking at the air."

Gunn chuckled. "You should have gotten a larger dog. They don't bark as much, and they're good for protection."

"I can't return him now." She tossed a kind look at the creature. "He is sweet, you know." Then she smiled at Gunn. "It's so nice of you to visit. Thanks so much for the flowers. I really appreciate it."

"Anytime," Gunn said cheerfully. "I just wanted to check in on you and see how you're doing."

"I'm coping. But it's hard to get closure, you know?" She sighed.

"Because they haven't found the driver?"

She nodded. "The police said it's still an open case, but I have the feeling they've got their hands full with everything else going on in the city. What's a hit-and-run, when there are riots and murders?"

Gunn put his hand on her shoulder and squeezed. "Don't give up, Amanda. I'll have a word with the Chief of Police; see if I can light a fire under his ass."

Amanda smiled thankfully. "That would be great."

"Don't mention it."

She took a breath and pointed to the coffee machine. "Can I make you a coffee?"

Gunn made a dismissive hand movement. "No, no, I've gotta go. Lots of stuff to do. But while I'm here, I just wanted to ask you something."

Amanda lifted an eyebrow. "Yeah?"

"I was told you received a box with all of John's personal stuff from the office."

"Yes, they sent it over just last week."

"You wouldn't happen to have seen his datebook in there?"

She nodded. "Oh yes, it was in there. I put it in his study."

"Do you mind if I take it with me?" He smiled. "It's just that before his death he'd set up some appointments and for some reason I can't find all the details, and I'm supposed to take over for him. And you know how he always made notes in his datebook. I think it might come in handy for me not to walk into those meetings unprepared, right?"

"Well, sure. You can have it. I don't know why they even sent it. It's of no value to me. I'll go get it."

"Thanks."

Amanda left the kitchen, while Gunn waited impatiently, tapping his foot on the floor. Apparently the dog took it as a sign to play. Diggi ran toward him, yapping again.

"Shut up, you idiot dog," Gunn hissed under his breath and stared the puppy down.

But the puppy tilted its head to the side, then jumped at Gunn's leg and got hold of his pants, digging his teeth into them.

"I hate dogs!" Gunn growled and kicked the dog with his other foot, so that the poor creature slithered along the polished tile floor in Hamish's direction.

Diggi yowled.

*Jerk!*

Hamish bent down to the puppy and stroked his hand over its back. The poor dog flinched, but Hamish brought his other hand to under its head and caressed its neck, soothing the creature.

Moments later, Amanda reappeared in the kitchen and handed Gunn a large, weathered datebook.

"Here you go, Robert. I hope you find what you're looking for."

"I hope so, too. Thanks so much again. And don't be a stranger. Next time you're near City Hall, call me and we'll have lunch." He smiled and walked toward the hallway.

"I'll do that."

Hamish followed him out. When Gunn reached his car and got in, Hamish ran to his own car, so he wouldn't lose him. He needed to have a look at that datebook and figure out what Gunn was looking for.

Back in his car, and following Gunn back into the city again, Hamish pulled out his cell phone and dialed Tessa's number.

She picked up after the second ring. "Hamish?"

"Can you talk?"

"Yes, we just got Mother settled. Dad's making tea. What is it?"

"Is there any reason why Gunn would want to get his hands on Yardley's old appointment book?"

"His appointment book?"

"Yes, he just went to see Amanda Yardley and asked her for it. She gave it to him. He said something about some meetings Yardley had set up before his death, which Gunn now has to attend. He claimed he needed to see any notes that Yardley may have made."

"That sounds fishy to me," Tessa replied.

"That's what I thought, too." He paused, thinking for a moment. "Listen, I'm going to stay on his tail and see what else he's up to. If I can't make it back to relieve Enya, I'll send somebody else to stay with you tonight, okay?"

"You won't come back?" There was panic and disappointment in her voice.

"Don't worry, you're not gonna get rid of me that easily. I'll be back, but I might be late, and I won't leave you unprotected. If Enya needs to rest and I'm not back, tell her to get Aiden to come and watch you."

"Not Manus?"

"No, definitely not Manus!" Hamish growled. He didn't want that womanizer anywhere near Tessa. "Aiden is my best friend. I trust him more than anybody." Besides, Aiden loved his wife and would never touch another woman. "But I'll try to be back as soon as I get something concrete on Gunn."

"Okay."

There was a click on the line. Yes, he would definitely try to be back sooner rather than later.

# 25

Despite Hamish's promise to come back later that evening and relieve Enya, he didn't. Instead, Aiden showed up at Tessa's apartment. Enya assured her that Aiden would keep her safe before she left. According to Aiden, Hamish had been busy breaking into Gunn's office at City Hall to go through his stuff, and was planning to do the same at his home, just as soon as he and his wife were fast asleep.

It was odd how quickly she'd gotten used to his presence and how alone she felt when Hamish wasn't with her. She shouldn't feel that way. After all, she knew this was all temporary. Once the danger was over, once the demons were defeated, Hamish would leave, too. There was nothing between them, just two kisses, both stolen in moments of despair and fear. Kisses that—according to his own words—meant nothing to him.

She tried to tell herself that they meant nothing to her either, but she would be lying. She'd enjoyed those brief moments of intimacy. She'd dreamed about those kisses, relived them again and again, though she knew there would be no repeats.

Sighing, Tessa got dressed in her yoga clothes. A session at the studio might help her relax and shake off the worries of the last few days. She walked into the living room, where Aiden was lounging on the couch, a coffee mug in his hand.

"Morning, Tessa, hope you slept well," he said. "Want some coffee?"

She shook her head. "Not before my yoga class. Coffee before you're doing a downward dog isn't a good idea."

"Got it," he said and put his mug aside. "What time does your class start?"

"In fifteen minutes."

"Well, we'd better leave then or you'll be late."

"It's just around the corner," she said and grabbed her yoga mat and her handbag. She pulled out her cell phone and looked at it. "Darn, battery is dead. I'd better charge it." She plugged it into the wall jack and laid it on the small side table.

"I'm assuming you don't want to be seen with me," Aiden said.

"Not that I don't want to show up with a handsome guy, but I'd hate to have to explain to the other women who you are."

"Hey, just checking. I prefer to remain incognito anyway." He motioned to the door. "Lead the way. I'll be right behind you."

She walked to the door and opened it, then looked over her shoulder, but Aiden had already cloaked himself. "I really don't know how you manage to avoid doors constantly getting slammed in your face when you're invisible."

He chuckled, but said nothing.

Her yoga mat under her arm, Tessa hurried down the stairs, then exited her apartment building. It was sunny outside, and she enjoyed the short walk to the yoga studio. But before she got there she realized she'd forgotten her water bottle.

"Gotta stop for water," she murmured for Aiden's benefit, and went into the convenience store next to the studio. She walked to the back of the store where the refrigerators were located and pulled a bottle of still water from one.

When she reached the cashier, she put the bottle on the counter and dug into her handbag for some change.

"How much?" she asked, but the guy was staring up at a TV, which was broadcasting the morning news. Tessa's eyes were instinctively drawn to the screen. A red bar with the words *Breaking News* was scrolling along on the bottom.

Oh no, not another shooting or riot, she begged silently. She'd seen too many of these breaking news stories in the last couple of months.

"This just in: the mayoral race has taken a new turn," the announcer started.

Instantly she was all ears. What outrageous statement had Gunn made now that warranted such as strong reaction from the media?

"Pictures of Councilwoman Wallace surfaced on various Internet sites this morning," the reporter continued, while a photo popped up next to him on the screen. "They seem to show Ms. Wallace injecting herself with drugs. The councilwoman could not be reached for comment. We will continue to monitor…"

But Tessa had heard enough. All she could do was stare at the photo. A photo showing her wearing a bra and shorts. A rubber tourniquet was wrapped around her bicep, and a hypodermic needle lay next to her. Her eyes had rolled back, she looked... stoned. This couldn't be her. It was impossible. But when she looked at the face of the woman in the picture, she was looking at herself.

"No," she choked out. "No, no."

The cashier turned his head to her, but Tessa was already spinning around and rushing to the door.

"Hey, you want that water or not?" he yelled after her.

She ran out onto the sidewalk when she heard Aiden's voice behind her. "Let's get back to your apartment, now."

Tears welling up in her eyes, she practically ran back to her apartment building. She fumbled for her keys when she got to the door, shaking. But then she felt Aiden's invisible hand on hers and his comforting voice in her ear.

"Easy, Tessa, you're almost there."

The thirty seconds it took to get from the front door to her apartment seemed to stretch forever. She braced herself against the wall once she was inside. Aiden, now visible again, was already pulling out his cell phone.

"We have a problem," he said to the person at the other end of the line and walked into the kitchen, lowering his voice.

A sob tore from her chest, just as her cell phone started ringing, startling her. She stared at the display. Poppy, her campaign manager. But she couldn't pick up. What would she say?

Then her gaze fell on her landline phone. Two messages. Automatically she pressed the button to replay them.

*"Honey, it's your dad. You've gotta call me. I know that photo isn't you. We need to talk. Please."* A beep ended her father's message.

Immediately the next message played. *"Tessa, are you there?"* It was Poppy. *"I just saw the news. It's all over the Internet. We've gotta get ahead of this. We need to work on a statement, come up with an explanation. Something plausible, or this will derail your campaign. Damn it, girl, why didn't you tell me? I could have helped you. Call me back now. We have to do something before this can't be contained anymore. I'll try your cell, too."*

Another beep. But the phone didn't remain silent. Immediately, it started ringing. Caller ID identified the caller as one of the news outlets in the city. Reporters were calling for comment. But she had none. She couldn't talk to them, because she only had one thing to say: "It's not me. That's not me in that photo."

Tears were now streaming down her face. Aiden looked blurred to her as he came back into the living room. Without a word he pulled the phone jack out of the wall outlet, silencing the ringing. Then he took her cell phone and switched it off.

Silence descended on her apartment. But everything began to spin. Her life was spinning out of control. Everything she'd worked for was slipping through her fingers.

"Who would do such a thing?" she cried out, staring at Aiden.

"We'll figure it out."

However, she couldn't help but see a sheen of doubt in his eyes. Did he believe that the woman in the photo was her? A bolt of adrenaline suddenly assaulted her, making her heart beat frantically. Hamish! Had he seen the photo yet? Was that why he hadn't returned yet? Because he thought her to be a drug addict not worth protecting anymore?

"It's not me," she repeated to herself. "That's not me."

# 26

Hamish had decided to get a few hours of rest at the compound after getting back from Gunn's house in the early hours of the morning, knowing Tessa would be asleep anyway. When he heard somebody knock loudly at his door, he reared up, still dazed.

"Hamish! Get up, you need to see this!" It was Pearce.

Hamish jumped out of bed, wearing only his boxer briefs. "What? Get in here!"

Instantly, Pearce entered, holding a laptop in his hands. "This is all over the news." He turned the laptop, and Hamish approached.

He blinked, looked at the image on the screen again, then back at Pearce. Adrenaline shot through his veins, and his heart began to thunder. "Shit! Which hospital is she at? Where the fuck was Aiden? I'm gonna kill him!"

"Stop, Hamish!" Pearce pointed at the lines of text below the picture that showed a half-naked Tessa shooting up what looked like heroine. "Tessa is at home. I checked with Aiden. She's fine. Nothing's happened to her."

His pulse started to beat a little slower. "Then what the fuck is this?" Because the woman in the photo was clearly Tessa. No doubt about it.

"The news says the photo may have been taken a while ago. But no matter when it was taken, this will derail her campaign. Nobody wants a druggie as a mayor."

Hamish grabbed Pearce by the collar of his shirt. "Tessa is no druggie, damn it!" No, it couldn't be true, though the evidence was damning. "There must be an explanation for this." There had to be. Had he been wrong about her? Just like he'd been wrong about Olivia? Was he doomed to fall for the wrong woman all over again?

Fall for her? Fuck! Was he falling for her? Had he lost his marbles? Hadn't he tried hard enough to stay away from her and not let her into his heart? Apparently he'd failed again. And now he was paying the price for it. She'd deceived him. Hidden something from him.

"Call Aiden. Tell him not to let her out of his sight even for a moment, not even to use the bathroom. I'm on my way."

Hamish had never showered and gotten dressed this quickly in his life. Nor had he ever disregarded the rules of traffic as blatantly as he did now. By the time he reached Tessa's apartment building, two traffic cameras had caught him running red lights. But he would pay those tickets gladly.

He parked around the corner, noticing that a news van had already pulled up in front of Tessa's building. The vultures were circling their prey. Making himself invisible, Hamish jumped out of the car, entered through a tradesmen's entrance in the back of the building and ran up the staircase to Tessa's floor. At the door, he took a breath. Without ringing the door bell, he marched into the apartment and made himself visible.

Tessa, her face tear-stained, shot up from the couch, shrieking. Aiden, who'd been pacing, spun around, clearly relieved to see him.

"Leave us," Hamish ordered his fellow guardian.

Aiden nodded and left the apartment the same way Hamish had entered it.

For a moment there was silence between them. His eyes strayed away from Tessa's face to her arms, which were bare. He realized that this was the first time he was seeing her in a short-sleeved top. He homed in on the inside of her elbows, checking for the telltale bruising that drug addicts who used needles exhibited. Her arms were pristine—pale, but unblemished.

"That wasn't me in that photo," Tessa said, her voice cracking.

He searched her eyes. Was she telling the truth, or was she lying just like Olivia had lied to him? Could he really trust anything a human said? Could he trust Tessa?

"I don't want you to lie to me. If it was you, I'll help you get through this. But you have to be honest with me." He didn't even know why he was offering his help. To do what? To get her clean? What for? Now that her reputation was tarnished in the eyes of the citizens of Baltimore, her chances of becoming mayor were practically nil. His work here was done. The demons wouldn't bother her again now that she'd destroyed her own career.

"You have to believe me." She took a few steps closer, her eyes pleading. "Please, Hamish. I've never taken drugs. Never in my life."

He dropped his lids, avoiding her gaze, and stared at his boots instead. "Are you saying we're all blind and the woman in the photo isn't you?"

"It must be photoshopped. It can't be me! It's impossible!" Her voice took on a high-pitched tone.

"At least admit it," he begged. "So I can help you." Because despite everything, despite her deception, despite the blow she'd just dealt her race, despite the huge advantage she'd just handed to the demons, he still felt something for her.

More tears shimmered in her eyes. She pointed to the laptop that sat open on the coffee table. "Her face might look like mine, but her body doesn't."

Tessa suddenly gripped the hem of her yoga top and pulled it over her head, then tossed it to the floor.

"Tessa, what are—"

She wore a simple white cotton sports bra underneath. But that wasn't what had shoved his words back down his throat.

"Oh my God," he choked out and bridged the distance between them in two steps, reaching for her.

Her stomach was covered in scars. Small round scars. He'd seen enough scars in his long life to know what they were: burn marks.

"The woman in the picture has flawless skin," Tessa continued, tears now streaming down her face. "She's perfect, and I'm not."

Hamish touched her stomach, but she shrank back.

"No, don't!" she cried out on a sob.

"Tessa, I'm so sorry. I should have never doubted you." He reached for her then and pulled her into his arms, stroking one hand over her back, trying to soothe her, but her sobs kept coming. "Please forgive me." He pressed a kiss on top of her head. "Please, Tessa, I should have had more faith in you. But..." He hesitated, but he needed to let her know how he felt, and why he'd reacted the way he had. "I loved a woman once. Her name was Olivia, and I thought she loved me, too. But it was all a lie... And then I met you, and when we kissed, I felt something so strong..."

Tessa lifted her head from his chest and looked up at him. "You told Enya it meant nothing to you."

"Because I didn't want to admit it to Enya or to myself. But it meant everything. That kiss awakened something in me that I thought had died for good with Olivia. I thought she loved me, but she deceived me. The demons, they were using her to get to me. And I didn't see it, because I was blinded by love."

She sniffled. No words came over her lips, but she was listening intently.

"The demons had their claws in her so deep that there was no way of bringing her back. She was already lost. I had to kill her, Tessa, I had to kill the woman I loved." He felt tears stinging his eyes. "When I saw the photo, when I thought that everything you'd shown me about yourself was just a cover, a lie, I thought that my heart would break a second time."

He took her face in both hands. "Tessa, I put chains around my heart so nobody would ever get inside it again. I wanted to be my own master again. The ruler over my own heart, my own emotions, my own destiny. Nobody was supposed to ever get close enough again. But then I touched you. And when I kissed you, those chains around my heart started to loosen. But when I saw that photo, I thought you'd deceived me, too." He searched her eyes for a sign that she understood. "Please forgive me."

## 27

Forgive him? There was so much more that she wanted to do, and his words had given her the courage to act. To be brave for once and demand what she desired.

"Then please kiss me, Hamish." Tessa raised her hand and laid it on his nape.

It felt like a dream in slow motion as Hamish dipped his face to hers, his eyes locked with hers and his lips parted. His breath brushed against her face, making her shiver in anticipation, because she knew that this kiss would not end with a stumbled apology or more awkwardness. She saw it in his eyes: the hunger, the need, the desire. And she knew he would see the same in her eyes.

His lips were firm and warm, and they took hers with a demand she'd never experienced before. This was how a real man kissed. A man who knew what he wanted; a man who took what was offered freely. She tasted him, tasted the powerful male, the warrior, the man who'd kept her safe these last days.

She welcomed his forceful invasion, his strong tongue exploring her, his lips touching hers, his arms holding her, making escape impossible. She wanted to feel his hard, muscular body pressed against her curves. Needed to feel his physical dominance, his preternatural power. She was drawn to it, to the way it made her feel: weak, yet safe and, first and foremost, desired. Desired by an immortal, a man who could have any woman. A man who'd had many before her. But it didn't matter now as long as he gave her what she needed. A taste of lust, of passion. A chance to forget all the terrible things that had happened. A chance to let herself fall and know he would catch her.

His passionate kiss was heating her insides, making liquid pool at the juncture of her thighs. Instinctively she undulated her hips to rub herself against him and find relief. She found more than that: a hard ridge that curved against his groin and pressed against his cargo pants. Involuntarily she moaned. In response Hamish dropped his hands to her ass and jerked her against him, rubbing his cock even harder against her.

But she needed to feel more. She needed him closer, needed to feel his skin, his heat. She pulled his Polo shirt from his pants and pushed it up. He helped her and broke off the kiss for a moment to pull his shirt over his head. While he tossed it on the floor, she got a glimpse of his chest. A light sprinkling of dark hair covered toned pectorals. It got thicker farther down, blazing a trail over his stomach and disappearing into his pants. As if she needed directions.

Her hands were already on his fly. She opened the button, but he stopped her by putting one hand over hers.

"It's been a long time since I've done this," he rasped, making her look up at his face.

"It's like riding a bike," she murmured with a smirk.

He chuckled. "Trust me, I know how it's done." He released her hand and pulled her flush to him, his chest crushing her breasts. "But if you continue like this, I'm not gonna last long." Then he reached for the clasp of her bra and unhooked it. "So why don't we start with you?"

Before she could protest, he'd relieved her of her bra and was caressing her naked breasts, while he sank his mouth back onto hers and continued his sensual onslaught. She gasped and felt bolts of heat shoot through her core. Oh God, how she needed his touch!

She suddenly felt herself lifted off her feet and knew they were moving, until she finally felt a wall at her back and Hamish pressing her against it. He ripped his mouth from hers and dipped his head, capturing one nipple with his lips and sucking on it.

Tessa moaned out loud, gasping for air.

His hands weren't idle either, both of them now sliding under her yoga pants, pushing them and her panties down to mid-thigh, then dragging them lower. She kicked her shoes off and freed herself fully from the garments.

When he brought his hand between her legs and finally touched her drenched folds, she lost all ability to speak. Warm fingers played with her, caressed her, explored her. Shudders of pleasure charged through her, making her shiver uncontrollably.

"Easy, lass," he murmured at her ear, before he proceeded to kiss a path down her neck and reclaim one breast with his mouth.

But how could she go easy, when he touched her like this, when his fingers and his mouth drove her insane with lust?

"Please!" she begged.

He understood as if she'd told him what she needed, and drove one finger into her.

"Fuck, Tessa, you're tight." He lifted his head from her breast and stared at her. "I'm not gonna last ten seconds inside you."

Her eyelids fluttered as he began to pump his finger in and out of her, while he rubbed his thumb over her clit.

Her cheeks were blazing with fire, while she stared into his eyes that now looked like dark molten lava, black with flecks of gold. "You're gonna make me come," she choked out breathlessly.

One side of his mouth lifted. "That's the idea, lass."

She loved the way he rasped that last word. It was like a caress.

"Now let yourself go," he demanded, pinning her with his eyes.

Her lips parted, and air rushed from her lungs. She felt the earth turn around her as if she were floating, when the first wave hit her. Like a tsunami, it crashed over her, pleasure and lust drowning her, making her gasp for air. She dug her fingers into his shoulders, holding on for dear life, her legs shaking, her knees buckling. But she didn't fall. Hamish was there to catch her.

Then his lips were on hers, and he kissed her without restraint. Harder than before. With more passion, more determination. She panted, and despite her climax only seconds earlier, she felt more need rise in her. But this time, the need was different. She wanted him to surrender to her like she'd surrendered to him.

She pushed him back to make enough space between their bodies to get to his zipper. Before he could protest, she lowered it and pushed his pants down. His gray boxer briefs stretched tightly over his erection, and a wet spot was showing where his cock had leaked pre-cum.

She hooked her hands under the waistband and lowered his briefs. His shaft sprang free.

"Fuck!" he hissed and reached for her, but she was already dropping to her knees, pulling his pants down all the way.

He helped her and kicked his boots off. A dagger fell to the floor, but she ignored it and brought her head level with his groin.

His hands were already on her biceps to lift her up, but she protested, "No!"

A ragged breath was his response. She lifted her eyes to look at him and saw him stare at her in disbelief. "Lass…" he groaned. But he released his grip and waited, the look in his eyes confirmation that he wanted this as much as she did.

She dropped her gaze to his cock then, and wrapped her hand around the thick root. She felt it pulse in her palm.

"Beautiful," Tessa murmured and moved closer.

The head was almost purple, so pumped full with blood that it looked ready to burst. It was time she took mercy on him. So she licked over it with her tongue, tasting his salty essence, before she wrapped her lips around the tip and slid down on him, taking him into her mouth.

~ ~ ~

He'd died and gone to heaven. There was no other way to describe what he was feeling right now. Tessa was on her knees in front of him, her lips tightly wrapped around his eager cock, one hand around its root, while she cradled his balls with the other.

"Fuck!" Hamish ground out and braced himself against the wall behind her, his knees starting to shake.

How long had it been since a woman had done this to him? Since a woman had sucked him like this? With such tenderness and such passion at the same time. And this wasn't just any woman. This was Tessa, the woman he'd desired from the moment he'd laid eyes on her. And now she was on her knees, worshipping him as if he were her master.

He knew what he was doing was wrong. But he couldn't get himself to stop her, because everything felt so right: her tongue sliding along the underside of his cock as she moved up and down on him, her lips sucking him with such skill, her hands caressing him with tenderness. Everything was perfect.

He looked down at her, watching her as she sucked and licked him with her eyes closed, her soft moans and sighs bouncing off his sensitive skin. He watched his hips move back and forth to demand more, to beg for more friction, to ask that she suck him harder, faster. He watched himself fuck her mouth the same way he wanted to fuck her pussy, with deep long strokes. But if he continued to allow her to suck him like this, he wouldn't get around to taking her the way he wanted to, because she'd finish him before he ever got a chance.

With the last ounce of his willpower, he pulled himself from her mouth and stepped back.

Tessa stared up at him, stunned. "Was I doing something wrong?"

He grabbed her arms and pulled her up. "You were doing everything right." Too right.

He spun her around so she faced the wall and grabbed her hips, surprising himself at the roughness with which he handled her. But his control was slipping rapidly, and he needed to be inside her now. He wouldn't make it to the bedroom.

He pushed her legs apart, dragged her ass back toward him and bent his knees, bringing his cock to her entrance. He felt the warm juices of her pussy coat his cockhead and pushed upward and forward, seating himself.

Tessa moaned and braced herself against the wall, while her wetness engulfed him.

"That's it, lass," he encouraged her and withdrew, only to slice back into her with more force. "Like that, yeah?"

"Yeah," she let out on a strangled breath, her hips meeting him on his next thrust. She turned her head to the side, looking back at him. "Take me."

He brought his face to hers and sucked her earlobe between his lips, giving it a gentle bite. He felt her shiver as a result and thrust harder into her, perspiration already covering his chest.

"I love fucking you, Tessa! I should've done this the day I met you in your office." He pounded into her, loving the way her muscles squeezed him like a tight fist. "I should've thrown you on that desk and taken you."

"Oh God," she said huskily. "Just make up for it now. For making me wait so long."

Her words were like a soothing balm on an open wound, eradicating any doubt that she wanted him as much as he wanted her. He brushed her hair back from her face and stroked his finger over her cheek. "Oh, lass…"

Farther below, his hips worked frantically, his pistoning cock driving in and out of her relentlessly, while he tried to hold back his imminent orgasm with all his remaining strength. He needed more of her, he needed to be inside her longer, to be joined with her.

"Fuck!" he groaned, because he knew he was losing the battle over his body. He blamed it on his long abstinence from women, though he knew that was only partially correct. It was all Tessa's fault, the way her body welcomed him, the way she responded to him, the way she surrendered to him.

When he felt his balls tightening, he brought one hand to Tessa's front and found her clit. The small organ was swollen, and he knew just what she needed now. He rubbed his finger over it, making rapid circles, while his cock kept pumping. He couldn't stop the approach of his orgasm now. His semen shot through his cock and exploded from the tip, filling Tessa's tight channel. Finally he felt her spasm around him, climaxing with him.

Hamish let out a ragged breath and dropped his head against the wall next to Tessa. She was breathing just as hard. He wrapped one arm around her waist, holding her to him. Suddenly he was all too aware of how he'd taken her. Like a savage. He hadn't even afforded her the comfort of a nice bed. But he couldn't even regret that fact. Because their lovemaking had been perfect.

# 28

Tessa suddenly lost the ground beneath her feet as Hamish lifted her into his arms and carried her into the bedroom, where he laid her onto the bed. Smiling, he joined her and pulled her on top of him, his arms wrapped around her, one hand in her hair, caressing her nape.

"I wish I could say I'm sorry about how rough I was and that I took you against a wall..." He put his finger under her chin and lifted her face so she had to look at him. "But I've never experienced anything hotter than taking you like that."

His eyes were blazing with lust again, almost as if he wanted a repeat right now.

Her heart beat rapidly. She hadn't felt anything more exciting in her life either. "I'm glad you did what you did."

"Even though a first time should be more... civilized?"

She chuckled, her cheeks still hot and probably red. But she felt no shame for what had happened, no shame for the wildness she'd exhibited. "I can't imagine you being *civilized*."

He moved, rolling them both over so he was now above her. "Are you saying I'm a beast?" He used his knee to push her legs apart to make space for himself at her center.

When his cock settled between her legs, she hummed appreciatively. "I love a bit of beast in a man."

He smiled and brushed a lock of her hair from her face. "Well, who would have thought that the prim and proper councilwoman was into rough and wild?"

"You think only men have a wild side?" she challenged him.

"Touché." He grinned down at her. "Guess I'm a lucky man." He pulled back his hips, readjusting his cock and let it slide against her without entering her.

Her breath hitched, and she tilted her groin in invitation, marveling at the fact that he was still hard. Or was he hard again?

"Make that a *very* lucky man," he corrected himself and kissed her softly. But to her surprise he didn't follow her invitation and instead rolled himself to the side, taking her with him. "Tessa, I didn't ask before, but there's something I need to know."

She stared at him, his expression suddenly serious. Did he still have doubts about her innocence? "About what?"

He lowered his hand and placed it on her stomach.

She swallowed hard.

"Please tell me how you got these." He ran his fingers over her scars. "I know they're not new. What happened to you?"

She rolled herself on her back and stared up at the ceiling, not wanting to look at him. "They're ugly, aren't they?"

He pulled himself up onto his elbow. "There's nothing ugly about you, Tessa. You're perfect."

She let out a bitter laugh, the wounds from the past opening again. She knew this would happen. It always did when a man saw her naked for the first time. She'd always evaded the question and made up a story, but she knew she couldn't lie to Hamish. She didn't want to. He'd been honest with her. Now he deserved the same honesty.

"I was perfect once. I was the perfect little girl. And my father loved me." She inhaled to take a pause. "He loved me too much."

She felt Hamish stiffen. "Did he—"

Immediately she shook her head, realizing he'd misinterpreted her words. "My father would never hurt me. I was his little angel. And I loved him. But my mother, she couldn't stand the fact that he was lavishing attention on me. She was jealous. So jealous."

"You were a child!" Hamish rasped.

"I was competition for her husband's love. She didn't understand that his love for me was different than his love for her. That both could co-exist. I don't think she'll ever understand that. So she punished me."

She suddenly felt Hamish's hand caressing her stomach with a tenderness she hadn't thought him capable of.

"By hurting you?"

Tessa nodded and closed her eyes. "Whenever she drank and was in one of her moods, she was cruel to me. Though she was smart, too. She always made sure my dad wasn't home when she hurt me."

"Oh God."

"She was a smoker back then. I can still remember what it felt like when her cigarette touched my skin. To this day the scent of burning hair and skin brings back those memories." Tears rose into her eyes. "She always warned me that if my father found out he wouldn't love me anymore. I wouldn't be his perfect little girl anymore. So I made sure he never saw the scars." A tear ran down her cheek. "I was a child. I didn't know. I believed her. Until I could take it no longer. Until it got so bad that I didn't care anymore if I lost his love." A sob tore from her chest. "I showed him what she'd done to me. And I waited for him to push me away." She met Hamish's eyes and saw rage reflected back at her. "But he took me into his arms and told me he'd make sure she would never touch me again." She sniffled. "He kept his word."

"And he stayed with her after all she did to you?" Hamish ground out. "He didn't go to the police?"

"He loved her. Just like he loved me. He couldn't choose. So he did the next best thing. He threatened her that if she ever hurt me again, he would divorce her in a heartbeat. After that, she stayed away from me. Never laid another finger on me." She wiped her tears away. "She's sick. Back then we just didn't know."

"I realized that something wasn't right between you and her, I just never thought..." Hamish blinked. "I can't even imagine..."

She touched his cheek and pulled him closer. She noticed the chords in his neck strain as he clenched his jaw. "I can live with those scars, because I know I'm safe now."

"The scars," he murmured and dropped his gaze to her stomach. Suddenly he reared up. "That's it. That's how we're gonna prove that the woman in the picture can't be you."

Tessa sat up. "No! We can't do that!"

"But it'll exonerate you completely! It'll save your campaign. All you need to do is get a few reputable journalists into a room and show them your scars. They'll realize that whoever circulated that photo just pasted your face onto the body of somebody else." Hamish's voice got more heated with every second.

Tessa jumped up and walked to her closet, ripping it open. "I can't do that to my father."

She heard Hamish get out of the bed and approach her. "Your father?"

"As soon as people see my scars, they'll realize that they're old. They'll know I was abused as a child."

She took a T-shirt out of the closet when she felt Hamish's hands on her shoulders. He turned her to him.

"Haven't you sacrificed enough?" he said, his gaze penetrating.

"I promised him, Hamish. He kept up his side of the bargain; I have to keep my word. If it ever came to light what my mother did, my father would be implicated, too. Don't you see that? Maybe the statute of limitations has run out, but that doesn't matter, because people will still judge him, condemn him for what happened under his roof. I love my father. I'm not going to see him destroyed."

She tried to turn back to the closet, but Hamish pulled her against his chest and stroked his hand over her hair. "Such devotion." He pressed a kiss to her forehead. "I'm sorry I suggested it. We'll just have to find another way."

Surprised by his words, she smiled. "Thank you for understanding. It means so much to me."

He winked at her. "How much?"

Her chin dropped. "You—"

But his laughter stopped her. His eyes twinkled with mischief. She slung her arms around him, thankful that he found humor even in the direst of situations, and kissed him. Then he moved his head back and took the T-shirt she was still holding in her hand and tossed it on a nearby chair.

"You won't need that." The heat in his eyes told her why. "Unless you want to dress up in something sexy and let me rip it off you—"

The ringing of the doorbell interrupted him. When she stepped out of his embrace, he stopped her.

"Let me check who it is, in case it's a reporter."

She watched him leave the bedroom, his toned butt muscles flexing with every step. Moments later she heard him speak into the intercom. "Yes?"

There was a crackling on the line, then, "It's Poppy. Where's Tessa? I need to speak to her."

Tessa was already in the living room. Hamish looked over his shoulder.

"She's been leaving messages," Tessa said.

"It's urgent! I need to see her," Poppy repeated through the speaker.

Tessa sighed. "Fine. Let her in."

By the time Poppy had reached the apartment door, both Tessa and Hamish were fully dressed again. Hamish opened the door for her and let her enter.

"Damn it, Tessa, why didn't you call me back? I left several messages," Poppy said, charging into the apartment without a greeting. "The press is going wild over this. We've gotta do something."

"Are the reporters still camped out in front of the building?" Hamish asked.

Poppy nodded. "It's a gauntlet out there."

"They won't leave me alone, will they?" Tessa asked.

Poppy put a hand on her forearm and squeezed it. "They want a statement. And we're gonna give them a statement, okay? An apology. Other politicians do it all the time. We'll say the photo was taken a few years ago when you had personal problems, and that you're very sorry, but that you've overcome that dark period of your life, yada, yada, yada."

"No!" Tessa interrupted. "I won't do that! That's not me in the photo! I've never done drugs, Poppy! Don't you know me at all?"

Poppy hesitated. "Well, we need to say something! How are you gonna prove that woman in the photo isn't you? Nobody will believe you."

"It's photoshopped! I know it's been doctored. It has to be!" Tessa insisted, annoyed that Poppy had even for a moment thought her capable of this.

"Even if it is photoshopped, how will you prove it?" Poppy tossed a strand of her red hair behind her shoulder and sighed. "We need to draft a statement."

"I have an idea," Hamish suddenly interrupted.

Tessa spun her head to him, hope blossoming in her chest. "Yes?"

"If I can get my hands on the original photo I might be able to find out where it came from. And I can examine it and figure out if it's been altered."

"Yeah, but how would you know where the original is?" Poppy asked with a large dose of doubt in her voice.

Hamish walked around the coffee table, where the laptop was still sitting and woke up the screen. Tessa followed him and looked over his shoulder.

"Photo credit, here!" He pointed to the screen.

"Meredith Durant," Tessa read. "I know her. She's from the Daily Republic." She turned to Poppy. "Did you see her downstairs with the other reporters?"

Poppy shook her head. "Nobody from her news outlet was there. Guess they figured they'd already gotten the scoop."

"Then I'll try her office," Hamish said.

"It's about fifteen minutes from here," Tessa said.

"She won't just hand you the original photo or disclose her source," Poppy interjected.

"I have my methods."

Tessa exchanged a look with Hamish. She knew what he was thinking. He would be using his cloaking skills to enter Meredith's office and snoop around.

"Go!" Tessa encouraged him.

"I've gotta get Enya here first so she can protect you," he protested.

"That's not necessary, Hamish. I think whoever sent me those death threats has just changed their tactic and decided to destroy my political career instead." For Poppy's sake she didn't say *demons*, though she knew it was them. "They're not gonna make another attempt. They've already achieved their goal. If I can't prove that it's not me in the picture, I'm finished."

She could see that Hamish was reluctant to leave.

"Please, Hamish. Besides, Poppy is here. And there are so many reporters downstairs. Nobody is going to be able to sneak past them and get in here."

Hamish inhaled. "Fine. But you're not leaving the apartment until I'm back. Do you hear me?"

She nodded. "Trust me, I have no intention of walking past those reporters and getting bombarded with questions."

Hamish tossed a serious look at Poppy, who nodded.

"I'll watch out for her," Poppy said.

Finally, Hamish nodded. "I'll be back within the hour, okay?"

Tessa smiled, when Hamish suddenly bent toward her and kissed her on the lips. Then he turned on his heel and left.

When the door shut behind him, Tessa sensed Poppy's eyes on her. "What?"

"*Pretend*-boyfriend my ass! That didn't look like pretend to me." She sighed. "Some girls have all the luck!"

## 29

Finding Meredith Durant's cubicle in the large, open-plan news office was no problem for Hamish, just as entering the building unseen and breezing past the security personnel had been child's play. And he was in luck; Meredith wasn't at her desk. Still invisible, Hamish went to work, leafing through the files on the desk. Meredith had made it easy for him. She was organized: each file was clearly labeled with subjects such as police brutality or names such as Yardley.

He picked up Yardley's file, curious, and opened it. It contained a copy of the police report of the hit-and-run, as well as handwritten notes by Meredith. He was about to close the file, when he noticed a question scribbled on the last page. *Accident or deliberate?* Did Meredith suspect that Yardley's death was murder? He raised an eyebrow. Or was this just another reporter fishing for a better, more sensational story?

He put the file back and went through the next few. There were several on the ongoing riots and demonstrations, then one on the mayor's race. This had to be it. He opened the manila folder and perused the contents thoroughly. It consisted of poll sheets, campaign schedules (both Gunn's and Tessa's), and interview notes. He even noticed a note with his own name on it. Below it Meredith had written a few questions, such as whether they could expect some sort of fairytale wedding after the election.

Hamish shook his head. Reporters! They'd found out that Tessa had a boyfriend, and already they wanted to get the exclusive on the next *it*-couple, as if he were JFK and Tessa were Jackie. Anything for a good story; anything to sell papers or increase clicks.

What he didn't find in the folder were photos, more specifically, the photo of Tessa that Meredith had published in today's online edition. Where the fuck was it?

He leafed through the file again, this time examining every scrap of paper, when in between the poll sheets he found a list that didn't belong there. It was a log. An email log, handwritten, with dates and the names of the senders, as well as the subjects. He ran his finger down the list until he saw it: an email from somebody named Zoel Monnadt—odd name—which Meredith had received late the previous night. The subject said photo. This had to be it.

He dropped the file back on the stack and turned to Meredith's computer.

Shit! She'd locked her screen. He'd have to get Pearce to hack into her emails, which would take time. Hamish was about to charge out of the cubicle in frustration, when Meredith's landline began to ring.

"That's yours, Meredith!" a woman in the neighboring cubicle yelled in the other direction.

Hamish peered over the cubicle walls and suddenly saw Meredith hurrying toward her desk.

"Damn it!" she ground out. "The phone's quiet all day, and then I leave my desk for two minutes, and it rings. How do these people time that?" She barreled into her cubicle and nearly fell over her own feet, reaching for the phone.

"Meredith Durant," she answered breathlessly. A moment's pause as she slunk into her chair. "Oh, thanks, yeah. I'm glad you caught me. Yeah, I've got it right here." She placed her hands on the keyboard and unlocked the screen, then quickly navigated to a folder and pulled up a report. She scrolled through it. "I got it." She tapped her finger on the screen. "The arresting officer's name is Schultz."

She listened to the caller, then nodded. "Yes, let's do that. I can meet you there." She was already rising from her chair. "In ten minutes? That's barely enough time to—" A frustrated sigh. "Fine! I'll be there." She rushed out of the cubicle, snatching her handbag on the way out—and forgetting to lock her computer screen in her hurry.

Bingo!

The moment Meredith was gone, Hamish jumped into action. He navigated to Meredith's email client and scrolled through the inbox. There: the email from Zoel Monnadt. It had an attachment. He clicked on it, and the monitor filled with the photo he'd seen online earlier. Meredith had cropped it, cutting off the lower part of Tessa's thighs and legs, most likely to size the photo in accordance with her editor's wishes. The photo properties told him that it hadn't been taken with a regular camera, but with a cell phone. It was all he could tell at this point. At first sight it didn't appear to have been altered, but perhaps Pearce would be able to find out more.

Looking around to make sure nobody could see what was going on in Meredith's cubicle, he pulled a USB stick from one of his pockets and inserted it, then copied the entire email including the photo onto it. As soon as the item was saved, he removed the stick and closed the email program. He would have liked to forward the email to Pearce directly from Meredith's computer, but that would leave a trail that might lead back to him and his compound mates. It was something he didn't want to risk.

As soon as he was outside, he raced back to his car, where he pulled a small laptop from a locked compartment and proceeded to send the file to Pearce. While it was uploading, he dialed Pearce's cell phone.

"Yeah, what's up?" Pearce greeted him.

"I'm forwarding you an email with a photo as we speak."

"I'm at my computer. It's just coming through."

"Good. I need you to examine the photo and figure out if it was altered. Can you do that?"

"Sure. Is that it?"

"I also need you to try and trace the sender."

"Zoel Monnadt. Odd name."

"Yeah, probably made up," Hamish agreed. "See if you can get anything on the name or the email address."

"Will do." Then he added, "Wow, that woman is Tessa's spitting image."

"You've never met Tessa."

"I've seen her file photo."

Hamish nodded to himself. It was standard procedure that all compound members were familiar with their colleagues' charges. He sighed. "But that photo in the news isn't her. I know it with 100% certainty."

"Wonder how they did it. I mean, she could be her twin."

Well shit.

Suddenly Diane Wallace's mumbled words started to make sense.

Hamish let out a curse. "Fuck!"

"What?" Pearce asked.

"Get me Tessa's adoption records."

"Why?"

"I have a hunch." And he hoped he was right.

"Okay. I'm on it."

"Thanks. I'm heading back to Tessa's now."

Hamish glanced at his watch. Forty-five minutes since he'd left her. Just another few minutes and he'd be back with her to assure her that he and his colleagues were doing everything to clear her name—and that with some luck they already had a lead.

# 30

Poppy blew out another exasperated breath, one of many Tessa had heard over the last fifteen minutes—every time Tessa rejected another of Poppy's suggestions of what should go in the statement.

"Damn it, Tessa, I'm just trying to help," Poppy said.

"I know, but I won't admit to something that's a lie."

"But we have to give the press something, otherwise they'll make up their own shit. You know how the press is. They're like piranhas. Just give them something! We can always amend things later when you can prove that it's not you in the photo," Poppy begged, her pen hovering over her notepad.

"And why would they believe me then if I lie now? No, Poppy! I thought you understood me. That's why I hired you— because you get me." She cast her old college friend an imploring look.

"I do get you. But sometimes we have to do things we don't want to do to survive. We might not like it, but we have no choice." She pointed her finger at Tessa. "*You* might not like it, but, girl, what choice do you have? At least try to save what you can. If you come out with a big, heartfelt apology, it might even help your campaign."

Tessa huffed. "How would claiming that I've taken drugs help my campaign?"

"It'll make you more human. It shows that you struggle with much the same issues as your electorate," Poppy explained.

"But it's not true. I'm not a druggie, and I won't admit to it."

"Tessa, just think this through—"

The ringing of a cell phone interrupted her. Poppy reached into her handbag and lifted her phone from it. She pressed a button. "Yes?" As she listened, her expression changed. "Oh, God, no!" She stared at Tessa, her eyes widening all of a sudden. "No, where? How bad is it? Where did they take her?" She nodded. "Okay, I'll be there as soon as I can." She disconnected the call.

"What's wrong, Poppy?" Tessa asked immediately, full of concern for her.

Poppy shot up from the couch. "My mother. She fell down the stairs."

"Oh my God! How badly is she hurt?"

Poppy shook her head. "I don't know. They couldn't tell me. She's at the hospital now. I have to get there." Then she hesitated. "But Hamish isn't back. I promised him I'd—"

Tessa rose and put her hand on her friend's arm, stopping her. "You have to go. He'll be back soon. I promise I'll stay in the apartment."

"Are you sure?"

"Positive. Now go. Your mother needs you." She motioned to the door.

Poppy collected her things and rushed to the door, looking over her shoulder at Tessa. "I'll let myself out. Go and rest until Hamish is back. I'll call you once I know more."

A second later Poppy was gone, the door falling shut behind her. Tessa sighed, hoping Poppy's mother was fine. As an only child, Poppy only had her mother left. Her father had died of cancer a few years earlier.

Tessa turned toward the kitchen. Maybe a cup of tea would do her some good. A frantic knock at the door made her whirl around. Had Poppy forgotten something in her hurry? She rushed to the door and ripped it open.

"Poppy, what—" The words got stuck in her throat.

Hamish had claimed she'd know demon eyes when she saw them. He was right, because right now, green demon eyes were staring straight at her. They belonged to a tall man of muscular build. But that was all she made out, before her survival instinct kicked in and she tried to slam the door in his face. She didn't succeed.

One of the demon's legs was already wedged between door and frame, preventing her from shutting it. She braced herself against the door with all her weight, but she knew immediately that it was futile. The demon kicked against the door, opening it fully and slamming her against the wall. The impact dazed her for a short moment, but it was long enough for the demon to enter and close the door behind him. She screamed. Maybe somebody would hear her; maybe Poppy was still in the stairwell, though if she'd taken the elevator down, she probably wouldn't hear anything. Or worse, maybe the demon had killed Poppy on his way in.

Oh God, somebody had to hear her. Anybody, please!

Her scream was cut short when the demon's hand wrapped around her throat and squeezed. She started choking, gasping for air. Was this how she would die? She tried to fight him, kicking her legs at him, hitting him with her hands, but he didn't release her from his chokehold. All her strength started to leave her, but suddenly he eased up on his grip, allowing some air into her lungs.

"No more screaming, you stupid bitch," he growled and pulled something from his pocket. A moment later, he slapped a broad tape over her mouth, preventing her from making another sound. Finally, he released her neck, but she knew her ordeal wasn't over. He grabbed her, lifted her up and carried her to the bedroom.

Oh God! This monster was going to rape her. Tears stung her eyes. But she had to be strong now. She had to get through this. She'd been through a different kind of torture before, and she'd survived. She would survive this, too. And if she could stall him long enough, Hamish would be back. And he would save her. She held onto that hope, while the demon tossed her on the bed.

"Never thought I'd get such an opportunity handed to me," he said, pulling something from inside his jacket.

Her heart almost stopped when she saw what it was: a rubber tourniquet and a hypodermic needle.

"Noooo!" she tried to scream, but the sound was muffled by the tape. She rolled to the other side of the bed, but he'd anticipated her and was already there. She pushed him with her hands, kicked him relentlessly, but he simply grabbed her legs and twisted her so she landed on her stomach.

He jumped on her back and pinned her down. "A veritable wildcat. Who would have thought that Councilwoman Wallace had so much fight in her? So very different from all the others."

She didn't know who he was talking about, and she didn't waste her energy trying to figure it out, because now the demon was wrapping the tourniquet around her right bicep. She tried to pull her arm away, but he was too strong. Stronger than any human. When the tourniquet was tightly knotted around her upper arm, the demon lifted himself halfway off her, but only to roll her back around so she faced him.

He pinned her arms with his knees, rendering her immobile. His green demon eyes stared down at her, and an evil laugh rolled over his lips.

"You're hard to kill. Twice already you've escaped your fate." He lifted the needle in his hand, drawing her gaze to it. "Not today." He grinned. "Your death will cement my superiority over the Great One. He was never supposed to be the leader. I was!" The last word was almost a shout.

Tessa's fear and panic ratcheted higher. Not only was he a demon, he was also crazy.

"But enough talking." He bent closer and pressed her arm deeper into the mattress as he lowered the needle. "They'll find you dead of a drug overdose, and nobody will even blink. Not after that nice little picture in the news."

She cried out against the tape over her mouth. Then she felt the sting of the hypodermic needle as it broke her skin and entered her vein.

"They'll think you killed yourself because you were found out…"

As the drug entered her bloodstream, she felt a lightness come over her. Everything began to blur, and the demon's voice grew distant.

"I don't leave loose ends, not like that weakling Zoltan… thought he could solve the problem without killing you…"

She didn't want to hear any more. She only wanted to sleep. To forget. To drift away. To a place where she was safe.

*Hamish…*

Darkness encroached, and all pain and fear vanished. She surrendered to it. There was no more fight left in her. It was time.

# 31

Upon his arrival at Tessa's apartment building, Hamish noticed several reporters still camped out in front of it in the hopes of catching Tessa and asking her to comment on her alleged drug use. Knowing that they probably knew his face from the incident at the Center for Drug Rehabilitation, he pulled around the back and parked close to the emergency exit. After reassuring himself that nobody saw him, he cloaked himself and exited the car.

He entered the building by passing through the emergency exit door. The corridor was dark. He headed for the stairs instead of the elevator and ascended quickly. On the landing to the second floor, he stopped briefly, then looked over his shoulder. It was dark here, too. A sense of foreboding made him look up to the ceiling. Fluorescent lighting. He reached for the light switch, praying his hunch was wrong. He flipped it, but nothing happened.

Shit!

He raced up the final flight of stairs and charged toward the door to Tessa's apartment. It was closed. Up here too, the light had burned out. Still invisible, he passed through the door, entering the apartment. He remained silent, didn't call out Tessa's name. The living room and kitchen were empty. Neither Poppy nor Tessa were where he'd left them. The door to the bedroom stood open. Treading lightly but rapidly, he approached and peered in.

His heart stopped. Tessa lay on the bed, a tourniquet around her right bicep, a hypodermic needle next to her arm. Her eyes were closed. She wasn't moving.

"Tessa! Oh God no!" he cried out and ran to her. He felt for her pulse, while he let his gaze roam. She was alone. No sign of Poppy or the demon who'd somehow gotten in. Because this had to be the work of demons. Tessa would never do this to herself.

Finally a pulse, but it was weak. He shook her. "Tessa, can you hear me?" But there was no response. Panic charged through him, but he knew he couldn't allow it to take a hold of him. He had to remain calm to save Tessa. "You're gonna be alright, lass, I promise you." Because he couldn't allow her to leave him.

He pulled his phone from his pocket and pressed Aiden's number, taking Tessa's hand while he waited for his friend to pick up. Her hand was clammy. How much time did she have left?

*Oh God, don't let it be too late!*

"Hamish? What's up?" Aiden's voice came through the cell phone.

"Where is Leila?"

"Right here with me, why?"

"Put me on speaker."

"You're on."

Then Leila said, "Hey Hamish."

"Tessa is unconscious. Somebody injected her with drugs."

"Shit!" Aiden cursed.

"Do you know what kind of drug?" Leila asked in her calm doctor voice.

"Not sure. An opioid, most likely heroine or something else. What do I do?"

"Does she have a pulse?"

"Yes."

"Is she breathing?"

"Very shallow."

"Okay, listen carefully. She doesn't have much time. You won't make it to the hospital—at the best of times it's a good half hour from where you are."

Hamish wanted to scream.

"You need to bring her to the compound. I have Naloxene here. It's a morphine blocker; it'll work on any opioid. If I can inject her within the next fifteen minutes, she's got a chance," Leila said.

"Hamish," Aiden interrupted, "there's a portal only five minutes from Tessa's apartment building. I used it when I left her place earlier."

"I know which one you mean. I'll be at the compound in ten minutes. Get everything ready."

Hamish disconnected the call, shoved his phone back in his pocket and put the hypodermic needle into another pocket in case Leila needed to test what Tessa had been injected with.

Then he lifted Tessa into his arms and carried her out of the apartment, extending the cloak to her so she was invisible, too.

"Hold on, Tessa, please hold on." Just a few more minutes.

He ran down the stairs with her and headed for the emergency exit, pushing the door open when he reached it. The moment he'd placed Tessa on the backseat of his Mercedes, he raced to the location of the portal Aiden had mentioned. It was located in the basement of an old warehouse that the kids in the neighborhood were now using for skateboarding. Several youngsters were practicing. He stopped the car behind a stack of old pallets and got out. As soon as Tessa was back in his arms, he carried her toward the entrance, still invisible. He found the stairs that led into the basement and took them.

"Almost there, my love, almost there," he murmured to her when he finally reached the portal.

To a human it looked like a wall, but Hamish recognized the carving in the stone: a dagger. He pressed his hand against it and felt the spot warm under his touch. A second later, the wall was gone. He charged into the dark cave that had opened up. With his mind, he willed the portal to close and concentrated on his destination. He held Tessa closely against his chest; everything seemed to spin around him, but he knew it was only an illusion. In reality, he wasn't moving. A few seconds later, it was over. They'd arrived. The portal opened up. Hamish stepped out of it.

Aiden and Leila were waiting for him with a gurney.

"Put her on here," Leila ordered.

Gently he laid Tessa onto the hospital bed. Leila was already checking her pulse. Hamish searched her face. When Leila nodded, he let out the breath he'd been holding. Leila pulled a hypodermic needle from her lab coat and removed the cap. As she swabbed Tessa's skin and stuck the needle into her vein, she said, "Naloxene works very quickly. If she has opioids in her bloodstream, this will block them." She pushed the liquid from the needle into Tessa's arm slowly and then pulled it out. "We'll know within the next fifteen minutes. Now let's get her to the medical room. I need to hook her up to the monitor to get her vital signs."

Hamish held onto Tessa's hand, while they pushed the gurney down the long hallway and through the double doors into the room that Leila had equipped as a mini medical center. Several monitors, a crash cart, and other equipment Hamish didn't recognize stood along one wall, while an operating table and steel cabinets took over the other side of the room. A large sink was located in one corner, a decontamination shower next to it. The University Medical Center Hospital wasn't any better equipped than their compound.

Hope finally blossomed in Hamish's chest. Tessa had a chance now. Thanks to Leila. Hamish lifted his eyes and looked at Aiden's mate, who was now placing sensors on Tessa's chest and an oxygen monitor on her index finger. Then she put an oxygen mask over Tessa's nose and mouth.

"I don't know how to thank you, Leila." He felt unshed tears sting his eyes.

Leila smiled. "I'll do everything I can. But she's not out of the woods yet."

Hamish squeezed Tessa's hand and looked down at her pale face. "I can't lose her." He was certain of it now. His heart wouldn't survive it. She meant too much to him.

He felt Aiden's hand on his shoulder and turned his head to his best friend. They exchanged a wordless look, and he realized that Aiden understood what was going on inside him.

Suddenly, a loud high-pitched noise blared through the compound, accompanied by flashing strobe lights overhead. Through speakers high up in the ceiling, a computer voice announced, "Intruder detected. Portal breached. Intruder detected. Portal breached."

"Shit!" Hamish cursed. Had a demon followed him because he'd been careless, only concerned with getting Tessa to the compound as quickly as possible?

"Demons!" Aiden grunted. "Fuck!"

"They must've followed me." He tossed a look back at Tessa, torn between staying with her and responding to the intruder alarm, while Aiden was already running toward the door.

"Go!" Leila shouted. "You can't do anything here anyway."

When Aiden pushed the double doors open, Hamish charged after him, drawing his dagger.

"Let's get those fuckers!" he ground out and ran to catch up with Aiden.

# 32

Disoriented, Wesley felt his feet touch solid ground. He exhaled sharply and pressed a hand to his heart. It was beating like a jackhammer. He felt like he'd been tumbled around in an industrial-sized dryer. At least his racing heart meant he was still alive. However, now his ears were ringing as if an ambulance were chasing him.

Shit, if this was what Stealth Guardians went through every time they used one of their portals, then he wasn't envious at all. He'd take a first class flight on a commercial airline anytime. Or on Scanguards' private jet.

Suddenly dim light illuminated the dark space he'd been thrown around in, and he realized that the portal had opened in much the same way as it had when he'd gotten in. For a moment he couldn't see anything. Shit, had the damn thing even worked, or was he still in the woods in Sonoma? Would his vampire friends at Scanguards, the security company he worked for in San Francisco, have a right old laugh when he returned, having to admit he'd failed in locating the Stealth Guardians?

His boss, Samson, an over two-hundred-and-fifty year old vampire, had been skeptical when he'd told him he wanted to investigate these preternatural creatures after encountering one in the woods of Northern California. But Samson had relented after Wesley had made his case, arguing that in today's volatile world it was good to have allies. He wanted these Stealth Guardians and the vampires of Scanguards to work together in defeating evil.

And he had no intention of disappointing Samson.

Wesley now took a step forward and let his gaze roam. Grinning, he pumped his fist in the air. "Yes, I did it!"

Because he wasn't in the forest anymore; he was in a building. Thick stone walls, a stone floor, sconces on the walls that provided light. Outside of the portal, the sound grew louder, indicating that it wasn't his ears ringing, but some sort of alarm that had gone off.

He didn't need to speculate whether it was meant to alert the occupants of the building to his arrival. Two men were already barreling down the long corridor toward him.

Crap, make that *armed* men, because unless his eyesight was failing him, they both held weapons in their hands, some kind of dagger or machete. When they saw him, they seemed to run even faster.

"Shit!" Wesley hissed under his breath.

It didn't look like either of these guys had any intention of giving him time to explain why he was here. They looked like the kind who killed first and asked questions later. Not a good scenario. But Scanguards had taught him to play the cards he was dealt, so he prepared himself for his not-so-friendly welcome committee.

He collected his strength and called the air to him, intending to throw up a shield, but nothing happened. He tried again, but the air didn't stir, didn't listen to his command.

"Change of plans," he mumbled.

Frantically, he looked around for an escape route, and saw the reason why his witchcraft wasn't working: along the walls, ancient runes were carved into the stone. Though he couldn't decipher them, he knew they were meant to shut down a witch's power. As long as he was within these walls, he was, in effect, powerless.

"Fuck!" he cursed, but it was all he had time for, because one of the men, clearly a preternatural as identified by his aura, had reached him and now slammed him to the ground with two-hundred pounds of muscle and rage.

"Fucking demon!" the man yelled.

A dagger came toward Wesley's neck, but he was able to divert it with his arm. Searing pain shot through him, and he realized the blade had caught him.

"Argh!" he cried out, but the knife was already coming at him again.

"Die, you fucking demon!"

"Fuck! I'm not a demon!"

But his attacker wasn't listening, his face a mask of rage and hate. He made another swipe with the blade, but before Wes could fend him off, his attacker was ripped off him by the second guy.

"Shit, Hamish, let go of him! He's a witch!"

Wesley breathed heavily, staring at both men and using the momentary truce (or whatever it was) to scramble backward, away from the blade's reach.

The man who'd attacked him, the one called Hamish, stared back. "A witch?" He let his eyes wander over Wesley, then ran a hand through his dark hair. "Shit!"

But if Wes had thought this might mean their encounter would now turn civil, he was wrong. Hamish jumped at him again and pinned him against the wall. "And how the fuck did a *witch* get into our compound?"

Wesley managed to jerk his thumb to the left. "Portal?"

"No shit!" Hamish hissed, while more footsteps could be heard echoing through the corridor.

"Aiden? You got 'em?" somebody called out.

The man addressed as Aiden looked over his shoulder at the two men coming their way. "We've got ourselves a witch."

"I'll be damned!" one of them responded.

Suddenly they were all crowding around him. The one they called Hamish still had his forearm pressed against Wesley's throat.

"Now tell me who you are and how the fuck you got in here," he demanded.

"As I said," Wesley gritted, "I used that portal. Can't you get that into your thick head, you numbskull?"

When Hamish bared his teeth, one of the other men put a hand on his shoulder. "Don't go all machete on him now. We don't hurt witches."

That little piece of information lifted Wesley's spirits a bit, though Hamish didn't seem to agree.

"Still doesn't explain how he was able to use the portal and breach our defenses," Hamish grunted.

"We'll figure it out," Aiden said calmly. "But you're under enough stress, buddy."

Whatever stress Aiden was referring to, it appeared that it had clouded the Stealth Guardian's ability to recognize Wesley's aura as that of a witch.

One of the others said, "Yeah, man, just heard about Tessa. Hope she pulls through."

Finally Hamish released him, and Wesley pulled in a few deep breaths. At least they weren't trying to kill him anymore. That was an improvement.

"So, fellas," Wesley started, "I suppose you wanna know what I'm doing here, huh?"

"Brace yourselves, guys," Aiden said to his friends, "looks like we've got a smartass on our hands." Then he narrowed his eyes at Wes. "You'd better make your explanation quick and to the point. As you may have noticed, some of us have a short fuse."

It wasn't hard to guess whom Aiden was talking about.

"I'm Wesley Montgomery from San Francisco. And if my research is correct, then you're all Stealth Guardians," he said, watching the four guys for their reaction. But they all had their poker faces on. "Okay, and none of you is the chatty kind either."

When several of them grunted in displeasure, he lifted his hands. "No worries, I get it. You're a little pissed that I didn't ring the doorbell. My bad." Still no reaction from the four. "I'm here because I was hoping to broker an alliance between you and Scanguards."

"Who's Scanguards?" Hamish ground out.

"A security company headquartered in San Francisco."

"All witches?" Hamish wanted to know.

Wesley shook his head and braced himself. "I'm the only witch in their employ. Most of the others are vampires."

Wes could have heard a needle drop in the silence that now descended. He suddenly realized that the alarm had stopped, though he hadn't noticed when.

Aiden shook his head and so did the other men. "Don't treat us like imbeciles. We know as well as any preternatural that witches and vampires are archenemies. So what do you really want?"

"Man, I'm telling you the truth. You can check it out—"

A shout coming from the end of the corridor interrupted him. "Hamish!" a man called out. "You've gotta come. Tessa is crashing."

"Oh God no!" All the blood drained from Hamish's face as he spun around and raced out of sight.

"So what should we do with him?" one of the others asked, gesturing to Wes.

"Lead cell for now," Aiden ordered.

"Hey, listen to me!" Wes protested. "I'm telling the truth!"

"We'll deal with you later. We've got more important things to worry about right now," Aiden claimed and grabbed him by the arm.

"Hey, watch out!" Wes pointed to the wound on his arm. "Can't you see that I'm injured? A little professional courtesy would be nice!"

"Let's go, witch! I've got a nice little cell with your name on it."

# 33

Hamish kicked the double doors to the medical room open and ran inside. Monitors were beeping. His gaze shot to the gurney where Tessa lay—not motionless like before. Her whole body was spasming violently, Leila frantically trying to hold her down. Her eyes locked with his as he approached the bed.

"She's having a seizure," she cried out.

"Oh God! No!" Hamish said, panic saturating every single one of his cells. "Why is this happening? Can't you do anything?"

"She's reacting to the Naloxene."

"What?" He took Tessa's head between his hands to hold her still so she wouldn't kick off her oxygen mask.

"It's a side effect of the opioid blocker. It happens."

"Fuck!" he cursed. "What now? Damn it, Leila, what now?"

Tears shot into Leila's eyes. "I don't know, Hamish! I don't know! I'm not a trauma surgeon." She looked around the room, appearing just as panicked as he. "I don't have anything else…"

The words clamped around his heart and squeezed painfully. "I can't lose her, Leila! I can't lose her." He looked at Tessa's face. "I can't bear to see her in pain."

The doors opened behind him, but he didn't look over his shoulder.

"She's not strong enough, Hamish!" Leila's words came out as a sob. "Not strong enough…"

"Then make her strong!"

The words had come from Pearce, who'd approached the bed behind him. Hamish looked at him. And just as Pearce opened his mouth again to continue, Hamish understood.

"Virta," Hamish said.

Pearce nodded. "It's worth a shot."

Hamish exchanged a look with Leila. A hopeful expression spread over her face. "It helped make me strong when I fought Zoltan in that farmhouse. You remember, Hamish, don't you?"

All too well. Leila had been nearly as strong as a Stealth Guardian, though the circumstances under which she'd received virta had been different.

"Do it!" Leila urged.

Hamish removed the oxygen mask from Tessa's face. "Leila, Pearce, hold her so she doesn't hurt herself." Because he'd have to concentrate on one thing and one thing only: to collect his virta— his preternatural power—and pour it into her.

He felt his body harden and his muscles tense as he called on his powers and commanded them to rise. For a brief moment he realized that he'd wanted to share his virta with her ever since he'd first laid eyes on her, though he'd never imagined it would happen like this.

As he bent over her and brought his face to hers, he prayed that he could save her.

"I love you, Tessa."

He sank his lips onto hers and willed his virta to leave his body and enter hers, holding her face with his hands so she couldn't move, while Leila and Pearce immobilized her arms and legs. His only thoughts were of Tessa now, of what she meant to him, of what could lie in their future if only she made it through this. He poured more and more of his life force into her, urging it to permeate every cell of Tessa's body and fight the effect of the drugs in her system. He'd give anything, even his life, to heal Tessa in this moment.

"She's stopped seizing." Leila's voice floated to his ears, but still, Hamish didn't let go of Tessa. He continued to pour his strength, his virta, into her.

He heard the beeping of the monitors returning to a less frantic pace. And he could feel it himself: her heart rate calming, evening out, her body stilling beneath him.

He felt Pearce's hand on his shoulder. "It's good now, Hamish."

Yet, he couldn't stop. He needed to continue, needed to know that he was giving her everything he could so she would survive.

"Her vitals are good," Leila said from the other side of the gurney. "She'll make it."

Suddenly he felt his body weakening, his knees buckling.

"Oh shit!" he heard Pearce curse.

His fellow Stealth Guardian ripped him off Tessa. Hamish tumbled backward and would have fallen had Pearce not caught him.

"Leila, a chair. Quickly!" Pearce ordered.

A moment later, Leila had pushed a chair next to the gurney, and Pearce was carefully lowering him onto it. But Hamish wasn't concerned with himself right now. Instead he lifted his eyes and looked at Tessa. Her skin shimmered golden, an aftereffect of the virta he'd shared with her. She'd never been more beautiful.

"Shit, Hamish," Pearce said, "you nearly brought yourself to the brink."

"She needed it," Hamish said, though he felt drained now, his virta at a level that was dangerously low. "I'll be fine." His power would be fully regenerated in a few hours. Being at the compound among his fellow Stealth Guardians would ensure that. He could draw from their collective virta and the power that lay within the stone walls of the building.

"You need to rest," Pearce demanded. "Come on!"

Hamish shook off Pearce's hand. "No! I'm staying with Tessa. She needs me."

"There's nothing you can do now," Leila said softly. "She's sleeping."

He reached for Tessa's hand, but Leila stopped him. "No, Hamish. You can't touch her now. She needs to rest."

He understood immediately what Leila was referring to. While Tessa shimmered golden, his virta strong in her, a touch from him would arouse her instantly and make her climax. "I know. But I need to be here when she wakes. She'll be frightened." He looked up at Leila. "She doesn't know you."

Leila nodded, a soft smile on her face. "Then stay."

He sighed in relief, and next to him, Pearce did the same.

"You've done well, Hamish," Pearce said.

Hamish glanced at him. "She can't die."

From the look his friend gave him, he knew Pearce understood. "She won't. And we're gonna get the bastard who did this to her."

Hamish nodded in agreement.

"I've checked on that email you sent me," Pearce suddenly said.

Hamish shot him a look, his body coiled in anticipation. "Yes?"

"That name that sounded so odd? Zoel Monnadt?"

"What about it?"

"It's an anagram. If you rearrange the letters, it spells Demon Zoltan."

"That sick son-of-a-bitch!" Hamish growled, his hands automatically curling into fists.

"He likes to play games. I also examined the photo, and it's not been altered. The photo is real. It wasn't photoshopped. Sorry."

Hamish nodded, letting the information sink in. It lent more weight to his hunch. "Did you get the adoption file I asked you for? I think I know how Zoltan did it. I just need confirmation."

"I hacked into the county records, but thirty-five years ago they had paper records. They're not digitized yet. I was about to go down to the county courthouse and let myself in to look for them, when…" He glanced at Tessa, then back at Hamish. "I'll go now."

"Thanks, Pearce." He hesitated. "For everything."

Pearce smiled. "What are friends for?" Then he turned and marched out of the room.

Hamish moved his chair closer to the gurney, still feeling physically weak. But he'd take that any day if it meant Tessa would live.

"What now?" he asked, lifting his eyes to Leila.

"Now we wait."

"Why don't you take a break, Leila; go see Aiden. I'll call for you if her condition changes," Hamish said.

"Are you sure?"

He nodded. "And you might want to take some bandages with you. The intruder is injured."

Leila's chin dropped. "You didn't kill the demon who got in?"

"It wasn't a demon."

"Then who breached our defenses?"

"A witch."

"But… how is that possible?"

Hamish shrugged. "We don't know yet. We'll figure it out." He glanced back at Tessa. "Later." When he could think straight again.

Leila grabbed a bag with supplies and walked to the door where she looked over her shoulder. "If anything changes, if she wakes up, press that button." She pointed to a spot on the wall. "It'll send a silent alarm to the command center and to my cell."

Hamish nodded. A moment later he was alone with Tessa.

Her face looked peaceful now, not the contorted mask of pain and anguish it had been earlier during her seizure. The golden glow that covered her entire body made her look like an angel. And to him she was an angel.

"I love you, Tessa," he murmured. "And if you wake up, no... *when* you wake up, I'll show you how much." He sniffled. "I'm going to kill the demon who did this to you. I'm going to destroy Zoltan. I'm going to make him wish he'd never been born."

# 34

Wesley cursed. They'd stripped him of his backpack and searched his pockets, emptying them, before they'd tossed him into a dark cell lined with lead. Without any weapons, his cell phone, or his witch power, there wasn't much he could do. He just had to wait for his reluctant hosts to come back and let him explain why he was here and how he'd been able to use the portal.

He wasn't sure how long he'd been in the dimly lit cell, but it couldn't have been long, when he heard footsteps approaching. More than one person, as far as he could tell. He jumped to his feet and stared at the door, which looked as if it belonged in an old castle. A key turned in the lock, and the door swung open, letting more light into the cell.

A man was silhouetted against the light behind him. "We're going to take care of your injury."

He recognized the voice. It was Aiden. He stepped aside, revealing a smaller figure. A woman. Wes lifted an eyebrow and approached the door, taking a closer look. To his surprise, the woman was human.

"One false move, and I'll have you by the balls, witch," Aiden threatened.

The woman put a hand on his forearm in an attempt to calm him. They exchanged a look.

"He's injured and powerless, Aiden, I don't think he's going to try anything." She glanced at Wesley. "Right?"

Automatically, Wes shook his head. "I'm not gonna hurt anybody."

When the woman stepped into the cell, Wes remained motionless, knowing Aiden was watching him like a hawk. If he had to guess he'd say that Aiden and this woman were an item, considering how protective he was of her.

"Leila, be careful."

She didn't reply and walked closer. Then her eyes homed in on Wesley's injured arm. "It's too dark in here," she said, looking over her shoulder. "Let's take him upstairs."

"He's staying here!" Aiden ground out.

She turned slowly. "Aiden, please be reasonable. Let's take him up to the kitchen. I need warm water to clean out his wound anyway. He's not gonna be able to escape, no matter whether he's in the cell or upstairs."

Aiden grumbled something, before he finally said, "Fine." Then he pointed his index finger at Wesley and added, "But one wrong move—"

"I heard you the first time," Wes interrupted. "And the name is Wesley. It's offensive the way you say *witch* as if it were a four-letter word."

To his surprise, Leila chuckled. "Come on, Wesley, let's get you patched up." She walked toward the exit, waving him to follow her.

"And did I hear kitchen? You wouldn't by any chance have something to eat there? I'm kind of starving," Wes said as he left the cell. When Aiden narrowed his eyes at him, he pointed to his wounded arm, where blood had crusted over the incision. "A stiff drink wouldn't go amiss either. You know, to dull the pain."

One side of Aiden's mouth curled up slightly. "We drink Scotch here."

"Love me a good glass of Scotch anytime," Wes claimed. Anything to connect with his hostile host.

Through several corridors and up a couple of flights of stairs, Aiden and Leila led him to a higher floor. There, the walls were similar to the ones in the basement, but the floors had a much smoother surface, and the place was well-lit. It even smelled homey. From what he could tell, this was a massive building, several stories high, and several city lots wide. His own house in San Francisco could fit into this place at least five times over.

Finally, Leila opened a door and motioned him inside, Aiden following him. They had entered a massive open plan kitchen, which included a huge kitchen island with barstools, and a den with an eighty-inch plasma screen on the wall and ample couches in front of it.

"Not bad," Wesley murmured under his breath and motioned to the TV. "You guys know how to live." The TV was muted on his favorite channel. Drawn by the basketball game on the screen, he moved toward it. "Go Warriors!"

"So you really are from San Francisco," Aiden said from beside him.

Wes nearly jumped out of his skin. He hadn't heard or seen Aiden approaching. "Shit! Don't do that!"

"Just keeping you on your toes." He paused, then added, "Wesley."

Behind them, Leila cleared her throat, making them both whirl their heads to her. "Once you're both done with whatever this is, maybe I could get started on bandaging the wound? I have another patient, you know." She pointed to the barstool, while she walked around the island and took a bowl from a cabinet.

Wesley hopped on the barstool and watched her fill the bowl with warm water.

"So, Leila," he started when she returned to set the bowl on the island, before digging into the black doctor's bag next to her. "You're not a Stealth Guardian."

She looked up briefly. "No, I'm not." She pulled white gauze from the bag and dipped it into the warm water. "But I'm married to one."

Before he could react to that, she ordered, "Take off your shirt so I can clean the wound."

He complied, and she went to work. While she concentrated on cleaning the incision, Wes turned his head to look at Aiden, who was watching them, his arms crossed over his chest.

"So you two are together. I figured as much." When Aiden only grunted, Wes had to grin. "Guess you're not that different from my vampire friends at Scanguards. They are just as protective when it comes to their women."

Aiden took a few steps closer, dropping his arms to his sides. "Yeah, you keep saying that you're friends with vampires. How did that happen?"

Finally, somebody was listening.

"Well, funny you should ask."

Aiden tilted his head to the side.

Wes lifted one hand in apology. "Okay, not funny. My brother is a vampire."

"Your brother?" Aiden frowned. "But if he's your brother, he would have been a witch. Why would a witch—"

"To save us all. Ever heard of the Power of Three?"

"Yeah. What about it?"

Wes felt his chest fill with pride. "My brother Haven, my sister Katie, and myself, we were destined to become the Power of Three. But we were betrayed."

"Betrayed by whom?"

"By our mother. And later by another witch, Francine. She tried to harness the power for herself, and the only way to stop her was for one of us to die."

Aiden contemplated Wesley's words. "A witch's power can't reside in a vampire's body."

Pleased that Aiden understood, Wesley continued, "My brother knew that. That's why he sacrificed his human life."

"But how do the vampires play into that?"

"Long story."

"Give me the short version."

"Our mother was killed—and our baby sister Katie kidnapped—by a vampire when we were just kids. Back then, we didn't know who we were, or that our mother had stolen our powers. Haven became a vampire hunter to avenge her. He searched for Katie for over twenty years, killing every vampire that he came across. But then he was tricked by another witch." He shrugged. "It was my fault. But that witch, she'd found Katie. She was an actress at that point. The witch managed to get her hands on us, too. And that's how Scanguards got involved, because Yvette had been assigned as Katie's bodyguard. We all ended up imprisoned by the witch. We had to work together." He smiled. "And Haven, he fell for her. For Yvette. That's how we all became a family. I would trust every single one of the Scanguards vampires with my life. And I would give mine for them if I had to. They're my brothers and sisters."

He suddenly noticed that Leila had stopped tending to his wound, and looked at her. "Thanks." He glanced at his arm. It was neatly bandaged.

"You're really friends with vampires?" Aiden now asked, his voice still incredulous, yet much friendlier than before. "So there is hope for peace between your two species."

"They're good people. They protect the innocent: humans, witches, vampires. Doesn't matter. They don't care what the evil looks like and who's in danger; they don't discriminate. They'll protect those who deserve protecting." And Wes was proud to be part of them.

Leila exchanged a look with her husband. "Just like we do."

Aiden nodded slowly, then shifted his gaze back to Wesley. "How did you find us?"

"I wish I could tell you. I'm not quite sure about that myself. But I saw a preternatural creature, a man who was invisible. He disappeared in a portal in the woods of Sonoma and—"

"One of the lost portals," Aiden murmured.

Not knowing what he meant by that, Wes continued, "I found a dagger carved into the stone where I'd last seen him. I did some research and got lucky. I figured out what that man was: a Stealth Guardian. So I talked to my boss at Scanguards and asked him for permission to find you guys."

"For what purpose?"

"So we could help each other; you know, work together."

"Hmm."

Wes lifted his hands. "I know. It was a long shot. But I was able to use witchcraft to give the portal the illusion that I was a Stealth Guardian, so that it would open for me. It did. But once inside, I didn't really know what to do. I couldn't find any buttons or anything."

Leila chuckled.

"Because there aren't any," Aiden said, and tipped his finger to his temple. "You can only operate it with what's up here."

"With your mind?" Excitement shot through Wes. "That's amazing. Fuck! But..." He furrowed his forehead. "Then how did I land here? I didn't know how to operate the portal. It just started turning and throwing me around like a ping-pong ball in a dryer."

"Yeah, I guess it would feel like that to you. To anybody but a Stealth Guardian or a demon, the trip in the portal is disorienting," Aiden admitted.

"You mean it doesn't feel like that to you?"

He watched Aiden run his eyes over him, assessing him now. "I think you know enough already." Then he motioned to Wesley's arm. "And you're all bandaged up. Time to go back to your cell."

Wes jumped from his barstool. He had no intention of going back there. He'd have to stall the guy for as long as it took to gain his confidence. "I haven't eaten anything yet."

Aiden pointed to the fridge. "Don't expect me to prepare it for you. Help yourself."

Wes didn't wait for a second invitation and marched to the industrial-sized refrigerator, ripping it open. It was fully stocked. "Excellent." He went to work, pulling out various items, before saying over his shoulder, "You know, Aiden, that glass of Scotch you promised me would be nice just about now."

Aiden grunted, "Don't get too comfortable. You're not staying here."

Wes grinned to himself. A few glasses of whiskey with Aiden, and the guy might sing a different tune. After all, Wes could charm any vampire. How hard could it be to get a Stealth Guardian on his side?

# 35

The weightlessness was gone. Tessa was aware of her body again, in fact, she was aware of every single cell of it. She felt strong and full of energy. There was a beeping sound somewhere close by as well as a humming that sounded like an air conditioning unit. Only, she had no air conditioning in her apartment.

She blinked her eyes open. The light around her was blinding, forcing her to squint. Fluorescent lights above her, steel cabinets in her periphery, white glossy walls all around. A hospital room. Immediately, memories rushed back: the demon who'd attacked her, the hypodermic needle, the drug he'd injected her with. Had she made it? Had she survived against all odds?

She inhaled sharply, when she felt movement next to her. She spun her head to the side. Hamish! He lifted his dark head of hair from the edge of the gurney where he'd been resting it.

"Tessa." His voice cracked. "Finally."

"Hamish," she murmured, her throat as dry as the Sahara.

He leaned to the side and reached for something. "Here, drink," he coaxed, bringing a glass of water with a straw to her lips. She pulled the straw into her mouth, lifted her head off the pillow, and greedily gulped down the cool liquid until the glass was empty.

"I knew you'd come," she whispered.

He smiled, and only now did she notice that his eyes were red and swollen... as if he'd shed tears. Automatically she reached for him, but he drew back and rose.

"Tessa, as much as I want to hold you in my arms right now, we can't touch just yet."

She felt confusion spread at his strange words and searched his face for a possible explanation. "W—"

"I nearly lost you, lass. You were slipping away. There was only one thing I could do to save your life."

She swallowed hard, fear gripping her once more.

"I had to pour virta into you."

"Virta?" She didn't know what he meant. She'd never heard that word.

"My life force. The force that gives me my preternatural powers. I needed to make you strong."

She exhaled, her pulse beating frantically. "I'm a Stealth Guardian now?"

He chuckled. "No, my love, but you're nearly as strong as one for a few hours. Look at your arms."

She lifted them and shrieked when she saw the color of her skin. "I'm golden."

"It'll wear off soon." She noticed how he ran his eyes over her, desire and tenderness colliding in them. "But if I touch you while you're shimmering golden, you'll orgasm within a few moments. And as much as I want to give you that pleasure and feel you climax under my touch, we need to talk first."

In disbelief she kept staring at her arms. "Oh my God, I can't believe it. But why? How? I don't understand." She'd thought she knew everything about Hamish and his race, but there appeared to be so much more.

"Stealth Guardians want to make sure that their lovers are always completely satisfied. We can will our virta to enter our lover's bodies during sex and—"

Shocked, she sat up. "You had sex with me while I was unconscious?"

Immediately he shook his head. "No!"

"But you just said—"

"When you reacted badly to the opioid blocker Leila injected you with and crashed, I kissed you and poured my life force into you that way. It gave you the strength you needed to fight for your life. I couldn't let you die, Tessa." Tears brimmed in his eyes. "You mean too much to me."

His words made her head and her heart spin. Without thinking she reached for him and stroked his cheek. A tingling sensation spread over her body and traveled to her core. A flame of desire heated her insides and shot to her pussy. Her clit began to throb uncontrollably.

"Oh God!" she cried out, but it was too late to pull her hand back from Hamish's face. A wave of pleasure rolled over her as she climaxed harder than she ever had, the power of it making her sink back onto the gurney, while her spasms reduced her to a moaning woman in need.

"Tessa," Hamish ground out, hovering over her. "Damn it, when you do that, I can barely hold onto my self control and not take you right here." He glanced around. "But this is neither the place, nor the time." He ran a hand through his hair and reared back again.

"I'm sorry," she murmured, feeling her cheeks flame.

"Don't be," he said, "you've just given me something to look forward to." In his eyes, she saw a promise, and she intended to hold him to it.

"Me, too."

He smiled, then he pulled the chair close to the gurney again and sat down. "Tell me what happened," he said gently. "Everything you can remember."

"He was a demon. His green eyes... I recognized them immediately. I'll never forget that color. I tried to slam the door in his face, but he was so strong..."

"You opened the door for him?"

Tessa felt her heart beat into her throat as she relived the most frightening moments of her life. "I thought Poppy had forgotten something."

"Poppy left you alone, after what she promised me?" Hamish ground out.

"Don't be mad at her. She got a call. Her mother fell down the stairs, and she needed to get to the hospital. She didn't want to leave me alone, but I forced her to go."

Hamish nodded. "That explains why she wasn't at your place. At least she's fine."

"We don't know that," Tessa said, shaking her head. "Not even a minute after she left, there was a knock at the door. I thought it was her. I thought maybe she'd left something in her rush to get to the hospital. So I opened the door without looking through the peephole." It had been careless. "What if he caught her on the way in? And hurt her?"

"There was no evidence of a struggle anywhere in the stairway. More likely the demon waited for Poppy to leave and snuck into the building after her—before the front door could snap in."

"I'm worried about her. We need to check on her. Please." She shot him a pleading look.

Hamish sighed, then nodded. "I'll send Enya to her apartment." He looked at his wristwatch. "It's almost five in the morning. She should be at home if nothing happened to her."

"Thank you."

"I know this is hard for you, but I need to know what else happened. Anything you can remember about the demon, what he looked like, what he did and said."

"He kicked the door open and slammed me against the wall. When I tried to scream for help, he choked me, until I almost fainted." Even now she felt her airways constrict and had to gasp for air.

"Easy, my love, he can't hurt you anymore," Hamish murmured.

There it was again: he was calling her *my love*. As if it were the most natural thing in the world. As if he truly meant it.

She nodded, recalling the horror again. "He put tape over my mouth then, so I couldn't scream anymore. Then he tossed me over his shoulder and carried me into the bedroom. I thought he was going to rape me..." She stopped, then looked down at herself—and sighed in relief. She still wore the same clothes as earlier. The only difference was that somebody had put sensors underneath her top. Her eyes shot to the monitor, from which she heard a steady beeping. Then she looked back at Hamish.

"Leila, Aiden's wife, took care of you. She's a doctor, well, a researcher. But she did what she could. I brought you here..."

"Where is here?"

"Our compound. All Stealth Guardians assigned to Baltimore live here."

"Like in a commune?"

He smiled. "Kind of. We're protected here."

"And the demons?"

"Nobody, no demon, no human can find this place. It's invisible to all but us. It's safe."

She let out a breath, nodding. "The demon, when I saw what he pulled from his pocket—a hypodermic needle—I tried to fight him, but he was so strong. So strong."

"No human has ever been able to overpower a demon. Physically they're too strong. The only way a human can fight them is by outsmarting them."

"And Stealth Guardians? Are they stronger than the demons?"

"We're about equally matched. But as you know we have a couple of aces up our sleeves."

She immediately remembered the fight outside her apartment building. "Yes." She swallowed and continued, "He pinned me and then he started injecting me with the drug."

"Can you describe him?"

She shrugged. "Tall, dark hair, scary looking." She shook her head. "I don't know. All I saw were his demon eyes." Tears shot to her eyes again.

"It's okay, Tessa." He gave her a reassuring smile. "Did he say anything before you passed out?"

She frowned. Words were tumbling around in her mind. "A lot of things. I'm not sure they make sense."

"Try and recall what he said."

She closed her eyes for a moment. "He said they would find me dead of a drug overdose. And nobody would question it. They would all think I took my life because of the scandal." She met Hamish's eyes. Understanding shimmered back at her. "He said I was hard to kill. That I'd escaped twice already."

"So he's responsible for both the attacks: the duct falling, and the demons attacking us the night after your parents' party."

"I think that's what he meant. He said this time I wouldn't escape and my death would finally make him superior."

"Superior?" Hamish's eyebrows snapped together. "Did he say anything else?"

"Something about the Great One," she said, but couldn't recall the exact words.

Hamish slammed his fist on the gurney. "Zoltan himself. That fucking bastard!"

"Zoltan?" Why did that name have a familiar ring to it?

"Yes. I found out who sent that photo to the press. There was an email by somebody named Zoel Monnadt. Only the name turned out to be an anagram. When you shift the letters around you get *Demon Zoltan*. He sent the photo to Meredith Durant to discredit you and destroy your campaign."

Excitement raced through her when she realized something. "So you can prove that the photo was altered, right?"

To her surprise, Hamish shook his head. "The photo is real. I had Pearce check it out. It wasn't altered in any way."

"But—"

The doors to the medical center suddenly opened, and she spun her head toward them. A man in his thirties marched in, a file in his hand. She'd never seen him before and tensed automatically.

"That's Pearce. He's one of us," Hamish said quickly, easing her concerns.

"Hey, she's awake, huh?" Pearce said as he approached. "That's great news." Then he handed the file to Hamish. "From the county courthouse."

"Thanks," Hamish replied. "And did Manus bring Tessa's things?"

"My things?"

Pearce nodded. "Manus went to your apartment and packed some clothes and personal items for you." He looked at Hamish. "We put them in your quarters. We figured..." He didn't finish his sentence, but instead dug into his pocket and pulled out a cell phone. "We brought your cell phone. Your father called several times. He's worried."

"Did you speak to him?" she asked, surprised.

"No. We hacked into your voicemail." He shrugged. "Sorry, but we needed to know whether there was anything we had to take care of while you were out..."

She nodded slowly and reached for the phone. When she felt Pearce's fingers brush hers as she took it from him, she jerked back, not wanting to climax in front of a stranger.

A frown crossed Pearce's face, then he suddenly chuckled. "Oh, I see. You told her, huh?" He tossed Hamish a sideways glance, then smiled at Tessa. "Just so you know, that uh... thing that happens when you're shimmering golden... it only happens if the person who touches you is the same as the person who gave you their virta."

Heat shot into her cheeks. She felt exposed, bare. "Uh..."

"It's okay, Tessa," Hamish said. "There's nothing to be ashamed of."

She avoided his eyes and instead looked at the cell phone in her hand. "Is it okay if I call my father? He'll be worried."

"Go ahead," Hamish said. "Don't tell him about the drug overdose. Just say that you needed time to think."

Tessa nodded and dialed.

# 36

"Dad?"

While Tessa was talking to her father, Hamish waved to Pearce, and they moved a few feet away. Hamish opened the file. He kept his voice low as he asked his fellow guardian, "Have you had a look at this yet?"

Pearce shook his head. "No. I just grabbed it and came back as fast as I could. Took me long enough—the filing system at the courthouse is antiquated."

"Hmm."

Hamish was already perusing the pages: an application by Mr. and Mrs. Wallace, character references, financial statements, Tessa's birth certificate. He leafed through the file, until he came across a note from a social worker. He stabbed his finger at it.

"This is it," he said excitedly and exchanged a look with Pearce, who blew out a breath.

"Shit! How did you know?"

"A hunch." Then he reread the few lines the social worker had written. "... leaving behind identical twin girls aged thirteen months. Closest relatives unable to care for the girls... After initially being interested in adopting both girls, Philip and Diane Wallace decided to take only one. Sibling to remain in foster care until suitable adoptive parents can be found." Then a reference number below it, written in different ink—it had been added later.

"That's how the demons did it," Pearce said.

A gasp from Tessa made Hamish rush to the gurney. Tessa's eyes were wide with shock. She was holding the cell phone to her ear, tears brimming in her eyes.

Had something happened to her parents?

"Tessa, what's wrong?" Hamish asked.

She stared at him, then said into the phone, "Dad, I need to... I just have to let all this sink in." A short pause, then she added, "Yes, I love you, too." She disconnected the call and let the phone drop into her lap. When she raised her lids to look at Hamish, there was both hope and disbelief in her eyes. "My dad. He told me I have a sister."

Hamish nodded. "An identical twin." He lifted the file he was still holding. "I just found out myself. That's how the demons were able to stage the photo and make it look like it's you."

"Hamish, what if they hurt her?"

"We're gonna find her. I promise you." And once they found her, they could clear Tessa's name. He marched to the wall and pressed a button to call for Leila.

When he turned around, Tessa was already hopping off the gurney, ripping the sensors off her chest.

"What are you doing?" Hamish asked, approaching her.

"We have to search for her. I need to make sure she's safe."

"We'll take care of that. Don't worry. Once we find her, we'll be able to prove it wasn't you in the picture."

Tessa froze. "That's why you think I want to find her?"

"Well, why—"

She shook her head. "She's my sister, my flesh and blood. And because of me they did this to her. I'm responsible. I need to know she's safe."

Hamish stared at her. Cinead and his emissarius had been right. Tessa was good through and through. Her first concern wasn't for her campaign and how to make the allegations against her go away, but for her sister, a woman she didn't even know, but was connected to by blood.

At that moment, he wished nothing more than to take Tessa into his arms, because his love for her had just doubled, if that was even possible. But even though the golden shimmer was already fading, her reaction to his touch would still be that of instant arousal and subsequent climax. Not something he wanted to share in front of Pearce.

"I'll do everything I can to find your sister," he promised, locking eyes with her. "But you have to do something for me."

She nodded without hesitation.

"Leila will be here in a moment. She'll check you out, make sure you're a hundred percent. She'll bring you to my quarters. Make yourself at home there. Take a shower, get changed, rest. I'll be back as soon as we've put together a plan of action."

"But I need to help."

"You're helping me as long as I know you're safe and well. Please, I'll be with you as soon as I can."

The double doors opened at that moment, and Leila entered.

"That's Leila. You can trust her." Then he motioned to Pearce. "Let's go."

Minutes later they were all assembled in the command center: Manus, Logan, Pearce, and Enya. Sean and Jay were out on assignments.

Aiden was the last to arrive. "Sorry, guys, had to lock up the witch again."

Hamish raised an eyebrow. "What do you mean by again? Did he get out?"

"No. Of course not. Leila bandaged him up, and then we had something to eat and talked. Interesting guy. I think he's genuine."

"We'll discuss him later." Hamish looked at his colleagues. "First things first. We have a lead, and we need to act quickly."

With as few words as possible, Hamish conveyed to his friends what he'd learned from Tessa and her adoption file.

"Why didn't we see this?" Enya asked, shaking her head. "It's so obvious now."

"We weren't looking for it," Hamish said. "It doesn't matter now. What's more important is that we find Tessa's twin—both to make sure she wasn't harmed, and, first and foremost, to clear Tessa's name and ensure she still has a chance in the mayor's race."

Logan grunted. "They're ripping her to shreds in the papers because she hasn't made a statement yet. She's gotta say something to keep them at bay."

Hamish nodded. It reminded him of something. "We'll get her campaign manager on this. But first of all we have to make sure she's alright. Poppy left just before the demon entered Tessa's apartment. Tessa is worried that he might have hurt her. Enya, check on Poppy. Try her apartment first. If she's not there, try the hospitals to see where her mother was admitted and find her that way."

"Why don't we just call her?" Enya asked.

"I want to make sure first that she's not being held by one of Zoltan's demons. Once we know she's safe, Tessa will call her and ask her to put out a statement to buy her some time."

"Fine."

Hamish tipped his chin in Pearce's direction. "Go back to the county courthouse and look for the adoption file on Tessa's twin. There's a reference number in Tessa's file. I think it may lead you to her. Once you have that, we'll know who adopted her and what her name is. We can find her with that information." He pointed to Manus. "Take Manus with you. You can split up the work."

"And the rest of us?" Logan asked, pointing to Aiden and himself.

"I need to shadow Gunn," Hamish said. "Even though we now know for certain that the demons were behind the duct falling on the stage, they'd still need to have somebody helping them. My money is on Gunn. He has the most to gain by Tessa's death."

"Agreed," Logan said, "but I'll watch Gunn. You're not ready to leave the compound and—"

"I'm more than ready."

Logan took a step toward him. "From what Pearce told us, you poured so much virta into Tessa that you nearly collapsed. That was less than twelve hours ago. You haven't fully replenished your powers yet."

"That's bullshit," Hamish protested.

"If you go out there now and run into a demon, he's gonna have you by the balls," Logan countered. "And what are we gonna tell Tessa then, huh? Do you want her to mourn you?"

Hamish sucked in a sharp breath. "Shit!" His colleague was right. He needed a few more hours at the compound to restore his virta and become as strong as before. He sighed. "Fine, you take Gunn. Aiden, you'll stay at the command center as backup. If any of them need help, you'll jump in. In the meantime, keep an eye on the witch."

Everybody nodded in agreement, their assignments clear. As all except Aiden left the command center, Hamish rubbed his neck. Suddenly he felt the effect of the stress of the last few hours. He was drained. When he looked in Aiden's direction, he caught his friend's eyes on him.

"Why don't you see if Tessa needs anything? I'm sure she doesn't want to be alone right now."

"You sure you don't need me to stay?" he asked even though he wanted nothing more than to be with Tessa.

Aiden pointed to the door. "Go! I don't need a babysitter. Tessa needs you more. I'll call you as soon as any of them report in with news, deal?"

"Thanks, bro."

# 37

Tessa leaned back in the large soaker tub and allowed the warm water to soothe her. Against all odds, she was alive. And safe in an invisible building. Yet too many things were going through her mind. She had a sister. A twin. Why had her parents kept this from her? And why hadn't they adopted them both? They would have had the means. She could have had a sibling to grow up with, a best friend, somebody she could have shared all her secrets with, the good and the bad.

But she shouldn't dwell on what could have been. She had to look to the future. Hamish had promised her that he would find her twin. And she trusted him that he would make good on his promise.

Footsteps made her sit up in the bath. She hadn't heard a door opening. "Who is it?" she called out, noticing how on edge she still sounded.

Hamish walked into the bathroom. "I didn't mean to startle you. I'm sorry. I'm not used to opening the door to my quarters."

She relaxed back beneath the foam. "You shouldn't have to apologize. I'm just jumpy. I didn't expect you back so quickly."

"That's cause I haven't left."

"But I thought—"

"The team's grounded me for the next few hours, so to speak."

"Why?"

"Because of the amount of virta I poured into you."

She suddenly realized what he was trying to say. "It's weakened you, hasn't it?"

He nodded. "I'll have fully recovered in a few hours, nothing to worry about. In the meantime the others are starting the search for your sister. And Enya is checking on Poppy. We should have a lead on your sister in a few hours; as for Poppy, we might know much earlier if she's alright. Hopefully, she's at home."

Relieved, Tessa nodded. "Thank you. For everything… you're doing so much. And I feel I'm not doing anything." Leila had told her to just rest.

Hamish smiled. "There is something you can do for me if you want to."

"Yes?" she asked eagerly.

"Make room in that bathtub and let me join you."

Instinctively she looked at her skin. The golden shimmer had almost completely dissipated. Only a faint residue was still visible.

She heard Hamish chuckle and caught him gazing at her.

"I'll just have to work a little harder to make you climax, now that the glow is almost gone." He grinned. "That is, if you want that… We didn't get a chance to talk after we made love."

The memory of how fiercely he'd taken her made her insides ignite like kindling in a furnace. "No, we got interrupted…"

"Maybe we should talk now."

When she nodded, Hamish began to undress. There was nothing hurried about his movements; he was all confident male. He knew that she wouldn't say no to him. She could see it in his eyes, which stayed locked on her while he shed his clothes. Yes, she wanted him, now even more than before. Whether it was his virta that drew her to him, or the fact that she'd just escaped certain death, she wanted nothing more than to surrender to the immortal warrior who was now walking toward her, naked and self-assured.

Tessa scooted forward in the large tub, making space for him, and he slid into the water behind her, his legs spread to either side of her. When she finally felt his arms wrap around her and pull her against his chest, she sighed contentedly.

His breath blew against her ear like a caress. "There's something I need to tell you."

Her heartbeat accelerated. Whenever somebody started like this, it was rarely good news. She felt her chest constrict. "Yes?" she choked out.

Hamish pressed a kiss to her temple. Was he trying to sweeten the blow of whatever bad news he had?

"Things between you and me have been happening so fast, and it's all so new, but I want you to hear me out."

Still not knowing where he was going with this, she swallowed hard and managed to nod.

"I've told you that I'm an immortal, but what I haven't told you is that I'm at an age where the members of our race reach a certain stage in their lives. We call it *rasen*. Mating season. That's when we find a partner for life. For eternity. After Olivia betrayed me, I vowed never to get emotionally involved with another human woman."

She squeezed her eyes shut. So this was where he would tell her that because she was human, what was between them was just a fling. Just sex. Nothing else.

"I know that forever is a difficult concept for anybody. Many marriages in the human world end in divorce. We don't have divorce in our race. When we mate, it's for eternity. The kind of love that lasts longer than a lifetime doesn't come around very often. That's why we have to grab it with both hands when we see it. I felt it once. And I was betrayed. It's made me afraid..."

She felt tears rise to her eyes. "You don't have to say any more. I understand," she said softly.

"You do?"

She nodded, trying to be brave. "You don't want anything serious, because you can't trust women anymore."

"Tessa..."

"I'm okay with that. I think I've known from the moment you first kissed me that this would only be temporary." She sniffled. "You don't have to feel bad. I enjoyed sleeping with you, and I don't mind if that's all this is."

"Liar," he murmured at her ear.

"There's no need to make fun of me. So what if I'm attracted to you?"

"Just attracted?"

She sensed him pull her closer, his arms now almost like a vice. She shrugged. "And grateful that you saved my life."

"So you're not falling in love with me?"

"Don't worry, I'm not gonna be one of those pesky conquests you can't get rid of when it's over."

He shifted behind her, turning her slightly so she had to look at him. "You mean there's no hope that you might one day return my feelings?"

She shot up, making water splash over the sides of the tub. "What?"

Hamish reached for her, sliding his hand behind her nape. "Tessa, don't you understand what I've been trying to explain to you? I don't want a fling. I don't want just sex. I love you. I know this happened fast, but that's how it is in our race. We just know when it hits us."

Her chin dropped. She was hallucinating. Everything began to spin around her. Maybe she'd fallen asleep in the tub. Maybe Hamish wasn't even here.

"I know it's a lot to lay on you, particularly after what you've been through," Hamish continued. "But I wanted you to know how I feel. I don't expect an answer from you now. I'll wait for as long as it takes." He pinned her with his eyes. "Just tell me that I've got a chance to win your heart."

Her throat felt as dry as sandpaper. Was this reality? Had he really said that he loved her? That this immortal man wanted her?

"Oh, Hamish…"

The temptation to tell him how she felt was immense, but she had to remain realistic. Even if he loved her and even if she loved him back, how could there ever be a happy future when she would grow old and wither away, while he lived on? She closed her eyes, but couldn't hold back the tears.

Hamish took her head in both hands. "Tessa, what did I do wrong? Please, whatever I did or said, tell me how I can make it right."

She lifted her lids, looking at him through her tears. "No matter how we feel about each other, how can we ever be together? Have you forgotten that I'm not like you? I'm not immortal, Hamish. I don't have eternity. Only you do."

A sob dislodged from her chest, but it didn't get a chance to escape, because Hamish's lips were on her, kissing her tenderly. All too quickly he released her and pressed his forehead to hers.

"I'm an idiot, lass," he murmured. "Forgive me. I should have explained. I thought when I told you about Olivia, you understood. And you met Leila. I thought you knew."

She pulled her head back. "Knew what? And what does Leila have to do with this?"

He brushed a wet strand of hair from her cheek. "Leila is Aiden's mate. She's human."

Her eyebrows snapped together. "But if she's human, how… I mean, how can he be happy knowing she'll die…"

Hamish brushed his thumb underneath her eye, wiping away a tear. "Because she won't. By bonding with her, he's sharing his immortality with her. It's his gift in exchange for her love."

This time she couldn't stop the sob that tore from her chest. She threw her arms around him.

"Does that mean you're giving us a chance?" he asked softly.

Unable to speak, she simply nodded.

~ ~ ~

His heart beating an excited tattoo against his chest, Hamish captured Tessa's lips for a kiss. He was aware that she hadn't told him that she loved him, but he couldn't expect that much this soon. Knowing that Tessa wanted him and was thinking of the future was enough for now. Time would tell if they were truly meant for each other—he for his part knew she was the one.

Her lips tasted of the salt of her tears, and he promised himself right there and then that she would never have to cry again.

"Let me make love to you," he whispered against her lips.

"Yes."

He rose and lifted her out of the bathtub, setting her on the thick mat in front of it while he reached for a towel. As he dried Tessa and then himself, he didn't take his eyes off her. She was beautiful. The last time they'd made love, he'd rushed things, because he'd been so impatient to have her, but now he feasted his eyes on her, committing each square inch of her body to memory.

He lowered himself on his knees as he dried her legs, then dropped the towel. He was eye-level with her stomach, but the scars didn't repel him. They were part of Tessa, part of what had forced her to be strong. He pressed his lips to them and kissed her there, showing her that to him she was beautiful everywhere. She didn't shrink back, didn't hide from him. When he looked up, she gazed down at him, her eyes full of tenderness.

Wordlessly, he pulled her down to him and laid her on the white mat and settled into the space between her legs.

"I should have done this last time," he said, "but when you sucked me, you obliterated my self-control."

Her lips curved into a smile. "You felt good in my mouth."

"Let's see how good this feels." He lowered his face to her pussy and inhaled her aroma. "Hmm." When he pressed a kiss into the tiny triangle of hair at the apex of her thighs, he felt her shudder beneath him. He put his hands on her thighs and pushed them farther apart, lifting them over his shoulders to either side of his head. Pink flesh beautiful like a flower greeted him. Though he'd toweled her dry, she was wet there now, her nether lips coated with her arousal.

Greedily, he swiped his tongue over her slit, gathering her juices and tasting them, tasting her. A bolt of pure lust shot through him. She was everything he'd ever dreamed of and more. And licking Tessa would give him just as much pleasure as it gave her. Eagerly, he explored her, licked and sucked the gentle flesh she so openly offered him now. Her sighs and moans bounced off the tile walls of his bathroom, echoing in the large room.

Tessa shoved her hands into his hair now. The contact sent a shiver down his spine and into his tailbone. Automatically, his hips began to move, and he felt his fully erect cock rub against the tile floor, seeking relief. Thanks to the coolness of the tile, he didn't explode immediately, but was able to maintain his control, because what was most important to him right now was to satisfy the woman in his arms. Make up for the horror she'd been through.

And he loved doing it. Loved licking her pussy, playing with her responsive flesh, and feeling her writhe beneath him. Because it meant she was alive. And so was he.

He moved farther up, spread her with his fingers now, revealing her clit. The tiny organ was swollen—and glowing golden. It was the last spot of her body that still showed evidence of his virta. Unable to resist, he licked over it with his tongue.

"Oh God! Hamish!" Tessa cried out. "You've gotta stop! It's too... oh God, it's too much..."

Spasms made her body twist and turn, but he held her to him and swiped his tongue over her center of pleasure once more. She was already climaxing. He cupped her clit with his mouth and allowed the waves of her orgasm to travel over his lips.

A shudder charged through him. "Fuck!" he ground out. Long seconds passed, until Tessa finally stilled and relaxed and let out a final sigh.

"Hamish," she mumbled and caressed his scalp.

He lifted his head from her and sat up. When he looked at her face, she met his eyes.

"Do you think it greedy of me that I want you inside me now?" she asked.

He pulled her into his arms and rose, carrying her into the adjoining bedroom. "You can't possibly be as greedy as I am." He lowered her on the bed and rolled over her. Looking deep into her eyes, he adjusted himself at her center and thrust inside with one single move. "So greedy," he repeated, "that I don't even have the decency to let you rest after all you've been through."

But her eyes told him that she didn't want to rest. That she wanted him instead. That knowledge filled his heart with warmth, and his cock with even more blood.

"I'm following doctor's orders," she murmured.

"How so?"

"Leila said I should lie down." Tessa patted the duvet next to her. "I'm lying down, am I not?"

"Well, if you put it that way, we should definitely continue to follow doctor's orders." He withdrew almost completely from her welcoming sheath, then sliced back into her.

Tessa pressed her head into the pillow, arching her back. "Yes!"

At her enthusiastic praise, he grunted, "Yeah? Like that?" He began thrusting into her with more vigor, his hips moving more rapidly now, his cock demanding he take her harder and make her his. He didn't put up any resistance, knowing he was defenseless in Tessa's arms. Stripped bare. Devoted to her.

Feeling her hands on him, feeling how she caressed and explored him, made his chest swell with pride. And when she locked her thighs beneath his butt to force him deeper into her, he wanted to roar like a lion who'd been freed of his cage. Because Tessa had freed him of his. The links in the chain that surrounded his heart were falling away with every caress and every kiss she granted him.

This wasn't just sex. Maybe back at Tessa's apartment they'd had sex, but this here, in his bed, this was lovemaking. Every time their bodies came together, their gazes met, connecting in a way even more intimate than their bodies.

When Tessa's eyelids began to flutter, he knew she was close again.

"I'm right there with you, my love," he murmured and captured her lips, kissing her with all the love he felt in his heart.

She responded to him with the same passion and desire, her hips rising to meet him as he delivered thrust after thrust into her wet pussy. Not able to withstand another second of this sweet torture, he let himself go and allowed his semen to shoot through his cock, exploding from the tip.

He moaned into her mouth and greedily lapped against her tongue, not wanting this to end, when he felt her interior muscles squeeze him and wring the last of his seed from him as she climaxed with him.

Only when her spasms subsided, did he allow himself to collapse. He braced himself on his elbows and looked at her face. A sheen of perspiration covered her skin and made her look even more radiant than before.

He parted his lips, wanting to say something, to tell her how he felt, but no words came over his lips. For the first time in a long time he was… happy.

# 38

"Hamish?"

It wasn't Tessa's voice that drifted to him. Hamish stirred and opened his eyes. He must have nodded off with Tessa tucked into the curve of his body. For a moment he felt groggy, but then he heard the crackling of the intercom next to his bed and reached to press the speaker button.

"Aiden?"

"Yeah. Enya just called in. She checked on Poppy."

Tessa suddenly shot up.

"She found her sleeping peacefully. No sign of demons."

Tessa released a sigh of relief. "Thank God!"

"Thanks, Aiden," Hamish added.

"No problem. She's staying out in the field and joining up with Pearce and Manus to see if she can help."

"Sounds good. Thanks." He let go of the speaker button and pulled Tessa back against his chest.

She turned her face to him. "I'm so glad she's alright."

Hamish brushed a lock of hair from her forehead and pressed a kiss to it. "See, Zoltan didn't get her after all."

"Zoltan... I've heard that name before."

"Of course you have. I mentioned him earlier in the medical room. Don't you remember?"

She shook her head. "I heard his name before that."

"You mean when he attacked you, he told you who he was?" Even for Zoltan that seemed a little unorthodox, though he knew that the new leader of the demons was cunning. There was a purpose behind every move he made.

"No, he didn't. He mentioned Zoltan."

Hamish stared at Tessa. "Mentioned him... as in how?"

"The demon said that Zoltan was a weakling for letting me live."

"Are you sure you heard him correctly? You were frightened."

"I'm sure, Hamish. Please believe me. He said he was supposed to be the Great something or other."

"The Great One?" Hamish helped.

She nodded emphatically. "Yes, the Great One. What does that mean?"

"It's the title of the leader of the demons. But Zoltan is the new leader," Hamish elaborated.

"The demon who attacked me said that *he* should be the leader. Not Zoltan. And that by killing me, he would prove that he was stronger than Zoltan... no," she corrected herself, "not stronger. *Superior* to Zoltan."

Hamish let the words sink in. "If this is true, then the demons are fighting a turf war amongst themselves. And you're caught in the middle of it."

"That's bad, isn't it?"

"Hmm... I'm not sure yet what it means in the long run. Right now though we have to be even more vigilant. If Zoltan really only wanted to destroy your political future, but his rival wants to seize the reins by killing you, then we have to fight on two fronts."

"Haven't we already been doing that?"

Slowly he nodded. "Unknowingly, yes."

"Then we're better prepared now that we know, right?" Tessa hypothesized.

He smiled and pressed a kiss to her lips. "Yes, thanks to you, my love." He swung his legs out of bed. "Come, let's talk to Aiden. Are you hungry?"

She tilted her head to the side, before she answered, "Actually, I'm famished."

A few minutes later they were both dressed and walking hand-in-hand through the corridors. At the door to the kitchen, Hamish stopped and looked at Tessa. "If you're uncomfortable about my colleagues knowing what's happening between us, I won't let on." Although that ship had sailed already, given the things he'd done and said in front of his friends when Tessa had been fighting for her life. But he wasn't ashamed of the tears he'd shed while her life had hung in the balance.

Tessa smirked. "I think they know." She lifted herself on her tiptoes. "And it's not making me uncomfortable."

He kissed her, before opening the door to the kitchen. The smell of pancakes wafted to him, and he realized only now how hungry he was.

"Leila, I hope you're making enough for all of us," Hamish said as he walked in with Tessa by his side. But it wasn't Leila who stood at the stove flipping pancakes. Leila was sitting at the kitchen island, Aiden next to her.

"What the fuck is the witch doing out of his cell?" Hamish ground out.

The witch spun around, a plastic spatula in his hand. "Making my famous coconut banana pancakes. Want some?" He grinned. "And again, name's Wesley. I wish people would remember that. It's not that hard. I've already memorized all of your names."

Hamish glared at the insolent man.

"Hamish, give the guy a break," Aiden said calmly, shoveling food into his mouth.

"Sit down," Leila added, "and have some food. He's a really good cook."

"And that gives him the right to have the run of this place?"

Aiden jumped up from his barstool. "Don't talk to my wife like that!"

"Damn it, Aiden," Hamish grunted. "This is against every rule of the house! You can't just let a prisoner run free."

His friend braced his hands at his hips. "Like you haven't broken any rules lately." His gaze drifted to Tessa.

Ah shit! He'd broken a whole bunch of rules, but at least the rules he'd broken wouldn't put the compound in danger. He pointed to Wesley, still locking eyes with Aiden. "We don't know whether we can trust him. He was able to breach our portal. Who knows what he's planning?"

"Right now I'm planning to make another batch of pancakes," Wesley interrupted. "Who wants some?"

As if in response, Hamish's stomach growled. Traitor!

"Ah," Wesley said triumphantly. He heaved two pancakes onto a plate and slid it over the island. "Syrup is on the counter." Then he looked at Tessa. "And your lady friend?"

"I wouldn't mind one or two," Tessa replied.

"Two pancakes, coming right up," Wesley said, and turned back to the stove.

"Take a seat, Hamish," Aiden said and hopped back on his barstool.

Knowing he'd lost this round, Hamish helped Tessa onto the barstool next to Leila, then took the seat next to her. "Did you watch him the entire time he was preparing the food?" he asked Aiden.

"Yeah, why?"

"Just making sure he's not poisoning us."

Wesley huffed indignantly.

"It's safe to eat," Leila said, rolling her eyes. "And it's delicious, by the way. Thanks, Wesley."

Wesley tossed a look over his shoulder. "Appreciate it."

Hamish reached for the plate and pushed it in front of Tessa. "Here, Tessa, have mine, I can wait. You must be starving."

She smiled at him gratefully, then took her first bite, chewing contentedly. "Hmm. These are good." After another bite she said casually, "I didn't know that you keep witches as prisoners. Well, I didn't know that witches existed."

Aiden chuckled with a sideward glance at Hamish. "I'll let you explain that."

Hamish sighed. "We don't normally. Witches are our allies. But when one breaks in here, we take issue."

At the last word, Wesley looked over his shoulder. "I wouldn't call it breaking in. It's not like there was a doorbell or something that I could ring. I explained it all to Aiden."

Hamish shifted his gaze to his friend. "Wanna fill me in?"

Aiden nodded. "I'm pretty sure he's genuine. He said he followed a Stealth Guardian somewhere in the woods of Sonoma, California, and found one of the portals. Apparently the person he followed told him to destroy some drugs a bunch of vampires had been producing. Anyway, I've sent a query to the compound loop to see which, if any, of our brothers has been running around Sonoma. If a Stealth Guardian can corroborate his story, then I'm willing to accept it. I'm waiting to hear back."

"Is that all you've got?"

"Nope. There's a lot more. Apparently Wesley here is friends with a whole bunch of vampires."

"You're fucking kidding me."

"Can't say I am. And guess what these vampires do for a living?"

"Suck people dry?" Hamish grunted.

"They run a bodyguard company. They protect humans and other innocents. From the preternatural. Kind of like us, huh?"

Hamish shot a look at Wesley, who was now putting more pancakes on a plate. "You're shitting me."

"Haven't checked it out yet, since we're a little short on manpower right now, but as soon as I can free somebody up, I'll send a guardian to San Francisco to investigate."

Wesley put a plate in front of Hamish, then a second opposite him, and hopped onto a barstool. "You should just let me call Scanguards and they'll talk to you."

"Scanguards?" Hamish asked.

"That's the company he claims to work for," Aiden elaborated. Then he looked at Wesley. "And we've discussed this already. No phone calls for you until we've thoroughly vetted you and have confirmed that neither you nor Scanguards are a threat to us."

Wesley dug into his stack of pancakes and shoved a fork full of them into his mouth. His stomach growling again, Hamish grabbed his fork and did the same. For a moment there was silence, and all that could be heard in the kitchen was the clatter of cutlery.

Hamish started to relax a little. He had to admit that Wesley presented no danger at present. His witch powers would remain inactive while in the compound, and with no way of getting out, he was at their mercy. After all, without witchcraft, a witch was merely as strong as a human. And Wesley knew that.

Hamish motioned to Aiden. "Any news from the guys?"

"Pearce called in earlier. They've got a name. Tiffany Jacoby."

Next to him, Tessa lifted her head. "My twin sister…" With a hopeful sheen in her lavender-colored eyes, she looked at Aiden. "Have they found her?"

"Not yet. I ran her name through the databases. The DMV had an address for her. Pearce and Manus are checking it out right now. But there was a different address on an arrest record I found in the Police Department's database. I sent Enya to check it out."

"Arrest record?" Tessa's hand trembled, and Hamish clasped it to calm her.

"For drug possession. Looks like she's been in trouble with the law a few times."

"Oh God, we need to help her."

The pleading tone in Tessa's voice made Hamish's heart ache. "We will. Just as soon as we find her."

She lifted her gaze to him. "I'm so worried about her. She's out there all alone. Who knows what the demons did to her."

That reminded him of something. He looked back at Aiden. "About the demons. It wasn't Zoltan who attacked Tessa and drugged her."

Aiden frowned. "What? But—"

"Tessa remembered what the demons said. And from what we've pieced together, it sounds like Zoltan's got a turf war on his hands. Apparently, *The Great One* wasn't planning on killing Tessa; though I think he was probably responsible for putting that picture in the papers to destroy Tessa's political career."

Aiden nodded. "Pearce was telling me that the email came from a Zoel Monnadt, and that it's an anagram for *Demon Zoltan*."

"Right. But the attacks on Tessa's life, they were perpetuated by a different demon. Somebody who wants to remove Zoltan from his throne." He was sure about this now. It made sense.

"I wonder whether we could use that information to stir up trouble in the demon world," Aiden mused. "Having them fight among themselves would take the heat off us for a while."

"It's possible," Hamish said. "Let's discuss it with the others when they—"

The ringing of Aiden's cell phone interrupted him. He picked it up from the counter and answered it. "Hey Logan."

Hamish pointed to the phone. "Put him on speaker."

Aiden complied. "You're on speaker. I'm with Hamish. Any news?"

"I'm with Gunn. The guy is so giddy right now, he can barely contain himself. He's practically celebrating his victory already."

"Bastard!" Hamish hissed.

"Oh I know," Logan agreed. "But he did seem a little surprised that Tessa hasn't made a statement yet. He's waiting for her to officially withdraw from the mayor's race. He's been making phone calls all morning trying to find out where she is. If he's really the guy helping Zoltan, then wouldn't he know that Zoltan tried to kill Tessa?"

"He might be creating an alibi for himself," Aiden said. "And by the way, we just figured out that the demon who tried to kill Tessa wasn't Zoltan, but a rival. Most likely Zoltan planted the drug story to undermine her campaign, but his rival went a step further. So Gunn probably works for the rival, who's been trying to kill Tessa all along."

"What do you want me to do then?" Logan asked.

"Stay on Gunn," Hamish ordered. "Once the others are back, I'll send Manus to relieve you. If anybody can lead us to the demons behind this, it's Gunn. Sooner or later, he'll be in contact with them."

"Not if they think that they succeeded and their work is done," Logan said. "For all they know Tessa is dead."

Hamish spun his head to Tessa, catching her apprehensive look. "Then we'll have to make sure the right people know that she's alive."

# 39

Hamish gave her an encouraging look, but Tessa dreaded making the call.

"Do I really need to talk to him? Can't I just leave a message with his assistant?"

"Gunn needs to hear your voice," Hamish said. "He needs to know you're alive. It'll prompt him to contact the demons, and then we'll be on them like white on rice."

They were still assembled around the kitchen island. The witch, who actually seemed like a rather easy-going guy, was stacking the dishes into the dishwasher, while everybody else was looking at Tessa.

"Okay." She took a deep breath and dialed Gunn's direct line.

"Yeah?" Gunn's tight voice bellowed through the line.

"Robert, it's Tessa."

Clearly stunned, Gunn blew out a breath. "Tessa." Then he seemed to catch himself. "So you're calling to concede, are you?"

"Concede? Dream on."

He chuckled. "Come on, Tessa, you know you've got no chance now. The press is crucifying you, and your prim and proper voters are deserting you by the thousands."

"They'll come back once they hear the truth."

"The truth? Tessa, wake up! You got caught." He laughed. "Who would have thought that under that holier-than-thou exterior you had a dark side? Not even I could have dreamt that up. Jesus, Tessa, drugs? You? You fooled us all. But thanks anyway. The election is mine now. And not even your crooked little campaign manager can fix this like she fixed everything else."

"I know what you're doing! You can't hide it much longer."

There was a sharp intake of breath on the other end of the line. "Watch yourself, Tessa. You're biting off more than you can chew."

"You fucking little shit!" she cursed, but the phone was slammed on the receiver. The call was disconnected. "Argh! That jerk! He's gloating!"

She felt Hamish's hand on her arm. "Let it go, lass, he's gonna get what's coming to him very soon. I promise you."

She sniffled. "Thanks."

He pressed a kiss to her forehead. "You've done well. You should talk to Poppy now and have her draft a statement. We can't afford any more of your voters deserting you."

She knew that. "What shall I tell her?"

"Have her draft an apology assuring your voters that you'll be coming out with a full explanation as soon as you've cleared up a few things," he suggested.

"An apology?" She shook her head.

Hamish cupped her shoulders. "I know it feels wrong, but until we've found Tiffany it's the best thing we can do. Have her draft it so it's as vague as possible, so you don't actually admit to anything, okay?"

She sighed. "Are you sure?"

"Trust me."

She did. "Okay. I'll—"

The door being opened stopped her. Manus marched in, followed by Enya and Pearce.

"Hey guys," Manus greeted them, before his eyes fell on the witch. "What the—"

"We've been through this," Aiden said. "The witch is no threat."

"Why does it smell like pancakes in here?" Enya asked.

"I'll make you some," Wesley offered immediately. "Anybody else?"

Pearce shrugged. "Sure."

Manus nodded. "If you're making some anyway."

Impatient, Tessa interrupted, "Did you find Tiffany? Where is she? Is she safe?"

A regretful smile passed over Manus's face. "Sorry, she was at neither of the two addresses we checked. There are no employment records we could find as of yet." He exchanged a look with Pearce. "Pearce will search for her social security records to see where she worked last. Maybe we can get a lead that way."

Pearce nodded. "We'll be canvassing the neighborhood, too. It looks like the address that Enya checked out was her last one. We'll start there. Maybe somebody saw something."

Tessa felt a sob work its way up her throat. She squeezed her eyes shut and pressed her lips together, trying not to cry. "He killed her, didn't he? Zoltan killed her."

Hamish pulled her into his arms. "If Zoltan didn't try to kill you, he has no reason to kill your sister." He brushed a hand over her hair. "We won't give up."

"Want some help?" Wesley suddenly said.

All heads turned in his direction.

"I mean, you do know that witches can scry for people, right?"

"Scry?" Another word she didn't understand.

"Yeah, it's like GPS."

Tessa looked up at Hamish. "Do you know what he's talking about?"

To her surprise, Hamish nodded. "Witches have the power to find people as long as they have something to guide them. You know, like a bloodhound with a scent."

"I need a bit more than a scent," Wesley amended. "I heard you say earlier that it's your twin you're looking for?"

Tessa nodded.

"Identical?"

"Yes, why?"

"Identical twins have identical DNA. All I need is a few drops of your blood, and I'll be able to scry for your sister."

Hope bloomed in Tessa's heart. Was this truly possible?

"Aren't you forgetting something?" Aiden suddenly asked, drawing Wesley's gaze on him. "While you're in here, you have no power."

"Ah, I was coming to that." He grimaced. "It would of course mean you'd have to let me step outside these four walls so I can access my powers."

"Ah, fuck," Hamish hissed.

Tessa gripped his biceps. "Please, Hamish, if this is how we can find her, let's do it."

"Tessa, once he's outside, he can use witchcraft against us."

She shook her head. "But if we wait, it might be too late. What if she's hurt somewhere? What if she's dying? I could never forgive myself for not having tried everything to help her. Please,

Hamish." She felt tears shoot into her eyes, and this time she was unable to hold them back. "If you love me, then please do this for me."

She felt Hamish's chest rise. He released a heavy sigh, then looked past her. "One false move, witch, and you'll feel my dagger in your heart."

"I get it, *Stealth Guardian*, and the name is still Wesley. Maybe it's time you used it." There was a definite smirk accompanying Wesley's reply. "Pancakes will have to wait."

Nobody complained.

## 40

"This had better work," Hamish grumbled under his breath.

He, Enya, Aiden, and Wesley were standing in an abandoned warehouse. Manus had been dispatched to join Logan in his surveillance of Gunn, while Pearce was staying back at the compound with Leila and Tessa.

Tessa had protested, but it was actually Wesley who'd been able to convince her to stay at the compound. "If you're with us, all the crystal will do is point to you, not your sister. And I won't be able to pinpoint her."

"He's right, Tessa," Hamish had confirmed. "You'll need to remain within the compound, where you'll be cloaked."

He kept his eyes locked on Wesley as the witch prepared everything. "The map?"

Aiden handed it to him, and Wesley spread it out on the dusty floor, kneeling beside it. He glanced up. "Baltimore, huh?" Then he wrapped the gauze with which he'd soaked up a few drops of Tessa's blood around a crystal he'd retrieved from his backpack earlier.

Hamish hadn't let him take anything else from his bag of tricks, just in case the witch was planning to pull a fast one on them.

"It shouldn't take long. If she's alive and anywhere on this map, the crystal will show her location." Suspended by a string, he held the crystal over the middle of the map and closed his eyes. A second later a soft humming echoed in the empty space.

Hamish exchanged a look with his two colleagues. They were both on high alert just like he. Should Wesley utter a spell directed at them, they would be ready; somehow, though, he was starting to trust that the witch meant them no harm. Witches had always been on the side of the Stealth Guardians. Their goal was the same as that of his own race: to destroy the demons. But just like humans, witches could be influenced by demons, and the fact that Wesley had managed to use one of their portals was nothing if not a little worrisome.

With his eyes still closed, Wesley continued to hum; the crystal on the end of the string starting to move as if drawn by an invisible force. Suddenly the crystal dropped to a spot on the map.

Hamish leaned in. "You sure about this?"

Wesley opened his eyes and nodded. "Why?"

"Because the crystal is pointing at the water."

Wesley looked at the map. "Next to a pier," he clarified. "Which means she's probably on a boat."

"I hope you're right."

"Well, let's go there and check it out," Wesley suggested.

Hamish tossed a look to Aiden. "What do you think?"

"We should be prepared in case it's a trap."

Wesley jumped up, hands at his hips, frustration rolling off him. "What else do I need to do to prove to you guys that I don't mean you any harm?"

"I meant a trap by the demons," Aiden clarified. "If they used Tiffany to stage the drug photo, they might still be watching her in case they need her again. We don't want to run into their waiting arms."

"Oh, yeah, right, makes sense," Wesley said.

Hamish nodded. "Okay, back to the compound. Let's pull any surveillance footage from the area and call Sean and Jay from their assignments for backup."

Enya asked, "What about Manus and Logan?"

"They need to stay on Gunn. We can't afford to miss it, when he contacts the demons," Hamish said.

Thanks to a nearby portal, they were back at the compound ten minutes later. Tessa was already eagerly waiting in the command center where Pearce was accessing surveillance cameras in the area.

"Do you have a location?" Tessa asked excitedly.

Hamish squeezed her hand. "Yes, we just need to make sure we won't get ambushed when we go in there and get her out."

"Oh God, I hope she's alright. I always wanted a sister. I don't want to lose her before I have the chance to meet her."

He locked eyes with her. "I'll do anything to keep that from happening."

The ringing of Tessa's cell phone echoed in the command center. She pulled it from her pocket and looked at the display. "It's Poppy."

"Haven't you spoken to her yet?"

"She didn't answer her phone when I called. So I left a message."

"Answer it, and put her on speaker." He turned to Pearce, motioning him to remain silent.

Tessa pressed the answer button. "Poppy, I was trying to get a hold of you."

"Tessa." A sound akin to a sigh came through the phone. "Sorry, but I was in the shower when you called. Are you alright?"

Tessa cast him a quick look. Hamish nodded.

"Yes, I'm fine," she replied. "But I wanted to speak to you about issuing a statement."

"Oh, okay. That's great. I'm glad you're finally coming around to it. I'll come by your apartment now and we'll draft something—"

"I'm not at home. Let's just do it over the phone—"

"Well, where are you then?"

"I'm at Hamish's apartment."

"Give me the address, and I'll meet you there."

Hamish instantly shook his head, but Tessa had clearly anticipated his reaction and was already saying, "That won't be necessary. Just write something along the lines that I'm sorry about what has come to light and that it isn't what it seems to be. And that I'll be coming out with a full statement addressing all the concerns raised in the next twenty-four hours. Can you do that please?"

There was a moment's hesitation on Poppy's part. "Yes, but what are we gonna do then? What will you tell them in twenty-four hours?"

"I'm working on that. Just trust me. Please. For old times' sake."

Poppy sighed. "Fine. But I really think it's better that we meet and go over all this. This is serious. Have you seen the latest news reports? They're coming up with all kinds of theories that paint you in a really bad light."

"I can't help that. But that's all I've got right now. Please, just issue the statement, and we'll go from there."

"Okay, if you say so. I'll take care of it."

"Thanks, Poppy." Tessa disconnected the call. "Phew!"

"Good job on holding her off. This will buy you some time," Hamish said. Then he turned to Pearce. "Anything?"

Pearce pointed to the monitor in front of him. "It's a marina. Not a lot of cameras in that area. There's one at the entrance, but not much else. Everything looks pretty normal; few people working on their boats. Not much to go by. The spot Wesley's crystal indicated seems to be one of the last three boats on this dock here. The F dock. I'd say check the last three slips."

"Okay. Any news from Sean and Jay yet?"

Pearce switched over to the second monitor and typed something on his keyboard. A message board came up. "They just checked in. They'll meet you at the marina."

"Good. You stay here, watch the women and Wesley. Notify me immediately if Logan or Manus call in with news about Gunn."

"I'm coming with you," Tessa said from beside him.

"No, it's safer for you to stay at the compound. If we encounter demons—"

"Tiffany will be scared. What makes you think she'll trust you? To her, you won't look any different than the demons. I need to be there. When she sees me, she'll trust me."

"Damn it, Tessa, you're gonna be in danger."

She shook her head. "You're going in cloaked, aren't you? So you'll cloak me, too. Even if there are demons, they won't see me. And I promise that this time I won't make a peep. They're not gonna get me."

Hamish expelled an exasperated breath. He knew her reasoning was correct. Didn't mean he liked it. But he couldn't think of any good argument that would make her stay at the compound, particularly since convincing Tiffany to come with them would be easier if her twin sister was there.

"Fine. But you do exactly what I say. One act of disobedience, and I'll haul your sweet ass back to the compound. Do we understand each other?"

Her eyes lit up. "You won't even know I'm there."

"Right!" He remembered saying the same to her when she'd complained about him accompanying her everywhere she went. And he liked it just as little as she had.

# 41

It was early afternoon by the time they reached the marina. Nervousness had crept into Tessa's cells during the drive. What if something went wrong? What if the demons were still there, holding Tiffany hostage, and were actually expecting the Stealth Guardians to make a rescue attempt?

"Are you sure they won't be able to sense us?" She searched Hamish's eyes. They were still sitting in the dark van that Aiden had driven with Enya in the passenger seat.

"Once we're invisible they have no way of detecting us unless we make a sound."

"Or if they have dogs," Enya added with a look over her shoulder.

"Dogs?" Tessa swallowed. "Why dogs?"

"Because they'll smell us."

Hamish put his hand on hers. "Don't worry, Tessa. Pearce is watching via the camera at the entrance. If he sees dogs anywhere near the area, he'll alert us."

She nodded, feeling reassured. "And the humans, they won't see us either, right?"

"Right. But you'll still be able to see us."

"But I'm human. How can I see you, if we're all cloaked?"

"There are different levels of cloaking. We can choose who sees us and who doesn't."

"Okay."

Hamish tossed a look to the front seats. "Ready?"

Both his colleagues nodded. Then he touched his earpiece. "Sean, Jay, you in position?"

Tessa couldn't hear the response, only Hamish's reply a few moments later. "Good, stay there. If you see anything suspicious, alert us and move in."

Once outside the van, Tessa looked around. The marina was of medium size. There were five fingers, or docks, with maybe three hundred boats tied up. She saw several people sitting on their boats, enjoying the afternoon sun. Others were working: cleaning the deck or making repairs. Several boats were just getting ready to leave their slip, while a couple of others were coming in from the water. She'd been to several marinas before, invited by friends, and recognized the goings-on as ordinary. Nothing and nobody seemed out of place. She just hoped she wasn't wrong.

Hamish made hand signs, motioning everybody to follow him. Trusting that they were all cloaked and thus invisible, she followed him in silence. All four of them were wearing tennis shoes, so as to make no noise on the planks. Tessa had borrowed a pair from Leila before leaving the compound.

When they reached the end of the dock, Hamish stopped and lifted his hand, indicating that she should stay where she was. He exchanged a look with Enya and nodded, then pointed to Aiden and then Tessa. When Aiden nodded, Hamish and Enya stepped on deck of a small sailboat by the name of *Jenny's Folly.*

Tessa watched them peer into the portholes, then inspect the lock. A heavy padlock hung on the door to the cabin. But it was no obstacle for Hamish. He moved forward, and Tessa saw his upper body disappear as he passed through the wood. A few seconds later, his torso and head dipped back out. He looked over his shoulder and shook his head.

No sign of Tiffany.

He and Enya moved to the next boat, while Tessa and Aiden followed. Again, Tessa remained on the dock, watching nervously as Hamish did the same as on the first boat. Damn it, had Wesley been wrong? Or had he tricked them after all?

When Hamish turned around again, and he and Enya stepped off the boat, Tessa felt a little bit of her hope fade. What if Tiffany had been here, but was gone now? After all, Wesley had scryed for her more than an hour ago. She could have left in the meantime, or the demons could have taken her somewhere else.

Silently she prayed. *Let me find my sister.*

Instinctively she followed Hamish and Enya to the plastic steps that stood on the slip to allow people to enter the boat. She felt Aiden's hand on her arm, holding her back and looked over her shoulder. She nodded. She understood that she couldn't follow them. It didn't make the waiting any easier. She peered past Hamish at the entrance to the cabin, and noticed one thing immediately. There was no padlock, but when Hamish tried to open the door, it didn't budge.

Locked from the inside!

Her heartbeat kicked up. This could be it. Again Hamish dipped his torso through the door, but this time he disappeared inside completely. Enya followed him a moment later. Something creaked, and Tessa noticed the boat rock a little from side to side, maybe as the result of Hamish and Enya walking around inside. Several minutes seemed to pass.

Then, another noise; hinges creaking. Tessa's head shot in the direction of the sound. A hatch was opening on that portion of the deck that pointed out to the water. A hand reached out. Enya's? Tessa's legs were already moving along the slip to get a better view, when somebody suddenly gasped, and the hand disappeared back inside the boat.

Tessa tossed a look over her shoulder. Aiden had already raced up onto the deck and was passing through the door hatch like his colleagues before him. The boat rocked again from side to side, and there were muffled noises.

Oh God, no. What was happening?

The door finally opened and Aiden waved her to approach. She practically raced up the plastic steps and onto the deck. Aiden helped her into the cabin. She nearly tripped when she stepped down into the darkened interior. Little curtains had been drawn over the portholes. But her eyes adjusted, and she finally saw what was happening.

Enya was holding a struggling woman down on the bench that had been pulled out into a bed. Tessa took a few steps closer.

"Tiffany?" she murmured, exchanging a look with Hamish, who nodded.

Tessa put a hand on Enya's shoulder. "Let go of her, Enya. She's frightened."

After hesitating for a second, Enya released the woman, who immediately scrambled into the corner of the bed, her legs pulled up to her chest, her arms wrapped around them. Frightened eyes looked out at them. But there was no doubt who Tessa was looking at: this woman was her twin sister. And she was scared out of her wits, shaking, whimpering.

"Withdrawal symptoms," Hamish murmured.

"Can she see us?" Tessa whispered back.

Hamish nodded.

"Step back, all of you. I'll take care of her," Tessa said. To her relief, the three Stealth Guardians honored her request and retreated toward the wooden ladder that led up to the entrance.

Tiffany's frightened gaze shot to Tessa. Tessa moved closer and slid her knee onto the bed, crawling toward her sister.

"Don't be afraid, Tiffany. I'm here to help you."

Her twin let out a sob and chewed on her fingernails, her gaze nervously darting around the cabin, then back to Tessa. Her eyes seemed to focus, and it appeared that only now did Tiffany really see her. A gasp escaped her sister's throat.

"No, no..." she whimpered. "No, I'm not crazy. No more." She sobbed. "Oh God, I'm never using again... no, no, please..."

Tessa crawled closer. "Tiffany, I'm Tessa. I'm your sister. Your twin sister. I'm here to help you."

"Sister..." she murmured as if she didn't understand.

"Yes, your twin sister. See, we both look the same. I'll take care of you now. You're safe."

Tiffany's eyes were glued to Tessa's face. She shook her head, but then she stretched out her hand. "My twin... my sister?"

Tessa reached for Tiffany's hand and brought it to her own cheek. "Yes, I'm your sister, and you'll never have to be afraid again."

A sob tore from Tiffany's chest, and she suddenly threw her arms around Tessa. "I'm so scared. Help me. I want to stop. Please. I want to live."

Tessa choked back her own tears and stroked her hand over Tiffany's hair. "I'm here for you. Everything will be fine. Nobody is gonna hurt you anymore."

When she felt Tiffany sag against her, she looked over her shoulder and met eyes with Hamish. "We need to get her to a hospital."

Hamish shook his head. "She's better off in a rehab facility. They'll get her clean, if that's what she wants."

Tessa nodded in agreement. "I know someone who can help us with that."

~ ~ ~

And hour later, the van was pulling up outside a clinic. Hamish was driving. Enya and Aiden were returning to the compound and Sean and Jay to their respective assignments, after making sure no demons were in the vicinity.

"We're here," Tessa murmured to Tiffany, who was clinging to her on the back bench, still shaking from the withdrawal. And most likely from fear as well.

Tiffany hadn't said much. All Tessa had been able to get out of her was that she'd broken into the boat to find refuge after she'd woken up in an alley, not knowing how she'd gotten there.

Hamish now pointed to a person waiting on the sidewalk in front of the building. "There's Gabriella." He looked over his shoulder. "Are you sure about this?"

Tessa nodded. "She's offered to help. Her center isn't open yet because of the incident, but she sits on the board of this one. We need her. Getting a place in a good rehab facility in this city is virtually impossible. The wait lists are too long. We can't wait. Tiffany needs help now."

Hamish nodded. "Okay, if you trust her."

Tessa smiled. "You said yourself that your colleagues don't believe she's involved in the incident at the center."

He sighed, then switched off the engine. "I'll help you with Tiffany." He got out of the car and waved at Gabriella, who instantly approached.

Hamish slid the side door of the van open and reached his hand in. Tiffany instantly shrank back. "It's okay, Tiffany, we're at a safe place now." He moved to the side so she could see Gabriella. "This nice lady will help us get you settled into a cozy, bright room. And your sister will be with you until you're ready to rest a bit, okay?"

Gabriella smiled gently. "Come on, honey, it's almost dinner time. I hear they're serving a wonderful roast tonight. And cherry pie for dessert." Her voice sounded like that of a fairy godmother.

Tessa gave her a grateful smile. "That sounds delicious, don't you think, Tiffany? I'm getting hungry. Shall we go in?"

Tiffany cast her a hesitant look. Then she nodded slowly. With Gabriella's and Hamish's help, they got her out of the car and into the building.

Gabriella guided them down a long corridor. She walked next to Tessa and leaned in. "I never believed the news reports. I knew there had to be an explanation. I'm so glad you called me."

Tessa smiled. "I'm so grateful that you were able to arrange this place for us on such short notice."

She made a dismissive hand movement. "You've helped the center so much. This is the least I can do in return."

Tessa squeezed Gabriella's arm. "I don't know how to thank you."

She shook her head. "I'm just so surprised. I mean, I didn't realize you had a sister, let alone an identical twin."

"Nobody knew." Well, nobody but her parents, the adoption agency, and apparently the demons. "I just found out myself. But now that I know, I want to make sure she gets all the care she needs."

"Your sister will be cared for by the best professionals here, I promise you that. In a few months she'll be a well-adjusted young woman just like yourself."

They reached a busy nurse's station, where they stopped. Gabriella approached the counter.

"Oh, Ms. VanSant, we got your call. I've set everything up. The doctor will be with you in about five minutes to examine the patient," the nurse behind the desk said with a smile.

"Examine?" Tiffany echoed and clung to Tessa.

Gabriella turned to her with a smile. "Just so we can make sure you're okay. You might be a little dehydrated and feverish. It won't take long. And then you can rest and eat something."

"It's alright, Tiffany, I'll stay with you," Tessa said.

The nurse behind the counter pointed to a seating area. "Please take a seat. I'll call you shortly." Then she reached for a clipboard. "And I'll need the person responsible for the patient to fill in a few forms."

Tessa took the clipboard. "I'll take care of that."

As they all sat down, she suddenly felt Hamish's hand on her arm. She met his gaze, and he pointed to a TV that hung on the wall. It was mute, but the closed captioning was switched on.

Poppy stood in front of the steps of City Hall, dressed in a chic pant suit and wearing wide-rimmed sunglasses, as she read a statement from a piece of paper. Tessa followed along by reading the captions.

*"...that these allegations will be dealt with in due time. Ms. Wallace asks that you be patient as she clears up these misunderstandings. We will release a statement that will answer all your questions within the next twenty-four hours. Thank you."*

Poppy turned on her heel, ignoring the microphones that were being shoved in her face, asking for more details, and dove back into the building.

Tessa sighed and exchanged a look with Hamish.

"Everything will turn out alright now," he said.

"I don't know how to thank you for what you've done."

There was a twinkle in his eyes. "I do," he murmured, leaning in so only she could hear it.

She felt her face flush.

Hamish grinned. "But first, let's take care of your sister."

# 42

It was almost midnight when Hamish returned to the compound, Tessa by his side. He put his arm around her waist as they walked toward his quarters, realizing how exhausted she must be after spending the last few hours at the rehab clinic.

"You were very patient with your sister," he praised her.

Her smile was tired, but genuine. "She needs family. I'm going to talk to my parents to ask if she can live with them after she's out of rehab. Only until she's back on her feet. Maybe I can find her a job, get her some training, I don't know. Something. I want her to have a chance at a good life."

"One thing at a time, lass. It will take a few months before she's out of rehab. Based on what the doctor was able to get out of her, she's been using drugs for a long time. It's not an addiction that's easy to kick. We need to be patient." But he was proud of Tessa for standing by her sister's side, supporting her. "You did good today. When Tiffany looks at you, I can see hope in her eyes. We'll get through this."

"We?"

He opened the door to his quarters, and they entered. "Yes, we. I'll be here to support you in this."

"Even though you have no obligation to do so?"

He let the door close and put his hand under her chin, tipping it up. He looked deep into her lavender-colored eyes, the ones he'd grown to love and that he would grow to love even more. "You have no obligation to take care of your sister either, yet you didn't hesitate for even a second when you realized she needed you. I'm very proud of you."

"She's my flesh and blood. Finally I feel like something that's been missing has been given back to me. She's a part of me, even though I don't remember her. I'll have to get to know her again."

Hamish ran his hand through her hair. "I know this might not be the right time to talk to you about this, but you'll have to go public about her. And soon. Tomorrow. Or you're handing the election to Gunn."

Tessa sighed. "She's so vulnerable. I don't want to parade her in front of the press. She needs some privacy now. So she can heal. Who knows what she remembers about the demons getting to her."

"Probably not much, which is good. There will be no need for her to ever find out about the demons." He took a breath. "And I wish I could give you both the time you need, but the truth needs to come out while it can still make a difference. The election is in three days. We have to act before it's too late."

"I wish I could sit with my sister until the election is over and be there for her, rather than having to make a statement to the press."

"Hmm." He contemplated her words. "Maybe you won't have to make a statement."

She looked at him, confused. "But I thought you just said the truth has to come out before it's too late."

"I did. But I have an idea."

"What idea?"

"Do you remember Meredith Durant?"

"The journalist who first published the picture?"

He nodded. "We'll send her an anonymous message telling her if she really wants to get the scoop on Tessa Wallace, she'll need to go to the rehab clinic in Bolton Hill tomorrow at eleven o'clock. She'll be expecting to find you there as a patient. Instead you'll be visiting your sister. I'll make sure the staff look the other way so she can sneak in. We'll make sure you and your twin sister are in an area where Meredith Durant can take photos without being noticed. She won't be able to stop herself from publishing such a huge story. Think of the career boost she'll get out of being the reporter who found out the truth about Councilwoman Wallace. Your sister won't have to endure any questions. And you won't have to make any statements. You'll be the woman who was only protecting her twin sister."

"You're sure that'll work?"

"Trust me. I've met enough journalists to know what they're after: an exclusive. She'll jump at the chance. By early evening tomorrow, Miss Durant will have published the story to their online edition, and the next morning, it'll be at every newsstand.

It'll give the voters enough time before the polls open in three days to realize that you're still their best choice for mayor."

"And what do *I* do in the meantime?"

"You take care of your sister. Stay out of the public eye. Enya and I will be with you whenever you leave the compound to visit your sister. And come Election Day, it'll be too late for Gunn or the demons to do anything else." And once they realized they'd lost, the demons would focus their attention on an easier target. While the danger would never truly be over, Hamish would always be by Tessa's side. Zoltan would have to realize that and direct his energy toward more attainable goals.

Finally, Tessa nodded. "Okay, we'll do it your way. Tomorrow."

He kissed her, knowing it was the best solution.

~ ~ ~

Everything had played out exactly how he'd planned it.

They'd returned to the compound after a long visit with Tiffany, who was still suffering from withdrawal symptoms. She'd been complaining about severe cramps and nausea, and had even thrown up while Tessa comforted her. Hamish had watched from a distance how Tiffany's lithe body was wracked by fevers and chills, how muscle spasms made her movements unpredictable. But he also saw Tessa's compassion in action. She walked the walk. If she treated her constituents the same way as her sister, this city would be in good hands once she became mayor.

And by the looks of it, nothing stood in her way now.

With Tessa by his side, Hamish entered the kitchen of the compound where Leila was cooking aided by Wesley. The rest of the gang, minus Logan, was lounging in front of the TV.

Hamish approached the witch and offered him his hand. "I haven't had a chance yet to thank you for your help."

Wesley grinned and shook his hand. "Pleasure. I'm glad you guys found Tessa's sister. I hope she pulls through alright."

"She's in good hands," Hamish confirmed. "I'm sorry I was suspicious of you at first."

Wesley shrugged. "It's all water under the bridge. I hope this means we can talk about an alliance between Scanguards and the Stealth Guardians."

"I'll send a message to our ruling body just as soon as things have settled down a little," Hamish promised. The least Wesley deserved was a hearing with the Council of Nine. He'd earned it.

When Manus sidled up to them, Hamish asked, "Hey, anything on Gunn?"

Manus grinned. "When the news about Tessa's twin broke about an hour ago, he was livid! That man has a temper, I tell you. He was screaming bloody murder. I had to get out of the way so I wouldn't get hit by the vase he tossed at the wall. I sure was glad when Logan relieved me." He reached for the whiskey bottle on the counter and poured himself a glass.

"Did you get the impression that he'll try anything else before the election?" Hamish asked, glancing past him to where Tessa leaned against the wall, staring at her ringing cell phone as if contemplating whether to answer it or not.

"He'll have to or he's finished. I mean it's still early—the TV stations are just now picking up the story, but it's already all over the Internet. Just wait until every voter in Baltimore reads about it…" Manus chuckled. "That reporter practically turned Tessa into a saint. I mean, I'm not saying she isn't, but I don't think I've read such a positive news story since the mayor's death."

Hamish nodded. He'd assessed Meredith Durant correctly. She hadn't disappointed him.

His gaze drifted back to Tessa. Instantly he was alert. She was talking on her cell phone, seemingly quite agitated. Without hesitation he walked over to her.

"No, I'm not giving a statement."

Hamish mouthed *"Who?"*

Tessa put a hand over the phone's mic. "Poppy," she whispered.

"Let me handle this."

Tessa lifted her shoulders, but appeared happy to hand him the phone.

"Hey Poppy, it's Hamish."

"Hamish? Can you talk some sense into Tessa? I'm her campaign manager. I shouldn't have had to find out about this via the Internet!" Poppy was clearly annoyed. "And now she doesn't want to come out and comment on the news article."

Hamish sighed. "I'm sorry, Poppy. I do understand your frustration. But Tessa has asked for privacy for her and her sister. It's a difficult time for both of them."

"Difficult time? Are you kidding me? The election is in two days! If she doesn't come out and speak to the voters, she'll lose the election after all."

"I'm with Tessa on that." He locked eyes with Tessa, who gave him a grateful smile. "She'll lay low until the election. We've done everything we can. Now it's in the hands of the electorate."

"At least have her meet with me. We need to go over stuff. We need to make plans," Poppy insisted, her voice turning more high-pitched with every second.

"We'll see you on election night at City Hall. Night, Poppy." He disconnected the call and silenced the phone.

Tessa sighed. "Thanks for doing that. It's really hard to say no to Poppy. She's always so insistent. But I just don't want to face the press right now. I'm exhausted, and I need my energy for Tiffany."

Hamish pulled her into his arms. "I'm here for you." He kissed her, until he heard hollering from his colleagues.

"Get a room!" Aiden demanded.

Hamish released Tessa's lips and smirked when he noticed her flushed cheeks. "Normally I don't like to take orders from Aiden, but I'm in a compliant mood today…"

# 43

It was time.

City Hall was buzzing like a beehive. More police than usual were on the premises to deal with the increased amount of visitors who had come to hear both candidates speak on election night. In addition to the usual security that required every visitor go through a metal detector, City Hall employees were at hand to direct people to the areas where they could get refreshments and sit down.

Only invited guests were allowed on the premises tonight. But according to Tessa, this didn't just mean the official guests selected by the acting mayor and the city council. Every city employee had received two passes to hand out to friends and family.

But this wasn't an event Tessa could skip. Tonight she had to be here. Preliminary exit polls showed that she was doing well, and if everything continued this way, she would be the one on the podium at the end of the night, giving an acceptance speech. Hamish felt his heart fill with pride. He knew she was right for this city. But he also knew that it meant that a future together, if Tessa wanted that, would be complicated.

In his mind Hamish went through the security arrangements he'd made for Tessa to make sure that she would be safe in tonight's melee. Sean was standing sentry at the main entrance, Jay at the side entrance used by staff and catering personnel. Both were cloaked, armed, and equipped with communication devices so they could alert the rest of the team if they saw a demon enter. Aiden was roaming through the halls, uncloaked, to look for anything suspicious. Manus, Enya, and Logan were shadowing Gunn, cloaked. Only Pearce had stayed back at the compound with Leila and Wesley.

While Wesley had offered to help, Hamish and his colleagues had voted against it. They'd already broken enough rules by not keeping him locked up or notifying the Council of Nine of his presence yet. Hamish was planning to deal with that issue after the election, when everything had settled down.

Hamish turned to Tessa, who looked radiant tonight. She wore an elegant red shift dress with a scoop neckline. They were alone in her office on the third floor of City Hall, where they were waiting for his team to check in and confirm that everybody was in position.

"Ready to mingle?"

She inhaled deeply, her chest lifting in the process, drawing his gaze to her breasts.

"Maybe you should have worn something a little less revealing," he mused, hating the idea that every man here tonight would be leering at her.

Tessa chuckled softly and put her hand on his chest, running her fingers down the lapel of his jacket. "I'm wearing this for you."

He rolled his eyes. "For me you should be wearing nothing but a skimpy bra and tiny panties."

Her eyelids fluttered in a most tantalizing fashion. "I'm wearing that underneath."

He pulled her to him, so her breasts were crushed to his chest, and her hips were aligned with his. "You do know how to get me all hot."

"I'm a fast learner," she murmured and brushed her lips to his. "I thought you liked that."

"I love it."

"Then show me later how much," she suggested and freed herself from his embrace.

She walked toward the door, and he followed her with his eyes.

"You coming?"

"Almost," he said and adjusted his rising cock, willing it to go down. This was neither the time nor the place. "Let's go before I forget all my manners."

~ ~ ~

With Hamish by her side, Tessa reached the gallery that overlooked the large rotunda in the middle of City Hall. Below them, chairs and a podium had been arranged for the speeches later in the evening: one concession speech, and one acceptance speech. She and Gunn would be on the podium, but who would give which speech wasn't decided yet. The ballots had closed an hour earlier, but not all districts had reported in with their results yet.

"I'm nervous," she admitted.

Hamish slid his arm around her waist. "I understand. But everything looks good. The exit polls favor you. And Gunn would be stupid to try anything tonight with so many witnesses. But if he's crazy enough to act, our guys will take him out before he can hurt you."

She smiled, grateful for everything Hamish and his colleagues were doing for her. But she was thinking of the future, too. "And what if I really win? What then?"

"Then you'll bring order and justice back to Baltimore."

"And the demons? Will they give up?"

There was no hesitation in Hamish's voice, when he replied, "Never truly. They'll always be looking for an opportunity, but even they know when they're chasing a lost cause. Zoltan will figure out very quickly that I won't leave you unprotected, not even after the election."

"But how will that work?"

He drew her closer to his side and brought his lips to her ear. "I was going to talk to you about that later, after the election. But since you're bringing it up…"

She turned her face to look at him. "You mean I'll always need a bodyguard-slash-pretend-boyfriend?"

"I was hoping that I could be more than that." His chocolate-brown eyes seemed to sparkle. "And if I have anything to say about that there will be no *pretend* anywhere in sight."

Her heart made an excited somersault. "Are you…" She swallowed hard. "You mean…"

"I—"

"Tessa!" Gunn's grating voice interrupted and made her spin around.

Dressed in a dark gray suit, Gunn made an impressive figure. He was alone, though she knew that Enya, Manus, and Logan had to be close by. But they'd cloaked themselves so not even Tessa could see them.

"Robert, good evening," she said as calmly as possible, though his presence unnerved her.

Gunn briefly nodded toward Hamish, then looked back at her, his face a mask of indifference. Just how good of an actor was he?

"Interesting little charade you pulled off this week," he started.

"It wasn't a charade."

"Wasn't it? Kind of weird that first Durant and her biased rag write about you being a druggie, and then three days later, she retracts it all and comes out with a sob story about what a good sister you are, taking care of a junkie sibling that you just pulled out of a hat. Well played." But the last two words weren't meant as a compliment; they sounded more like a curse.

"I don't like your insinuation that this was staged. We both know who planted that false story about me using drugs to boost his own campaign," she retorted.

Gunn narrowed his eyes. "You're accusing me of having anything to do with that?"

She made a step toward him, incensed by his lies. "Who else had anything to gain by seeing me fall on my face?"

"As much as I'd like to take credit for that brilliant move, I'd like to think that I'm smarter than giving you an opportunity to turn into Mother Theresa." He huffed. "I'm sure your Miss Smartypants campaign manager cooked it all up for you. Maybe *I* should have hired her instead."

"As if Poppy would have worked for somebody like you."

She felt Hamish's hand on her arm, and realized only now that her voice had risen.

"Yes, Mr. MacGregor, you should hold her back, or she might hurt herself. And we wouldn't want that, would we? It would be a shame to disappoint all her voters." Gunn turned on his heel and stalked down the hallway, disappearing around a bend.

Tessa forced down a curse. "That vile, no-good—"

"Don't Tessa, he was just riling you up. He knows he's lost." He took her hand, leading her toward the stairs.

As they descended into the rotunda, she glanced at him. "Do you believe what he said? That he didn't do it?"

"He's a very convincing liar, and he's desperate. He's capable of anything."

She nodded to herself. "That's the feeling I got, too."

Upon reaching the first floor where the crowd was mingling, Tessa let her eyes roam. Her assistant Collette was coming straight at her, smiling.

"There you are," Collette greeted her.

"Hey, Collette," Tessa replied. "You look nice tonight." Her yellow dress looked beautiful on her.

"Thanks, so do you. And thanks again for giving me your spare tickets. I brought my son and my parents." She pointed toward the crowd. "They're so excited to know that I might soon be working for the new mayor."

"The results aren't in yet," Tessa cautioned her.

Collette smiled. "But it's looking very good. We're all keeping our fingers crossed."

"Thank you! That's so sweet. By the way, have you seen Poppy yet?"

Collette turned her head to the side. "I just said hi to her. She went to the ladies room just a second ago." She pointed to the corridor next to the stairs with a sign saying *Ladies Restrooms* above the open doorway. "In there."

"Thanks!"

"I'll see you both later," Collette said and walked away.

"Do you mind if I go see Poppy? She's probably still pissed at me for not returning her phone calls."

Hamish hesitated. Then he pressed his finger to the mic in his ear. "Where's Gunn now?" There was a short pause, then he nodded. "Okay, you can go to the ladies room, but only there. I'll be out here watching the entrance."

"I'll be back soon."

Tessa turned around and walked to the open doorway and into the corridor. At the end of it, it made a right turn leading to several doors: the ladies room, a janitor's room, and a couple of mechanical closets. She pushed the door to the ladies room open and entered.

# 44

Standing only a few yards away from the entrance to the corridor that led to the ladies room, Hamish glanced around. More and more visitors were streaming in. He got a glimpse of Sean standing near the entrance, critically running his eyes over every person who entered through the metal detectors. Lifting his eyes, Hamish gazed up to the gallery. Several people were walking around up there, some with drinks in their hands. He noticed Gunn shaking somebody's hand. Good, he was far away from Tessa.

"Excuse me, young man," a woman suddenly said.

Hamish turned his head to look at the lady, who looked to be in her mid-sixties. "Yes, ma'am? Can I help you?"

She pointed to the ticket in her hand. "You look like you know your way around here. My daughter gave me this ticket and said she'd meet me at the entrance and show me where I could sit, but I don't see her."

Hamish glanced at the ticket. "There's general seating only. You know, first come, first serve."

"Oh, Poppy didn't mention that." She gave a long suffering sigh.

"Poppy Connor?"

The woman took a step closer. "Yes. She's the campaign manager for Councilwoman Tessa Wallace. I hope she wins. I mean, that Gunn, I don't like him." She put her hand over her mouth. "Oh dear, you didn't vote for him, did you?"

Hamish shook his head and smiled. "I'm with you on that. So, you're Poppy's mother."

She nodded proudly. "Do you know her? She's so bright. But I've barely seen her since she's been working on Tessa's campaign. She's always so busy."

Hamish smiled, glancing back to the corridor. "Yes, I'm sure." Then he motioned to the area where rows of chairs had been arranged in front of a podium. "You might want to grab a good seat while you still can, Mrs. Connor."

"You're right, I'd better go."

"And I hope you're feeling better after your fall," he added automatically.

She'd already turned away and now spun her head back to him. "My fall?"

He nodded. "Yes, a few days ago. You were in the hospital."

Mrs. Connor's forehead furrowed. "I just got back from Aruba two days ago. And I can assure you, I didn't fall anywhere. I'm not that old." There was a sharp tone in her voice. With a huff, she whirled around and marched toward the chairs.

Nothing in her gait suggested that she'd recently taken a fall and had to spend time in the hospital. Then why had Poppy left Tessa alone in her apartment to go to the hospital to take care of her?

Poppy had lied.

"Ah shit!" he cursed.

He spun around and started running, his finger on his mic. "It's not Gunn, it's Poppy."

~ ~ ~

Tessa stepped out of the stall and walked to the sink, about to turn on the water, when she noticed that pieces of glass from a broken champagne flute lay around the sink. Annoyed about people's carelessness, she moved to the second sink and started washing her hands.

"I know you're still angry with me, Poppy," she said. "But I needed a few days to myself."

The stall door opened and Poppy came out. Tessa looked up and saw her friend's reflection in the mirror.

"What's with the sunglasses?" she asked.

Poppy sighed. "Pink eye, would you believe it? Brilliant timing!"

"Sorry, that really sucks."

Her friend shrugged. "Can't do anything about it now." She moved to the second sink and reached for the faucet, while she continued, "I'm sure it'll go away."

"Don't, there's glass," Tessa said, turning her head, but it was too late.

Poppy had already reached into the sink. "Ouch!"

"Damn, let me help you," Tessa said quickly and reached for the towel dispenser when something caught her eye. She shot a look at the white sink. Streaks of green mixed with the water and ran down the drain—drops of green blood dripping from Poppy's hand.

Tessa let out a shriek. Poppy's eyes shot to her. For a split second they both stood there, frozen.

"No hiding it now," Poppy said, her voice suddenly as cold as ice.

An instant later, Poppy charged her and slammed her against the tile wall.

"No!" Tessa cried out, fear freezing the blood in her veins. "Oh my God, Poppy, you're a demon!"

Pinning her with superhuman strength that made escape impossible, Poppy brought her face within inches of Tessa's. "Well, surprise, surprise."

Tessa gasped for air, Poppy's vice grip cutting off her supply. There was nothing she could do other than appeal to whatever humanity was left inside her. "Please, Poppy, I'm your friend."

"Friend?" Poppy scoffed. "The friend who always got everything she wanted! While I was just the hanger-on. The less pretty one. The less desirable one."

"That's not true, Poppy!"

"Not true?" Poppy hissed and ripped her sunglasses from her face, tossing them aside. Green demon eyes glared at her. "Tell me, am I prettier now, huh? Do you think I'll get the right guy now?" Poppy shoved her harder against the wall.

Pain radiated down Tessa's ribcage. "Poppy, you don't have to do this."

"But I do! Don't you get that? They blackmailed me into it. Those demons, they saw me. They saw what I did. And they used it to make me do their bidding." She threw her head back and grunted toward the ceiling.

"Did what? Please let me help you!"

"You can't help me! Don't you understand?" She sounded anguished now. "I was the one who hit Yardley. I was behind the wheel when I shouldn't have driven that night. I wasn't seeing clearly, and he just crossed the street." She shook her head furiously. "It was his fault! Yardley came out of nowhere. He just ran into my car."

"It was an accident. You could have just called 9-1-1."

"Damn it, Tessa, don't you get it? I was drunk that night. Way over the limit. And they saw it. The demons. I didn't realize at first what they were. I went along so they'd keep silent. I would have lost everything I'd built for myself."

Tessa shook her head, tears brimming in her eyes. "So you helped them."

"They told me to write those notes. So you would get out of the race and let Gunn win. They want him to lead this city, not you."

Tessa swallowed as Poppy confirmed everything Hamish and his colleagues had already assumed. Only it hadn't been Gunn helping the demons, but Poppy.

"You made the duct fall..."

"I had no choice."

"You always have a choice."

Poppy glared back at her. "You should have heeded those warnings I sent and just got out of the race. But no, you had to continue; you had to play the tough one. So I had to act."

Maybe she could stall Poppy long enough until Hamish came looking for her. "Then why did you get me a bodyguard?"

"Because I needed to make sure nobody suspected me, least of all you... I needed an alibi."

"Why go to Faldo of all people?" It made no sense. Or did Poppy not know that Faldo worked for the Stealth Guardians?

"Given Faldo's criminal history, I figured if anything went wrong, I could always blame him."

"But Hamish saved me."

"Yeah, that was bad luck. And I'd planned everything meticulously. I even wore that terrible blouse with the silver sequins to make sure nobody noticed how I made the duct fall."

That confirmed what Manus had suspected. "How could you do that? Why didn't you come to me? I could have helped you."

"Helped me?" Poppy shook her head and let out a bitter laugh. "It was too late already. I was in their clutches, and they drew me deeper. I had to do what they wanted. It was me or you."

But there was a glint in her eyes, and Tessa knew not everything she'd done had been against her will.

"At first, maybe," Tessa dared to say. She remembered what Hamish had told her once, that when humans surrendered to the demons and accepted their fate, they turned into demons themselves. "You're a demon now. You didn't fight it."

"I gave up fighting. I mean, why not? All those times I had to stand in your shadow and take the crumbs you left for me, the cast-off boyfriends, the second-rate jobs... I was never your equal." An evil grin spread over her face. "But now I'm better than you. Stronger."

To prove it, Poppy grabbed her and flung her against one of the stalls. The door gave way, and Tessa stumbled inside, hitting her knees on the toilet as she tried to brace her fall. She scrambled to get up and turn around, and just as she did, Poppy blocked the door, a pistol in her hand.

"Time to say good-bye, Tessa," Poppy said.

"No!" Tessa screamed and barreled toward her.

But she never made contact. Poppy was ripped back. A shot went off. Stucco rained down on them.

~ ~ ~

Hamish slammed Poppy against the sink, surprised by her physical strength. When he saw her face, more specifically her eyes, he knew why. She'd already surrendered to the demons. She was a demon herself now. Beyond redemption.

"Fuck!" he cursed.

Poppy glared at him, pushing herself away from the sink, one hand bleeding green, the other holding the gun, pointing it at him. She clearly didn't know that the bullets couldn't kill him. It appeared her demon master hadn't yet had the chance to initiate her and equip her with the right weapons.

Nevertheless, he had to disarm her so she couldn't hurt Tessa, who was now scrambling out of the stall.

"Get down, Tessa!" he ordered.

Poppy shifted her gaze and with it, her gun, now aiming it in Tessa's direction.

"Bad choice," Hamish hissed and jumped in front of the nozzle of the gun.

It went off. He felt the bullet graze his arm. Wrong weapon and a bad shot, this was his lucky night. He jumped her, slamming her to the ground, kicking the gun out of her hand. She swung at him, but she was a good fifty pounds lighter than he, and had no combat training.

"Who sent you? Zoltan?" he ground out.

She rocked her head forward to use it as a bowling ball, but he was faster and veered back, shifting his position so he could reach into his boot. With his weight shifted to one side, she was able to kick him off, but he'd already managed to pull his dagger from the sheath in his boot.

She lunged for the gun, but he pounced, bringing her down to the ground once more, this time face down. He pulled her head back by her hair, causing her to give a high shriek, and pointed the dagger at her throat.

"Which demon sent you? Name him!"

She kicked out underneath him, but even Poppy had to know that she was defeated.

"What's his name?"

"I don't know," she finally grunted.

"Then you're no use to me."

He eased up on her hair and leaned backward. When she lifted her head, he did the only thing he could do with a demon: he sliced her throat open.

Green demon blood spilled on the linoleum floor as Poppy slumped to the ground.

At a sound behind him, Hamish spun around.

Tessa stood in the door to one of the stalls, her hand pressed over her mouth, her eyes brimming with tears.

He jumped up. "Are you hurt?"

Wordlessly, she shook her head, her gaze fixed on Poppy's lifeless body.

"I had to kill her," he explained. "She'd already surrendered to them. There's no way back from that."

Tessa nodded, but tears started streaming down her face. He pulled her into his arms, holding her close to stop her body from trembling.

"She said the demons blackmailed her," Tessa choked out between sobs. She lifted her head. "She was the driver in the hit-and-run that killed Yardley. She was drunk."

"Oh God. That's how they got to her."

Tessa nodded. "What are we gonna do now?"

Hamish heard footsteps outside the door. "Hush." He made himself and Tessa invisible.

The door was pushed open and Enya charged in.

"Hamish?"

He uncloaked them. "Thank God you're here. We've gotta get rid of the body."

"Help is here," he heard Logan say from the door as he and Manus charged in.

Enya pointed to the door. "There's no way we're gonna be able to get her past all those people out there. She's swimming in demon blood. We can't cloak that."

"Enya is right," Logan agreed. "We need to make sure that nobody gets in here." He turned to Manus. "There should be a sign we can hang in front of the door that says *Cleaning in Progress*. Find it!"

Manus charged outside.

"How did you figure out it was Poppy?" Enya asked.

"I ran into her mother," Hamish said. "I found out she never took a fall like Poppy said." He looked down at Tessa, still in his arms. "She had no reason to leave you alone in your apartment other than to make sure the demon got to you. She probably let him in through the emergency exit door on her way out."

"She wasn't a demon then. Her eyes, they were still—"

"It takes a while until a human turns completely to the dark side. But that final act, giving the demon access to you, so he could kill you, was probably what sent her over the edge." He remembered something now. "When she made the statement on your behalf, remember? We saw it at the clinic. She wore sunglasses. She'd probably already turned by then."

"I thought she was my friend." Tessa's voice was thick with tears. "We've known each other since college."

Manus reentered the ladies room without opening the door. "Look what I found in the janitor's closet." He lifted his hand that held a gray plastic tarp. "If we wrap her in this and make sure all demon blood is concealed, we can cloak the body and ourselves and carry her out of here."

"Brilliant idea," Hamish said.

"There are also cleaning materials in the janitor's closet," Manus said with a look at Enya.

She huffed. "Well, that's just great! You get to dispose of the body, and I get to play cleaning lady."

"I'll help," Hamish said. "After all, I was the one who made the mess."

# 45

"Congratulations on becoming mayor," Leila greeted Tessa, when she, followed by Hamish entered the kitchen of the compound.

Everybody else was already assembled. After disposing of Poppy's body, Enya, Manus, and Logan had returned to the compound, while Sean, Jay, and Aiden had stayed until after the race had been called for Tessa. After Tessa's acceptance speech, she'd left with Hamish by her side, making a stop at her apartment to pick up more of her things.

She'd told Hamish everything Poppy had said in her final moments. Her betrayal had been a shock, nevertheless, Tessa felt sad about the loss of her friend. How had she not seen what was going on inside of Poppy? How had she missed the signs?

"You okay?" Hamish murmured next to her.

She glanced up at him. "I will be."

"Tessa did it," Aiden said, putting an arm around his wife. "We should celebrate."

Tessa was about to decline, still feeling too agitated from her escape from death, when a female voice from the door interrupted.

"Celebrate what? The fact that this compound constantly ignores our rules? Or maybe that your security protocols are so loose that a witch was able to breach your defenses? Or maybe the fact that you just don't give a damn that no human charges are allowed here? Enlighten me!"

The woman who stood in the door wore black leather pants, a black T-shirt, and a black leather jacket. Her tall boots reached to her knees and gleamed as if somebody had polished them for hours. At her hip sat an ancient dagger. Long red hair fell over her shoulders in soft waves.

Instinctively, Tessa reached for Hamish's hand.

"And you are?" Hamish asked.

"Virginia Robson, newest member of the Council of Nine."

A few mumbled curses sounded behind Tessa.

"Oh crap," she heard Manus choke out.

"To what do we owe your visit?" Hamish asked diplomatically.

She narrowed her eyes at him. "You must be Hamish. I would have expected better from you than bringing a human charge into the compound." Her jaw tightened. "Not to speak of letting a witch run wild here." Her gaze shot to the couch where Wesley stood as if frozen. "But all this is about to change. I'm here to clean up."

Tessa felt a shiver run down her spine and Hamish's arm come around her waist, pulling her to him.

"Starting with the human," Virginia continued. "She has no right to be here. You've compromised the security of this compound by having brought her here. We'll have to abandon this place and relocate everybody." She stepped closer to Hamish. "You'll answer for this before the Council of Nine."

"He didn't do anything wrong!" The words were out before Tessa realized that she had enough courage to oppose the intimidating woman.

"What did you say?" Virginia hissed.

"I have the same right to be here as Leila, Aiden's wife."

Virginia tilted her head to the side, perusing her with suspicion. "Are you telling me that you're Hamish's mate?"

Tessa swallowed. To get Hamish out of trouble, she'd say whatever she had to. "Yes."

Virginia narrowed her gaze on Hamish. "And why has the Council not been informed of this?"

Tessa noticed how Hamish gave her a sideways glance. He seemed to hesitate for a moment. "It only just happened. I was about to inform the Council but we had to deal with a demon attack instead. I apologize for my tardiness."

Virginia pressed her lips together, clearly annoyed that her accusation didn't stick.

"Very well. I suppose congratulations are in order." But her voice didn't sound very congratulatory.

"Thank you," Hamish said, his voice just as icy. "If you don't mind then, my mate and I would like to retire. It's been a long night."

"Not so fast!" Virginia snapped and pointed to Wesley. "There's still the matter of the witch."

"Name's Wesley," Wesley introduced himself, a charming smile on his lips as he approached.

"Stay where you are!"

~ ~ ~

When Virginia's hand went to her dagger, Wes stopped walking. For now. He didn't mind strong women, and if this gorgeous redhead wanted to give him a few orders and tell him what to do, he wasn't at all opposed to it. For all he cared she could strip him naked, tie him up, and ride him into oblivion. And he wouldn't protest. No, he'd encourage her, spur her on.

"Whatever you want," he said, running his eyes over her. "Anything, really."

What a body! Long legs that looked strong and toned. A slim waist, flaring hips, firm boobs. Just the right curves everywhere. And then that hair. Flaming red. Just what he liked best. He'd always associated red hair with passion and lust, and instinctively been drawn to women whose hair looked like the smoldering embers of a fire.

He shifted his gaze to her face. Hazel eyes with flecks of green glared at him, her luscious plump lips pressed together in obvious contempt.

"You'll be interrogated. In the meantime, you'll be locked up."

Hamish cleared his throat. "Wesley helped us with our mission. Without him, we might have never been able to thwart the demons' plan to destroy Tessa's political future. He's no danger to any of us."

Virginia tossed a dismissive look at Hamish. "That remains to be seen. Anybody breaching our defenses is a danger. And you and your compound mates should have notified the Council of Nine immediately when the breach occurred. We had to find out from a guardian at another compound." She made an all encompassing motion to the other Stealth Guardians in the room. "This has not gone unnoticed. Together with the previous infractions of your motley crew, you've exhausted the Council's patience."

"Oh," Wesley murmured to himself. Because of him the Stealth Guardians were in deep shit. He sighed. "Listen, Virginia, I—"

"That's Ms. Robson to you!" she snapped.

"Ms. Robson then." He shrugged. "Listen, it's really not their fault. Don't punish them for what I did."

Within the blink of an eye, her face was only inches from his. "You, witch, listen to me. I'm the one giving the orders. If you think you can wrap me around your little finger like you've clearly done with these dimwits, you're wrong. I'm your worst nightmare."

Nightmare? More like a wet dream. But maybe it was better not to come back with that kind of response just yet.

Instead he grinned. Virginia wouldn't be an easy conquest, that was certain. She would be a challenge, but he didn't mind. She was worth it. Worth the extra effort to get her into his bed.

And he didn't care how long it took before she was beneath him, panting in ecstasy, because one thing was certain: he was in lust!

# 46

Hamish shut the door to his quarters behind Tessa and leaned against it, watching how she placed her handbag on the coffee table in the sitting area.

"Phew, that woman is a piece of work," she said and turned to him.

He jerked his thumb over his shoulder. "What just happened out there?"

She raised her eyebrows. "Well, you saw it. She was accusing you left, right, and center."

Her protectiveness of him was downright endearing.

"So you figured you'd propose to me, hmm?"

Tessa's chin dropped. "Propose?"

"Yep. Couldn't leave it up to me, could you? No, you had to take the reins, Ms. Mayor, didn't you? Is that how it's gonna be between us? You bossing me around until you get what you want?"

"But I didn't want her to punish you. I mean…"

She stopped herself, because Hamish couldn't keep a straight face any longer. A smirk spread on his lips.

"You, you—"

"Did you mean it? That you want to be my wife?" he interrupted before she could hurl an insult at him.

Her cheeks flushed, and her chest rose, making him all too aware of how sexy she looked in that red dress.

"I… I, uh… earlier at City Hall you were saying something…"

He'd never seen her so nervous. "We were interrupted."

She nodded slowly, her throat working as if she was trying to swallow down a lump.

"It's an easy question, Tessa. Don't I deserve an answer? Did you mean it?"

"Yes." The word was so quiet that he almost didn't hear it.

"Does that mean you love me? Truly love me?"

"Yes."

"Then tell me."

She lifted her lids and looked straight at him. "I love you. I don't know how it happened."

"The *how* doesn't matter, lass. But the *how much* does." He took a few steps closer, but he didn't reach for her. Not yet. "There's something you need to know. When a Stealth Guardian bonds with a human, it's not without risk."

"Risk?" she echoed.

"Only a bond of true and pure love will endure. If the love isn't true and pure the bond will kill us. Both of us. Not immediately, but within a few months. We would have to watch each other wither away, regretting our decision every day. That's why no Stealth Guardian enters into a bond lightly."

"Is that what you were trying to tell me earlier?"

"That, and more. I love you, Tessa. And I want a bond. I want you in my life. But if you're not sure whether your love is real or just a momentary infatuation, then you need to turn me down."

"Is that a proposal?"

"Guess it is." Even though he said it casually, his entire body was coiled in tension.

She walked to him and put one hand on his chest where his heart beat excitedly. She lifted herself on her tiptoes, bringing her lips close to his. "Then it's a yes."

His pulse raced. "Aren't you afraid of what could happen?"

"When I'm with you, I'm never afraid." She chuckled. "Now, are you planning to kiss me anytime soon? Or do I have to seduce you?"

He cleared his throat, while farther below his cock was hardening. "You did mention earlier that you were wearing something for me…"

"Actually, I lied."

She reached behind her back and lowered the zipper. When she brushed the dress over her shoulders, then down her hips to let it pool around her feet, he discovered the extent of her lie. Tessa wasn't wearing a stitch of clothing underneath her red dress.

"Fuck me!" he mumbled under his breath, his cock now tenting his pants.

"How about you take off that suit," she murmured and turned.

He watched her walk to the bed, while he started undressing. His shoes went first, then his jacket, shirt, and tie. By the time he was lowering the zipper of his pants, Tessa was already lying down on the bed, one knee up, one arm stretched above her head. She looked like a pin-up girl. Pure seduction.

Impatiently, he rid himself of his pants, boxer briefs and socks and stalked to the bed, his eager cock leading the way. He gazed down at Tessa, drinking in her beauty with his eyes. She was perfect in every way. Perfect for him.

He lowered himself onto the bed and pulled her into his arms. Gently he brushed his fingers over her lips, then her chin. "Making love tonight will be different than the times before."

"How?"

"Remember when you had my virta inside you? Tonight I will pour it into you while we make love. And you'll return it to me by placing your hand over my heart. It'll create a circle that binds us together forever."

"Will I glow golden again?"

He smiled. "Yes. So don't plan on sleeping tonight, because I have no intention of giving you a break once your skin shimmers with my virta. I'm very insatiable that way."

She ran her fingers along his chin to his neck. "Don't you think that warning comes a little late?"

"It's not a warning, it's a promise," he replied and captured her lips, pouring all the love he had for her into the kiss.

~ ~ ~

Hamish's kiss was more passionate than the previous nights they'd made love. She felt his power, his strength almost immediately. And she felt something else, too.

Around them the room seemed to disappear in a cloud of fog and air. It swirled around them as if they'd gotten caught in a storm. She felt weightless like she was floating in outer space, yet at the same time she felt cocooned in a bed of cotton wool.

She felt Hamish's hands on her, caressing her, his mouth on hers, his tongue exploring her. Strong thighs pushed her legs apart, making space for the man who owned her heart. As he settled at her core, she pulled him closer, one hand on his nape, one around his waist. She needed him, needed to feel what he could give her: his love and his strength.

She'd never been so sure of anything in her life as of the love that now crackled between them like electricity. Little sparks ignited the air around them, like lightning illuminated the night sky. She knew instinctively that it was their passion, their desire for each other that made the storm around them gain in strength.

Then she felt Hamish's cock at the apex of her thighs, the bulbous head nudging forward, parting her nether lips. She moaned out loud at the intense sensation. When he thrust deep into her, all air rushed from her lungs, and she locked her heels below his butt to hold onto him.

Hamish released her lips and looked deep into her eyes, his breath ragged. "I love you, Tessa. More than my life."

She felt tears shoot into her eyes and her heart fill with joy and the knowledge that they had a future together. "My love," she murmured.

As he began to pump into her, his tempo accelerating with every second, she could feel it already: his virta. It began at the point where they were joined and started radiating outward, until all her cells were saturated. She felt her entire body becoming more aware of everything around her, as if her senses were sharper now. And she felt an energy charge through her body that filled her with a power she'd never experienced before.

"It's time," she heard him say all of a sudden.

A moment later, he'd rolled them, and Tessa found herself above him, straddling him, his cock still deep inside her.

"Ride me. Bond with me," he demanded and took her hand, placing it over his heart.

Her hips began to move, rocking up and down on his cock, when she felt a tingling sensation travel up from her core and down her arm.

Hamish looked at her, his eyes full of desire and the love she could now feel physically. "Yes, Tessa, yes."

The tingling reached her fingers and tiny sparks now exploded from them. As they connected with Hamish's skin, his body spasmed and his back arched off the mattress.

"Oh God," he cried out, just as she felt his cock explode inside her and fill her with his seed, igniting her own orgasm.

Their moans mingled with the churning air and fog around them, while the sparks of lightning painted a more beautiful picture than any fireworks display. Passion and desire mixed with love and adoration, while their hearts became one.

"For eternity," Hamish murmured and pulled her to him for a kiss.

"Forever, my love."

And forever couldn't start early enough.

## 47

Zoltan paced in his private study, a cave between his private quarters and the great hall where his demons assembled to receive his orders. The study was reserved for discussions that weren't meant for public consumption.

Many things were bothering him.

Tessa Wallace had won the election, destroying his plan to have Gunn rule the city and throw it into even more chaos with his divisive policies. But for now, it was a matter he had to put on the back burner. More pressing things were demanding his attention.

Somebody was after his throne. After Vintoq had alerted him to the rumors that were circulating, Zoltan had gone up top and waited for Tessa and her Stealth Guardian lover at City Hall.

He'd disguised himself in his usual fashion so none of his own demons would recognize him, and donned his special contact lenses so no Stealth Guardian would be drawn to him. He saw two guardians, in fact the two he'd fought once at a farmhouse in Sonoma. But he was certain they weren't alone, their comrades most likely nearby in their invisible forms. Knowing that he would be outnumbered, he'd confined himself to watching. If one of his demons was there to kill Tessa Wallace, who was leading the polls, Zoltan would find him. And then he would have his traitor.

While roaming, he'd spotted Tessa's campaign manager—wearing sunglasses indoors. It had set off an alarm in his head. But before he'd been able to investigate further, she'd disappeared into the ladies room and Tessa had followed, her Stealth Guardian bodyguard blocking access to the area.

He'd waited around patiently, sipping champagne while he watched the guardian run into the restroom minutes later. When he came back out with Tessa by his side a good twenty minutes later, she'd looked shaken. As they'd passed him, Zoltan had looked down, averting his eyes out of habit, and spotted a drop of green color on the Stealth Guardian's shoes. Demon blood.

He didn't need to be a genius to put two and two together. The campaign manager was a demon he'd never met. A youngling still beholden to the demon she'd served as a human. The demon who wanted his throne.

A knock at the door interrupted his musings. "Come in."

The door opened and Yannick, one of the demons responsible for protecting the circles which allowed for the casting of a vortex, entered. "You asked to see me, oh Great One."

"I need you to do something for me."

He bowed his head.

"From now on I want to be informed of everybody's movements. Whenever any of my subjects go up top, I need to know about it. Keep a log. Present it to me daily."

Yannick tossed him a questioning look. "But, oh Great One, how…"

"Find a way!" he snapped. "Or would you rather lose your head?"

The demon scurried backwards. "It'll be done as you wish, oh Great One," he hastened to reply.

"And not a word to anybody about this! Now leave!"

Yannick charged out of the study. When the door fell shut with a loud thud, Zoltan exhaled a curse. "Whoever you are, I'm gonna find you. And then you'll be sorry you ever crossed me."

But in the meantime, there was lots of work to do. After all, the Stealth Guardians were never idle. It was time to adjust his game plan so he'd be one step ahead of them when it came to the next battle.

# ABOUT THE AUTHOR

Tina Folsom was born in Germany and has been living in English speaking countries for over 25 years, the last 14 of them in San Francisco, where she's married to an American.

Tina has always been a bit of a globe trotter: after living in Lausanne, Switzerland, she briefly worked on a cruise ship in the Mediterranean, then lived a year in Munich, before moving to London. There, she became an accountant. But after 8 years she decided to move overseas.

In New York she studied drama at the American Academy of Dramatic Arts, then moved to Los Angeles a year later to pursue studies in screenwriting. This is also where she met her husband, who she followed to San Francisco three months after first meeting him.

In San Francisco, Tina worked as a tax accountant and even opened her own firm, then went into real estate, however, she missed writing. In 2008 she wrote her first romance and never looked back.

She's always loved vampires and decided that vampire and paranormal romance was her calling. She now has over 32 novels in English and dozens in other languages (Spanish, German, and French) and continues to write, as well as have her existing novels translated.

For more about Tina Folsom:

www.tinawritesromance.com
http://www.facebook.com/TinaFolsomFans
Twitter: @Tina_Folsom
Email: tina@tinawritesromance.com

Made in the USA
Columbia, SC
18 December 2017